The BEGINNING

Prelude to the Apocalypse

Bruce S. Campbell

Clovercroft Publishing

The Beginning

Published by Carpenter's Son Publishing, Franklin, Tennessee.

Published in association with Larry Carpenter of Christian Book Services, LLC. www.christianbookservices.com

Cover Design by Todd Goodwin

Interior Design by Adept Concept Solutions

Printed in the United States of America

978-1-942587-02-6

Dedication

This book is dedicated to
all questioning people everywhere.

Is the supernatural real?
We must choose between two possibilities!

With special thanks to my wife and friends,
for all their help and editing.

And to my friend Rendy,
who gave me the idea in the first place!

Contents

CHAPTER 1

First Things

Public Notice—July 8, 1959: Yesterday, a newborn white male was left on the steps of the chapel of Cabrini High School. The all-girls' school, formerly known as Cabrini Orphanage and Convent Chapel, is at 3400 Esplanade Avenue, New Orleans, Louisiana.

The child was found at 7:00 a.m. on July 7. A police spokesman commented, "If the mother steps forward now, she will not be charged with any crime." All leads will be explored. The authorities have asked the community to get involved by calling in any information no matter how trivial to help solve the case.

The school gave no comment on the suggestion that the mother could be one of the students. Sr. Trinita, the headmaster, said that the baby was in good health and that arrangements were being made with authorities.

The baby was wrapped in a gray wool blanket. The child has blue eyes, brown hair, and a small, spiral birthmark on the right forehand. The basket he was found in is common brown wicker with two oscillating handles that fold toward the center.

A folded, lined piece of notebook paper was pinned to the blanket with the words, "His name is Enoch Kingu Galah. Please take care of him." The name may be of Indian or Semitic origin. If you have any knowledge of this baby or know the mother, please contact your local authorities.

—Staff writer, the *Times Picayune*

This is my story and background. How do I explain my path to the supernatural from such humble beginnings? I scarcely believe it myself. I was a skeptic; I refused to believe what my eyes told me. In my later years, the fullness of the bizarre, unnatural, and strange began to encroach on my life. I didn't ask for it. It was thrust on me, and I had no say in it.

You must travel the road with me and decide for yourself. Are these the writings of a raving lunatic, or are they real? The names and some of the circumstances have been changed to protect the innocent. A global threat looming on the horizon is either the work of men or another, more-ominous reality. Will the world end in my lifetime? Am I a key player in the end of the world or the pawn in a global conspiracy to dominate the affairs of mankind?

I'm not sure about my beginning. I was told by my foster parents that I had been left on the steps of Cabrini Girls' School. The tattered, old article from the newspaper was the only piece of personal history I had. No hospital had a record of my birth; there were no clues as to how I'd ended up on the steps of that school. I always wondered why my mother had left me, what had made her throw me away. I wondered if she was one of the girls from the school. Sometimes, I would just get mad and think, *What idiot would leave a boy at an orphanage that wasn't an orphanage and wasn't even for boys?*

I tried not to think about it as I grew up, but it was always in the back of my mind. They gave me the name on the note pinned to my blanket. Since that was July 7, I always celebrated my birthday on that day. I always hated my name because it was just plain weird. Enoch Kingu Galah! Who would name a kid that? I've never seen the note or the blanket. The police took it years ago as evidence in case they ever found my mother.

My foster parents told me I had a great name because I was named after a Bible character who had been taken by God, without dying. I didn't have much use for a God who had given me such a bum deal. I wished God would take me out of my miserable name. John or Tom or Steve would have been just fine with me. I liked to imagine my strange middle name meant I had descended from a mysterious line of ancient kings. In my imagination, Kingu meant "King of the Universe." I would wear a blanket as a cape and run around my room pretending I had superpowers.

I don't remember much of my early years except constant moving; I never stayed in any home or place too long. New beds, new rooms, and new people were a constant of my life. I was taken from New Orleans to Detroit for three years, from second through part of fifth grade. That was the only place that gave me some stability, you know, like family. I often chuckled at its funny name, The Evangelical Home for Children and the Aged. The big building that housed the chapel was full of old, smelly people in wheelchairs who always made me feel uncomfortable when they stared at me.

However I ended up there, it was the closest thing to a family I had experienced. Except for a traumatic beginning, it wasn't too bad, and I enjoyed having boys my age to play with. We lived in four cottages—two for girls and two for boys, about ten to eleven kids and a housemother in each. We boys were not allowed to interact with the girls except on the way to chapel every morning. I never paid much attention to the priest. We mostly doodled and fidgeted until it was over. After chapel every morning, we went to school across the street.

I had some difficult times at the orphanage. Mrs. Blackburn was our housemother, strict and mean, and we all feared her. On my first day, she grabbed a boy by the hair and pulled him out of the shower. She shook him like a rag doll and threw him onto the white tile floor. She barked, "You splashed water all over the floor on purpose! Now clean it up!" He sat on the floor naked, sobbing, as he wiped up the water. I was terrified and angry. The shower curtain had been slightly open, and water had splashed off his back. He hadn't noticed water had gotten on the floor. That was the first time I felt injustice. I imagined myself pushing her down the stairs. I thought she was an evil witch.

One time while at the dinner table, I was lost in my thoughts. A piercing voice brought me back to reality. "Billy asked you to pass the peas!" she screamed at me. It took me a moment to focus. I tried to explain I hadn't heard him. She grabbed me by the hair and yanked me up from the table. After slapping me several times, she made me stand in front of all the kids with my nose to the wall. I stood there sobbing, my nose stuck to the wall, until bedtime. This was during a time when child abuse was not a well-recognized matter. In those days, we had no advocate, just a short, stocky woman who represented the law. I'll never forget the cruelty I saw in that old woman.

I began having nightmares soon after I arrived at the home. I imagined evil things under the bed. I would sometimes see dark figures in the shadows of the room and hear whispers at night. I'd pull the covers over my head and pray to God that they wouldn't get me. I wondered if there was any real security in the world even before I knew what *security* meant. I felt insecurity as if it were alive. It was like a breathing, dark presence that was going to swallow me whole. I felt I would rot in its belly, being slowly digested by acid for all eternity.

Quite a few strange incidents occurred while I was young. Although the events could be explained naturally, they happened in a supernatural way. As a child, I believed unseen forces were out to get me. Toys would sometimes turn on when I would reach for them. On a number of occasions, lightbulbs would blow out when I entered a room. The kids in the cottage noticed these things and said I was cursed. They were just teasing, but I thought they were right. Later, when I was grown, such supernatural incidents increased in frequency and intensity.

My dreams and the strange happenings made me think the orphanage was haunted; I wanted to believe it was the home rather than me. I ran away from the home several times with no idea of where to go. I just started walking and walking, hoping I could walk to New Orleans. Of course, I was always caught and taken back to the orphanage. One time, I walked up to a house and asked an old couple if they could give me a ride home to New Orleans. They called the police; back to the orphanage I went. I knew I'd been left in New Orleans, and I had to get back.

The kids in the home were like family to me in spite of my reputation for being strange. Billy Bonds was my best friend. In the summers, we would laugh and play and chase bees for hours, trying not to get stung of course. We spent one whole afternoon burning ants with a magnifying glass Billy had found at the bottom of the toy bin. In the winters, we mostly played in the cottage, a tri-level house with a partial basement that served as our play and activity room. Ground-level windows there let in a lot of light, and we would color and draw to our hearts' content. We loved to have contests to see who could draw the weirdest monster or the most souped-up hot rod. Most of the time, I won the monster contests because my drawings were the scariest. I usually just drew things I'd seen in my nightmares.

Christmas time was the best time of the year. We were taken to Christmas parties held by charities all over the place. People seemed to think about us orphans just at that time of year. We were showered with toys and gifts and taken on many sleigh rides and hay rides. I sat on quite a few Santa's laps to collect the next gift-wrapped surprise. I could almost catalogue the various colors of the Santa's fake beards. Some were bluish and thin while others were coarse and white. I didn't care they were fakes because I was getting toys.

One Santa had a real beard. While sitting on his lap, I studied it to find the elastic, sure I would find the flaw, but it seemed every hair went right into his skin. I wondered if he had glued every hair to his face. I wanted to yank it to see if it was real but thought I better not. I wondered if he was the real Santa Claus for a minute, but I decided he was just an old man with a white beard. None of us ever let on that we knew they were fakes.

Incidents happened at the two Christmas parties I attended. After I received a gift, I stood next to the Christmas tree. Every bulb on the tree blew out at once. Several adults asked me what I had done to burn out all the bulbs. I hadn't touched the tree and was terrified, thinking that it had tried to kill me. The adults decided the circuit had been overloaded and told me not to worry about it. Another time, I reached for a present under the tree and the tree fell on me. I hadn't touched the tree. Nonetheless, the Christmas presents helped distract me from the fear always with me.

When we got back to the cottage, we would divide our loot and trade with each other if we didn't like our gifts. Sometimes, wrapped gifts would be delivered to the cottage and we would choose a box after carefully considering its size and weight. We would laugh and tease each other if we got a stupid gift such as doll. I mean, really? Who would buy a doll for the boy's cottage? You definitely didn't want to get a girly gift in our group!

One of the kids got a Barbie doll one time, and we promptly tore off her clothes to see what was underneath. We laughed and carried on, pointing to the bumps on her chest. The red-faced housemother heard the ruckus. We got a stern reprimand from her, but we couldn't stop giggling. In total frustration, she grabbed the naked Barbie and her clothes and stomped up the stairs, at which point we burst into laughter so hard that my sides started to hurt. The fun times were a great distraction from the nightmares and strange happenings that plagued my life.

I learned many things at the orphanage. I learned about cruelty and kindness and friendship. I learned about loss and anger, and I learned how to laugh! I never recalled laughing before third grade. It had been as if I hadn't existed. I was backward and shy. I was told I never spoke before second grade. I knew how to talk but just wouldn't. I was tested for mental deficiencies many times, but it was determined I suffered emotional rather than physical problems.

I had strange dreams all through the time I was there. I remember dark, shadowy figures telling me I would never fulfill my purpose. Voices of people who seemed to wear clothes made of light would calm me down when the dark people would talk to me. In my dreams, I couldn't look at the light people because they were too bright, but I was glad they were there. The dark people were like shadows, smoke, and they whispered and laughed at me. They told me that they were going to kill me and that they would peel my skin off. My dreams felt real; I had no control over what happened in them.

In one particularly terrifying dream, I was being chased by the shadowy people and a coffin with spikes on the inside. It kept opening and shutting like a huge jaw waiting to impale me in its evil grasp. Suddenly, a hand of light touched me on the shoulder and a voice said, "Do not be afraid. I will not allow them to hurt you." I woke up in a sweat.

I rarely talked about the nightmares with anyone even though I could remember their every detail. I thought I must be weird to have so many nightmares. I wasn't allowed to watch TV for two months one time after I woke up screaming. The housemother thought I must have been seeing too many scary things on TV.

In the fifth grade, I was told that the last foster parents I'd had in New Orleans had made arrangements for me to go home. I hadn't been with them long when I was taken to Michigan. I barely remembered them; I wasn't sure what was going on at the time. Once again, I was going to a new situation.

I'll always remember those days at the orphanage. I was sad and glad to be going back to New Orleans. I was going to miss Gary, Billy's brother, but most of all Billy. We were best buddies for the whole time I was there. When odd things happened, Billy always comforted me and told me not to be afraid.

The day I was leaving, Billy was nowhere to be found. A station wagon pulled up to the front door of the cottage, and the housemother told me my ride was here. She placed my meager belongings in the back of the car. "Where's Billy? Where's Billy?" I turned and saw a running boy in the field. "Eeenie! Eeenie!" He always called me that. He practically knocked me over when he jumped on me. "I don't want you to go!" Tears were running down his face. I felt a profound sadness like I had never known. I felt my heart breaking. In that moment, I didn't care about New Orleans or even finding my mother. I couldn't talk. Tears flooded down my cheeks. I couldn't keep from sobbing as I waved to him and the others as we drove away. We had promised to write and call and move in together when we were big, but in fact, we never saw each other again.

CHAPTER 2

Hopes and Dreams

Back in New Orleans, I moved into the Wellington's house on State Street. They were good people for the most part and seemed to accept me into their home. My foster mother was very religious and taught me Bible stories and took us to church. Mostly, church was boring to me, and I didn't want to go, but I had no choice.

The highlight of my preadolescent days was our next-door neighbor, Aaron Levy. He was a rabbi who seemed to accept me with none of the usual suspicions that accompanied foster kids or Gentiles for that matter. I called him Mr. Aaron or Mr. Rabbi, as was proper in the South. I never knew why it was proper in the South to call adults by their first names and put "Mister" or "Miss" in front of them. I think Mrs. Blackburn would have slapped me silly if I had ever called her "Miss Bertha."

I liked the rabbi even though my foster mother didn't approve of my going to his house. He filled my head with imaginations about my origin. One day, he asked me, "Enoch, do you know what your last name means in Hebrew?"

"You mean my name has a meaning? I just thought it was a joke or something."

"Not at all, son. In the old days, every name had a meaning. Your name might describe your character or maybe what work you did or sometimes what hopes and dreams your parents had for you. Your name might mean 'valiant warrior.'" He chuckled. "Valiant warrior ... he, he! Have you ever seen a valiant warrior baby?"

I started to laugh as I envisioned a medieval, diaper-clad baby trying to carry a lance on a horse, his little bobblehead struggling to stay upright in his oversized helmet. "No, I've never seen a baby warrior before," I replied, still chuckling at the thought.

"That's right, son. A baby cannot be a warrior, but his name might mean 'valiant warrior'. You see, names set a tone and a direction for a person's life. My name, for instance, Aaron, has had a great impact on my life. Aaron was the high priest during the time of the exodus. He was part of the Levites and was the brother of Moses. So is it any wonder I should become a rabbi?"

"Please tell me what my whole name means!" I blurted. I was giddy with excitement to hear of the great nobility of my name. Mr. Aaron said, "Hold on just a minute, son. I'll be right back."

A few minutes later, he emerged from his library with a large book. He carefully turned the pages and intently stared at the words in the book as if searching over a great treasure map. I sat there, imagining my name would have some great, heroic meaning that would become my destiny. Perhaps I was a valiant warrior or a great prince who would save the world or at least a damsel in distress. My head swam with anticipation as I anxiously waited to hear the mystery of my weird name. "Uh huh, mmm, yes, yes. g-a-l-a-h! Here it is. Are you ready?" he asked.

"Yes, yes, please, please!" I begged.

"Well, I had to get the spelling just right ... So here it is. It meeaannns ... 'revelation ... to uncover, to be revealed, a hidden mystery or secret that unfolds like a book.' It also means an Australian rose-breasted cockatoo!"

We burst out laughing. I'm sure we were laughing for different reasons, though. My childish laughter centered on the fact that a bird would be named with what I had thought were two naughty words. If I had said those two words in the same sentence in earshot of my foster mother, I would've had my mouth washed out with soap. Believe me, it takes only one mouth washing to teach you to hold your tongue.

After I stopped laughing, I asked, "Does this mean I'm Jewish or some nasty bird?"

"You don't much look like a rose-breasted cockatoo, so I guess you must be Jewish."

I laughed again at the mention of the bird's funny name. I tried to imagine its strange anatomy. "Please don't tell Mrs. Wellington I might be Jewish. I don't think she could bear it."

He laughed and assured me it would be our little secret. "Now listen, son. My first name was given to me in honor of a great heritage, just as your first name was given to you in honor of a great heritage. God took only two men in history for Himself, Elijah and Enoch. Both were righteous men who walked with God. Whoever gave you your name did so by the will of God, for God knows all things, and nothing is a surprise to Him. When you get older, you can decide for yourself if you are Jewish or Christian or agnostic. You must freely choose to serve God and live according to His statutes. God does not force us to serve Him but allows us to choose by our free will. I trust, young Enoch, when you are of age, you will consider carefully all things and make the right choice."

As I reflected on Rabbi Levy's words, I realized I had heard the word *revelation* in my dreams. I didn't know what the word meant at the time. I wondered how dreams could say words I didn't understand. I thought it odd that a child would hear talk best suited for adults. At the time, I hoped my name would be some clue to my beginning, but Mr. Aaron's talks back then held little relevance for me.

I didn't understand Mr. Aaron when he would talk about deeper concepts such as life and God. My mission was more urgent ... to find out as much as I could about myself.

"How about my middle name, Mr. Aaron?"

He looked puzzled. "Enoch, I don't believe you have ever told me your middle name."

I thought for a minute and said, "Enoch K. Galah!"

"Yes, yes, son, but what does the *k* stand for?"

"Don't laugh!" I insisted. "It stands for Kingu!"

He looked puzzled again and said, "Hold on. Let me check my book." He flipped through several pages while muttering softly. "No ... No ... uh uh, nope. Sorry, son. I thought it might be a subroot of or a description of *king* in some way, but it doesn't fit any Jewish words. The *u* on the end is puzzling, but I will keep researching. For now, I guess you'll just have to be a hidden mystery king."

I always left our talks with my head spinning with imagination. He told me stories of floods and angels and giants and men so strong they could carry away great gates of cities. I had heard some of these same stories in Sunday school, but he had a way of bringing his stories to life. I always felt better around him, as if we had a connection deeper than just a friendly neighbor and a kid next door. He always said that God didn't make mistakes and that we were destined by God to meet. He often told me, "God, like your last name, is a mystery that is revealed in many ways. God can be seen in flowers and trees and birds and animals, but most of all, God can be seen in man, who was created in His image."

The religious people I knew were tormented by the fear of God. They were driven by unseen forces of guilt and shame as far as I could see. Sometimes, it was more about their feeling good about themselves than giving the love and mercy they preached. I always got the feeling that foster parents took kids in from some great sense of religious guilt that hung over their head, like the hammer of God just waiting for them to step out of line so He could crush them.

This God thing was a mystery to me. Everybody wanted to do good deeds so they would be okay with God. They all wanted to be careful not to upset God's law. I began to turn from the idea of the supernatural and God to the idea of reasoned logic even at an early age. It may have been in response to the poor examples of religion I had encountered. It could also have been a deep desire to avoid the possibility of the supernatural. I thought, *If God's real, I might have to face Him one day.* I just wanted to live life my own way and not be subject to God's wrath.

One day, I ran smack into the wrath of God by leaving a piece of cheese in the wrong sink in Mr. Aaron's kitchen. A sheer look of horror came over his face as he screamed "No! No! No! That sink is *not* for dairy!" I ran out of the kitchen totally terrorized, feeling all the old torments from an earlier part of my childhood.

Later, he apologized for screaming at me. I tried to explain I thought the sink had a garbage disposal. He told me a long story about goats being boiled in milk and mixing meat and dairy and God's law or some such thing, but I didn't understand why God would freak out over cheese. I wasn't sure I wanted to be Jewish after that. It seemed you could never be good enough to make God happy. What did cheese have to do with right and wrong anyway? Incidents like that confirmed my desire to reject the idea of God.

At the time, I thought my existence and beginnings were mysteries to solve. You know, like those great mystery hunts in which you find clues that lead you to the next clue, and you eventually solve the mystery. I was beginning to feel I had a purpose in life. I didn't know what it was, but I sensed a great mystery would unfold. Little did I know how true that would be.

I began to search for people with my last name. Mrs. Wellington kept saying, "If God wants you to find your birth mother, He will not need your help." I think I just frustrated her with my constant badgering to get me all the phone books for the area. I searched them, hoping to find someone with the last name of Galah. It took only a few weeks of begging and pleading with everyone I knew to completely exhaust the New Orleans and greater surrounding Gulf Coast phone directories. Not a single reference! Not one person with my name. My name sounded foreign, as if it was from the Far East or something, and yet I was Caucasian. The more I searched, the less sense it made.

I continually hoped to find some further clues to my existence. I imagined my mother was beautiful and had had to give me up to save me from terrible people who wanted to kill me. I just *knew* she was not at fault somehow. I thought she must have put up a terrible fight to keep me but evil men had overpowered her and had taken me away. Maybe she was underage and had been forced by her evil parents to abandon me. Perhaps she died giving birth to me and a relative left me on the steps of that school. I played out every scenario in my mind I could think of until I was exhausted.

Strangely, I never thought much about my father; my thoughts always gravitated toward my mother. It seemed that a mother's love was somehow different from a father's. A few of my friends' parents had gotten divorces, and the courts always gave custody of the kids to the mothers. Some of my friends' fathers who had left because of divorce never even called them, but I never knew a mother to do that. It just seemed that a mother would do anything for her kids while the fathers went off to new families and gave little time to their original kids. Most of the kids saw their dads only occasionally or for a few weeks in the summer.

At the orphanage, some of the kids were not orphans. About half had parents who were living. Their mothers would pick them up on weekends, but I never saw any father picking up any kids. I found out the home took in children when mothers couldn't afford to take care of them. Even so, the mothers would come every week to see their kids. Billy and Gary's mother worked three jobs and paid the orphanage to see they were clothed and fed. She couldn't work all those jobs and be home to take care of them.

I continued for some years to dream of one day being reunited with my mother. Thoughts of picnics on the beach and trips to the lakefront amusement park filled my imagination as I idled away hours with the maternal presence I'd never known. I'd look into the faces of women everywhere we went, wondering if one might be the mother who had been lost to me. As time went on, my perspective became more distorted by the loss I felt in my heart. I had no need for God, but it seemed I was destined to deal with an inner longing for a great, noble purpose. As I became an adult, I decided that logic and science would be my God. I wanted nothing to do with religion, but I found myself being strangely attracted to the supernatural. I felt a presence always watching me. Even though I felt a strange pull, I wanted to believe in the natural only.

After I graduated from high school, I got a job as a painter and carpenter's helper. I moved into my own place and learned all I could about construction. I wanted to be the best carpenter possible, so I studied techniques and books to learn the math and terminology. At night, I took classes at Delgado Community College. I tried to work on the prerequisites, hoping to get a full degree at some point. I had a knack for woodworking and soon was put into a lead carpenter's role. By the age of twenty-one, I knew enough to venture out on my own.

I began by advertising my handyman services in the newspaper and began getting jobs. I liked being my own boss, but I soon realized I couldn't take on certain jobs without help. I tried several guys over the next few years but never found anyone who showed the same level of care I did on the job. Finally, I met a fellow named Jon who had been on his own for some time and knew the importance of quality work. We decided the best thing to do was to form a partnership.

In our first week of working together, I had several strange, near-miss accidents. The first involved a ladder that seemed to slide off a roof by itself. If I hadn't jumped at the last minute, the ladder would have hit me. We looked at each other and wondered how it could have fallen sideways for no apparent reason.

On another occasion, Jon and I were in front of a house when we heard a cracking sound above us. Jon pushed me aside just before a huge tree limb hit the ground right where I had been standing. Had Jon not pushed me out of the way, I would've been crushed, maybe killed.

At another job, one of my workers was sent up scaffolding to the top of a brick chimney on a house. Over the years, the mortar had disintegrated, and we had to tuck-point the bricks of the crumbling structure. As the worker got to the chimney to assess the work, he leaned against the chimney to stabilize himself. It crumbled and fell between the scaffolding where I was standing. I had a piece of plywood in my hands above my head, trying to cover a large window to protect it. At what seemed to be the perfect time, a gust of wind, pushed the plywood away from the window and up against the scaffolding. The force of the wind blew me backward, and the top of the plywood hit the scaffolding behind me. It wedged between the scaffolding and a gas meter at my knees. The massive brick chimney struck the plywood, which protected me. If the wind hadn't happened at that second, I would have been badly injured or dead. Every incident was explainable, but I wondered if something was trying to kill me.

Things like that happened on every job. I used to tell Jon he was the reason for all the near misses. I'd never experienced such accidents before he came along. We often laughed as I accused him of subversive, evil plots to get rid of his partner. We began to take every precaution to protect ourselves. We would tie down or lock down every potential hazard. We were so overcautious that our workers called us the Occupational Safety and Health Administration bosses. The truth is we were way more cautious than OSHA was.

I still had a number of near misses in spite of our cautious approach. We couldn't tie up our workers. Many times, I would somehow be protected from a hammer coming out of its holster or a nail gun or bundle of shingles sliding off a roof. At just the right time I would slip and avoid injury; something always happened at just the right time to protect me. I always passed it off as the normal dangers of construction sites, but I wondered about the odds of so many incidents happening just to me. None of the other guys ever had even one dangerous thing happen to them. They nicknamed me Typhoid Galah, the walking poster child for bad luck. They'd tease me endlessly about who was going to work with me any one day. One would say, "I'm not working with him today! You work with him." Another would say, "Not me! I value my life." They would go back and forth laughing and teasing me. The truth was that they were actually half-serious.

There was always something happening that seemed directed at me. Jon noticed the strange occurrences but never showed any concern. One day, Carl, one of my workers, had just turned off a grinder and had laid it on a board sitting on two sawhorses. As Jon walked in the door of the house with a two-by-twelve, the grinder suddenly turned on and flew off the board. It was heading straight for my head. The board Jon was carrying came through the door at just the right time to deflect the grinder from tearing up my face. It tore up the subfloor, skipping along until it pulled its own plug out of the socket. We all checked out the grinder. The switch was in the on position even though we'd all heard him switch it off. It lay dormant on the board for a few seconds and then suddenly turned on again.

After that incident, Jon told me he thought something funny was going on. He said he would pray and ask God to remove the Devil's constant harassment of me. I took what he said with a grain of salt; I didn't believe in religion, but I appreciated his attempt to comfort me. I hadn't ever thought about him as a religious guy.

CHAPTER 3

Things Are Getting Weird

I always loved the strange ambience of New Orleans; it was like living in a bygone era. Certain areas of the city, such as the French Quarter, were eerie and exhilarating at the same time. The architecture of wrought-iron balconies, old, double-hung sashes, and cracking plaster gave the area a serene, historic quality that could be felt elsewhere only in places like Europe. Different colors protruding through flaking chips of paint gave rise to imaginations of a place time had forgotten. Perhaps it was the intrigue of the incredible intricate millwork in the old buildings and houses that drew me to carpentry. I knew there would always be a need for a carpenter in an aging city of continuously crumbling buildings.

Jon was my friend and business partner for several years while I was in my late twenties and early thirties. It was during my work that I first became aware of realities outside the realms of reason and logic. The incidents escalated to more than just strange accidents.

I was working up an estimate for a renovation project on North Rampart Street. The old building had housed a gay bar on the first floor for some years; the floors above had been at the mercy of the elements for many years. The owner was toying with the idea of turning the upper floors into apartments to increase revenue from the building. We had met with him in his large uptown home on Rosa Park Street just off St. Charles. Like many owners of French Quarter properties, he rarely thought about them until there was a problem. His orders were for us to find the leaks and look into the possibility of turning the upper floors into apartments.

In the French Quarter, it was not unusual for floors above street level to be empty because the upper floors were hard to get to. The entrance to the upper floors might be on the side through a narrow passage or perhaps accessible only through a shop on the first floor. In some cases, the first-floor tenants had removed the stairs to create more retail space. It was always a challenge just to get to the upper spaces. Water was the greatest problem in these old spaces. It was hard to maintain the old buildings because usually, when rot or damage showed up on the first floor, the damage on the second or third floor was already substantial. Since no one visited the upper floors, such damage was never noticed until it was too late. Most of the owners of the buildings were third- or fourth-generation owners. It was the first-floor tenants who created income for the owners generation after generation.

Jon and I got the key to the side entrance from the owner of the bar. He showed us where the ceiling had buckled and the plaster was giving way near the front entrance. The dark stains of water damage were all-too-common sights in old buildings such as this one. We walked through the building like detectives, carefully examining the evidence, trying to find the guilty culprit that had destroyed this valuable landmark. Water stains and missing plaster on the second floor suggested that the roof needed a lot of attention. While exploring the upper floor, we went up the last flight of steps to the attic. If unchecked, leaks would destroy any future cosmetic work on the lower floors. We weren't able to access the attic due to a large and solid wood door.

"Enoch, this one's in bad shape! It'll cost a fortune to fix this mess."

I agreed with Jon's assessment, and I knew most owners didn't spring major cash to repair old spaces. "Yeah. I figure it's a long shot to pick up the renovation work, but maybe we can make some money on the water damage work."

We often gave estimates for old properties. Most of the time, the cost was prohibitive. We'd typically spend hours measuring and calling on material prices to get a cost. After much work, we'd hand the estimates to people just to find out that they'd just been curious about the cost, that they had no intention of actually having the work done. I wondered how people could think our time didn't have value.

When I came into a space that had been neglected for so many years, I knew the likelihood of getting a contract to actually do the work was low. Most of the time, people would do only what was absolutely necessary to keep the tenants happy.

"You're right, Jon, but we still need the work, so we have to keep doing it."

"How are we gonna get into the attic? The door's locked."

"Let's see if we can knock it open."

In unison, we both tried to slam the door with our shoulders to see if it was just jammed. After several attempts, it was clear the door wasn't going to yield.

"Ouch! My shoulder hurts. That was a stupid idea."

"We have to get in. We can't give him an estimate if we can't find the problem. Why don't you call him and see if he has a key?"

Jon called the owner. "Mr. Belisaire? This is Jon. I'm afraid we're going to have to get into the attic to find where the water's coming from. Do you have a key? Uh huh, yeah. Really? ... I see ... Well, the only thing I can think of is to use a crowbar ... Okay, Mr. Belisaire, but I can't guarantee it won't break the door, and we don't want to be held responsible for any damage. Yes sir, I understand. We'll get right up there with your permission."

"Mr. Belisaire said no one in his family has been in the attic in his memory," Jon said. "The key was lost over forty years ago, and his family hasn't lived in the building for generations. He said he's always been curious what was up there. He says to do what we have to do, so let's get at it."

We went to the truck. As we walked back up to the attic with a crowbar in hand, we heard strange sounds emanating from behind the large, heavy door. I had an eerie feeling. I asked Jon, "Do you hear that, or am I imagining it?"

"No. As vivid as your imagination is, I hear it too."

"You got the crowbar. Let's bust this puppy open."

Jon carefully placed the crowbar between the jamb and door and began to pull with his entire two hundred and sixty pounds. Placing one foot on the wall, he gave a final lunge and broke the door open with a great crash. The door slammed against some large object behind it. The door wedged in place as if it had been grabbed by the object. "Look out!" A rush of noise and foul odor blew into our faces after the door flew open, taking remnants of the shattered frame into the room. A roar of flapping wings, feathers—the sound of a thousand pigeons trying to escape our presence nearly caused us to fall back down the old, rickety stairs. "Shut the door quick! Shut the door!" Jon screamed. We swung wildly at the air hoping to frighten the flock long enough to shut the door. Jon grabbed the handle of the door but quickly let go when it wouldn't budge.

I was panicked. It was reminiscent of a scene from Alfred Hitchcock's *The Birds*. I picked up the crowbar Jon had dropped. Crouching low to the floor, I reached into the space with the crowbar and hooked the door. After a couple of attempts, I was able to pull it mostly shut, but the crowbar was still hooked to the other side. I kept a steady pressure on the door by pulling on the crowbar as if the pigeons could somehow pull the door open and terrorize us again.

We sat on a three-foot landing, stunned and shaking. Jon took in a sharp breath. "Wow! Can you believe that?"

I sat there breathing hard, feeling adrenaline coursing through my blood.

"That scared me to death! Feel my pulse. I might be dead!" His eye caught mine, and we began to laugh nervously. We sat there panting for some time until our breath and heart rates returned to somewhat normal. The uproar of disturbed pigeons had died off somewhat; we heard only the occasional flapping sound in the room. Jon slowly cracked opened the door, pushing the crowbar from my unwilling grip. As the door creaked open to a chorus of cooing sounds, he peered ever so carefully into the attic. Most of the pigeons had exited through the broken dormer windows, but a large group of the bravest birds were still perched on the rafters. Other nesting birds intently stared at us through holes in the walls. Each head moved in unison with cold eyes, suggesting we were invaders who had no right to be in their hidden sanctuary. We moved very slowly so as to not upset the delicate accord we had managed to strike between the birds and us.

The attic was very large; two dormers faced the street. The windows had long ago been broken, and the wood was either rotting away or missing. A number of old dressers and armoires were filled with holes from nesting birds. The chairs were mostly tattered remnants of frames. The cloth and seat stuffing had long since been removed for building materials by winged residents past and present. Although we briefly noticed some of the oddities in the shadows, we didn't 't want to be distracted from our mission.

We crept ever so slowly over the mounds of bird dung and feathers to assess the condition of the structure. The broken glass on the old sash were soiled brown with age and looked as if they were flowing down like melting wax. Most of the glass had long ago fallen out as the glazing had disintegrated. The few muntin bars on the sash looked like frazzled sticks instead of perfectly milled roman ogee shapes from a time gone by. It's amazing how adrenaline rush can heighten the senses and make everything more vivid.

The attic was not targeted for renovation, but we had to see where the water problems were coming from. We had followed the ceiling stains on the lower floors to their inevitable conclusion. It was obvious that every time rain was accompanied by strong winds, water came into the building through the broken windows. The tenants were baffled by the haphazard leaking and had told us that sometimes it leaked in the lightest storms and sometimes it didn't during the hardest storms. I looked out the windows. I could see the gable roof protruded out beyond the windows for about three feet, an unusual distance; only strong winds from a particular direction could carry the rain into the windows. Once inside, however, rain had an easy opportunity to do its destructive work.

I was satisfied by my reasoning and felt I had solved the mystery of the intermittent leaking. Jon and I discussed the dormers and the best way to repair the problem. The windows were too far gone to be repaired; they would have to be replaced.

Our total focus had been on the dormer problems. Since we were satisfied with our detective-like conclusions, we were free to explore the rest of the attic. I was curious about what had jammed the door and went to investigate. The door had wedged up against an old armoire. Its eight-inch curved legs had the old-style, ball-and-claw feet common to an earlier era. The front claw foot protruded just enough to have caught the bottom of the door and wedge it tight. I was glad to know there was a plausible explanation for why it had been so hard to close the door. The armoire, black with age, had two old mirrors in its doors. It was about seven feet tall with a fancy, curved top with intricate molding. It was narrower than usual, only about thirty-six inches, but it had a commanding presence.

I looked into the mirrors at the cracking and faded silver backing. It was more yellowish than silver and made me look like an altered image from an old horror movie. As I looked in the mirror, I began to see the shapes of backward letters and words behind me. The faded writing interrupted my thoughts and curiosity as to the age and potential value of the antique armoire. I turned to inspect the faded writings I hadn't noticed earlier. The ravages of time and missing plaster made the writings mostly incoherent gibberish, but one phrase was clear: "The Beginning ... End of Days! Prepare!" Other smaller writings under it looked to be some form of hieroglyphs. Circle symbols with crosses were under them. I noticed horizontal lines with hundreds of separation lines that formed rectangles. In the rectangles were shapes of triangles, circles, squiggly lines, and straight lines.

Other words were just partial due to fading and missing sections, but they were in English. I strained to read them. Inanna ... Destroy ... Witnesses ... Death ... War ... Apocalypse ... Horsemen. I thought some religious nutcase had had too much to drink and had taken it out on these poor walls. "Inanna. Who's Anna, and who wants to get in her?" I asked. Jon looked at me with one of those looks. He never approved of juvenile male humor.

As our eyes further adjusted to the darker areas of the attic, we noticed the reddish-brown words and symbols were everywhere. We often saw graffiti in old buildings. Vagrants, drug addicts, and homeless people often broke into abandoned spaces to escape the elements or to steal valuables. Abandoned properties would usually be stripped of copper wiring, fixtures—anything that could be sold for scrap.

The light coming in from the dormers revealed the original knob-and-tube wiring that hadn't been touched since it had been installed at the turn of the century. It was unlikely that any vagrants could have gotten into this space anyway. The walls to the dormers would have been impossible to climb even with the tallest ladders. The only other way to get into the space was through the door.

In many areas, plaster had fallen off the walls and revealed the wooden lath behind. A number of these laths were missing, and tufts of nest hay and cloth surrounded the openings. The nesting birds' heads were just visible as their disapproving eyes peered at us through the dark holes.

"Wow! This is freaky!" Jon's comment refocused my mind from revisiting scenes from Hitchcock's avian horror thriller. I silently agreed with Jon's assessment. "I've seen these symbols in a book from church. They're satanic!"

A cold chill ran down my spine. I had an unsettling sense of dread. "Jon, do you think some cult has been up here using this space?"

Jon looked intently at the painted symbols and said, "Not recently. This looks like it's been here a hundred years. Look how old and faded everything is. Do you think Belisaire's ancestors were Satanists?" I began to respond when Jon said sharply, "Shut up!"

"What is it?" I whispered.

"Look over in the shadows at those words on the wall, Enoch. It's your name!"

I froze as I peered into the darkness. I could just barely make out some words on the old plaster. Just below a spiral shape that matched the birthmark on my right hand, were the broken words "Beware E ... ch Kingu Galah." I felt frozen in place as I looked at the faded words. The plaster had fallen off at the area of a first name leaving what looked like an *e*, then a small missing section of plaster with a partial *c* and a 4 or maybe an *h*. The plaster was missing at the bottom half of the *c* as well as the left leg of the *h*.

"No, that can't be!" I said, quickly trying to dismiss the faded words. "You can't make it out. I think it says King of Gala or something! Look, that has to be an *o*; that's it! It says Kingo, not Kingu! I think the top just faded out! I ... I ... uh ... you know ... it ... it can't be!" I felt panic slowly rising. My explanation wasn't convincing even me. Above a pentagram were the faded words, "The Witness Will Come ... The Emissary Must Die!"

There appeared to be an old altar with what looked like black candles and bowls covered in bird excrement and thick dust. Under the altar were bones, feathers, and dark, reddish-brown stains that reminded me of dried blood. As we stared at the macabre scene, we heard wood cracking. Startled, we turned just in time to see the legs of the old armoire give way, causing it to ram into the open door. The large, old piece of furniture somehow managed to swing the door shut and block the way out at the same time. Pigeons literally came out of the woodwork. The room filled once again with flapping wings. "Let's get out of here!" I screamed. We clawed at the armoire like two wild bears to push it away from the door while waving our arms to fend off the birds. We practically fell over each other as we stumbled in a panic down the stairs and finally tumbled out the side entrance leading to the street.

Jon ran into the bar and threw the key to the barkeep. I was too shaken to talk, so Jon called the owner and told him we weren't able to do the project because it was too large. The real reason was the terror we felt at the thought of getting close to that attic.

I never stepped foot in the building again. For a long time, I couldn't even go to that area of the quarter. If I got within three blocks of the building, I'd feel ready to vomit.

That was the first time I had ever seen any fear on Jon's face. Prior to that, Jon and I had witnessed a number of strange happenings at renovation projects. Several times, we heard noises coming from rooms but were unable to find any causes for them. Pictures would fall off walls and things would move for no apparent reason. Jon often teased me, "You know, Enoch, this is all your fault. The Devil is out to get you." I usually couldn't come up with any great response to his intended humor. Through nervous laughter, I'd say something stupid to deflect my fear. The truth was that I couldn't think straight because his comments hit too close to home.

The incidents were increasing, and I rarely told Jon about the things that happened when he wasn't present. We never talked about the attic or the fact that my name had been written on its walls before I'd been born. I could close my eyes and see the images in my mind as vividly as the day we set foot in that space. I imagined the symbols and names had surely been painted in blood that had faded with time. I didn't know for sure if it was blood, but there was no way I was going back to find out.

No matter how hard I tried, I could never shake the images from my mind. I couldn't dwell on them for too long or the fear of their reality would get to me. In a panic, I would imagine the ceiling was going to collapse on me, or maybe a dark force would choke me, or the walls would consume me. Unlike the nightmares of my childhood, I couldn't wake up from these events. As was the case with the biting coffin's spiked jaws of my childhood dream, I felt unseen, dark forces were waiting to impale me in their grip. I felt I would've gone insane if it hadn't been for Jon. His humor helped me through some of the most difficult times. I was able to keep my composure and look for rational explanations for all that happened.

Jon was a big guy with a well-formed, protruding belly. His round face, deep-set eyes, and curly, sandy hair made him look like the quintessential contractor type. Although he was rough around the edges, he was a decent guy. Jon loved practical jokes and delighted in creating mischief on the job. He often told stories that kept us entertained through the day.

One day at lunch, Jon asked Carl, a black friend and coworker, if he had any spare quarters. Carl pulled change out of his pocket and gave it to Jon. "Nope, you don't have any. Hey Enoch, do you have any spare quarters?" I reached into my bulging pocket and produced about six quarters along with various other coins and dumped the lot in Jon's hands. "Nope, nope, too bad you don't have one either!"

Curiosity got the best of Carl. He asked, "What are you looking for?"

Jon replied matter-of-factly, "The new Martin Luther King quarter. They're going to be worth a fortune! If you find one, hold onto it for dear life!"

Carl responded, "I haven't heard anything about it. Why are they going to be worth a fortune?"

Jon gave Carl a funny look and asked, "Man, don't you ever read the papers? Martin Luther King was one of the greatest men of all time, and they're honoring him! Unfortunately, there's been a huge recall on the first run of quarters from the mint."

Carl, obviously intrigued, asked, "Why were they recalled?"

Jon retorted. "His lips keep getting hung up in drink machines!"

Carl, after a puzzled moment, began to laugh so hard he fell out of his chair onto the floor. I was shocked at Jon's political incorrectness. I knew Jon loved Martin Luther King and often spoke of his inspiration. The joke was offensive in its very nature, but my black friend was rolling on the floor in that Popeye's restaurant, unable to catch his breath. Like a spider spinning a web, Jon had a way of pulling you into one of his stories. Because we knew his heart, we could take his outlandish jokes.

There was no sacred ground for Jon. Where most people would get into trouble, Jon had a way of being loved no matter how outrageous he was. He tested people in ways I would never have dared to. I often wondered how he got away with it.

He'd even pull jokes on people we worked for. One time, we were working in one room out of eyesight of the homeowner, and Jon slapped the wall and said in a very loud voice. "Oh no! This is not good! This is a big problem!" The homeowner came running in. "What happened? What is it? What's wrong?" Jon, looking at his finger, said, "Look at this! It's a hangnail!" After a minute, we all began to laugh, and the homeowner left the room laughing while commenting, "Jon, you're impossible!"

Even the hardest, obsessive-compulsive disorder types would give in to Jon. I never understood some people's hovering. They would get so caught up in the fear of our making a mistake that they would hover over us, making it difficult to work. It was as if Jon made the possibility of something going wrong seem humorous rather than disastrous. He had a way of putting people at ease.

Jon's humor made the strange incidents we endured more bearable. It brought a normalcy to life for me. When the grandfather clock on one job spun backward when I walked by, Jon laughed and said, "I think someone pulled the chains too tight." I needed to hear that even though it didn't make any sense.

Another time, the needle of a large compass on a coffee table began to follow me as I walked around the room. I wouldn't have noticed if Jon hadn't said something. He was on a ladder covering the chandelier with plastic when he looked down. "Enoch, stop moving!" I'd been moving chairs away from the wall in preparation for painting when his command stopped me in my tracks. I didn't know if I'd knocked something over or if I was about to trip on a wall cord or something.

Jon said, "Take three steps to the left." I obliged, not knowing what he was seeing that I couldn't see. "Check it out! The needle on that compass is following you around the room." That familiar eerie feeling began to give me a slow sense of panic that I could feel rising like a simmering pot getting ready to erupt into a boiling cauldron. I felt a familiar sense of dread getting stronger. Just as the panic began to choke my ability to breathe, Jon said, "It must be your magnetic personality!"

His perfectly timed humor distracted me from the feeling of being in a bad episode of *The Twilight Zone*. It didn't seem that anything bothered Jon; he just cruised through life in such a way that made me wonder how he could be so unaffected. He was a religious guy, and he used to invite me to go to church with him, but I always declined. I hadn't been to church since I'd left foster care years earlier. I had little use for religion; I'd had a bellyful of it as a kid. I believed in God at one time, but I'd since decided none of it made sense.

But some of the strange occurrences of late were giving me pause to reconsider my hard-nosed views. Jon saw many of the same things I saw, but he never was affected in the same way. Other than the time we spent in that satanist attic, I never saw him panicked over the weird stuff we saw. That was the only time I ever remember Jon cussing. One thing I appreciated about Jon was that he never pushed his views or religion on me. If there was a God, I figured He must have sent Jon to me to keep me from going insane.

CHAPTER 4

Strange Meetings

It was just another day. Our crew met for morning coffee and breakfast at McDonald's. Juan sat next to Carl, and Oscar and Jon sat with me on the other side. Juan's family was from Mexico, and Oscar's family was from Honduras. Jon loved to tease all of us by finding some part of our lives or backgrounds to center in on. If you were Mexican, he'd tell you a Mexican joke. If you were black, he'd come up with a black joke. He'd never tell a black joke to a white person. I don't think there was a racist bone in his body. Now that I think about it, I believe all his bones were funny bones.

"Juan, you know, I've never actually seen your green card. I read the INS agents are sweeping uptown construction sites today. Do you have a green card?" He barely looked up from his paper to see if he had evoked a response from Juan. Juan wasn't biting. He just chuckled and took a sip of coffee.

"I hope none of those Mexicans killed in that bad accident on Friday were any of your relatives."

That got Juan's attention.

"What accident? What are you talking about?"

"Hold your horses. Let me see." Jon looked intently at the morning paper. "Blah, blah, blah, blah, blah ... Okay, apparently, a whole carload of 'em hit the guardrail out past Bullard on I-10 where they're digging canal and drainage ditches. The workers saw the whole thing. The investigation backed up traffic for an hour!"

"Any names in the paper?"

"Wait a minute! I can't read that fast!" Jon began to read: "'Perhaps one of the oddest accidents on record' ... blah blah blah blah blah ... 'After a number of phone calls came into 911, police arrived on the scene approximately eight minutes after the first recorded phone call ... When the police arrived, there was no sign of the reported accident. According to Sgt. John Hemmiter of the New Orleans Police Department, only state road workers were at the scene of the alleged accident.'"

"What happened to the car?"

"I don't know yet! ... Wait ... let me see ... uh huh ... here it is ... 'According to eyewitness accounts, the speeding car had a front-tire blowout causing it to swerve into the guardrail ... blah blah ... causing it to flip over into a ditch near the work area.'"

"Well, what happened to the people and the car?"

"My God! Be patient, man ... Apparently, the police asked the same question ... Just a sec ..." Jon began reading again. "'Sgt. Hemmiter interviewed state workers,' blah blah blah ... The bulldozer operator, one Mr. Boudreaux Bellefontaine of Lockport, Louisiana, an eyewitness of the accident, gave the following account: 'A carload of Mexicans landed in the bayou dat I was fillin up, so I pushed dat mound of dirt right over the top o' dat car.' According to reports, Sgt. Hemmiter, shocked, quickly responded, 'You did what? My God, man! Were any of the victims alive?' Boudreaux responded, 'Who*eee* Cherie, a couple of dem said dey was alive, but chew know how dem Mexicans lie!'"

After a stunned moment of silence, it began to sink in. We'd been had. We all began to laugh; he'd done it to us again! We'd been lambs led to the slaughter by a superior intellect. There was no end to his mastery of his art or for that matter our gullibility. Juan laughed hardest of all.

I marveled at Jon's bold humor. I would never have dreamed of telling a Mexican joke to a Mexican or a black joke to a black guy for fear of offending them. Perhaps I was never comfortable with ethnic humor because of my own mysterious heritage. I winced at jokes targeting Jews because I might have been one. I thought jokes targeting blacks or Hispanics were bigoted, racist. Jon, however, had no such inhibitions; he was fearless, and I admired that about him. I felt safe around him. He was like Teflon; nothing seemed to stick to him. Every problem, every incident slid off him; it was as if no power in the universe could affect him. He told me his faith was what kept him centered. I didn't care what centered him; I was just glad he was. I was going to need him more than ever that day.

We arrived at the job around 8:00 a.m., ready for work. It was December, and we were feeling the effects of the first true cold snap to hit New Orleans that year. As we were unloading our tools, Juan noticed a blanket covering a human-sized lump across the street between two shotgun houses A man in a long, dark coat with a black hat reminiscent of the 1940s was walking by. The quivering lump had caught his attention about the same time it had caught ours. It was not unusual to see homeless people in New Orleans, but rarely did they get out to residential areas. I felt sorry for the plight of anyone who'd spent a night in this miserable cold. I ran across the street just slightly ahead of the guys to see if I could help. We saw a huddled figure with his back resting against the pier of the abandoned house. The thin arms wrapped around legs and the shape of the head suggested the chin was huddled in front of the knees.

"Hello? Are you okay?" Oscar called out. We received no response from under the shaking blanket. We saw the tattered cloth of a pant leg and an old, pink tennis shoe in an area the blanket didn't cover. In spite of the pants, the frail figure and the pink shoe suggested a woman was under the blanket.

We weren't sure what to do. I looked at the stranger, hoping he would be brave enough to pull the cover off to reveal the person under. The stranger seemed cold and aloof. He had a black goatee barely visible under his turned-up coat collar. I caught a glimpse of his dark eyes; they gave me a chill to match the morning air. He stood there saying nothing while he stared at the blanket. We felt as if we were invading the personal space of someone who had nothing in life but the shelter of a tattered, old blanket to call home.

"Hello! Can we help you? Ma'am? Sir? Hello! Are you in there? We just want to help."

No response.

The stranger stepped to the side of the blanket and placed his hand on the round shape that was obviously a head. All movement ceased under the blanket, and the stranger turned and walked back to the street.

We looked at each other. Carl remarked, "That was odd!" Oscar finally got up the nerve to pull the blanket off the rounded shape of the head. The face of an elderly woman came into view. Her wrinkled, worn face gave evidence of a hard if not horrifying life. A type of sadness was in her blank, staring eyes that seemed to focus on an invisible object. Oscar touched her shoulder. "Ma'am? Are you okay?"

As if pushed by an unseen force, the woman collapsed to her side, her eyes fixed.

"Whoa!" Oscar jumped back with the frightful realization that she was dead. "Holy crap! Call the police."

I stepped out from the breezeway to the street to catch the stranger as a witness. I intended to call him back to the scene to verify what had happened in case the police needed corroborating stories. He was gone. It had just been a moment. Where had he gone? I ran up the street past several shotguns, hesitating between each house to search for the stranger.

"Did any of you guys see where that man went?"

"No, boss. He was just there a second ago. I didn't see what he looked like."

"What did he look like, Enoch?" asked Carl.

"Did anybody see his face?" I replied in unbelief.

"No, boss. I couldn't take my eyes off the blanket lady."

"Okay, he was white ... kinda ... well, darkish ... sorta ... with a black goatee ... uh, with a black hat ... C'mon, guys. He was right here ... You didn't look at him?"

"Sorry, man, not really."

"Nope."

"Me neither."

We fanned out to look for the stranger while Jon called the authorities. We came back after ten minutes of searching. There had been no sign of the stranger. We were all commenting to each other on the strangeness of the encounter when two New Orleans police cars arrived, lights flashing. We recounted the whole scenario to the police as best we could. We were trying not to overwhelm them with everyone talking at the same time. One officer carefully examined the body, probing and lifting corners of the blanket with a pencil. The other officer took down our names and numbers and told us, "The procedure in a situation like this is to call the coroner's office. The coroner will come out and rule out foul play. Only the coroner is allowed to touch the body. If we need any further information, you'll be contacted."

After our interview, we were told to go across the street to our job while they cordoned off the area. I had never seen a dead body much less had someone die in my presence. None of us could work that day. We stayed close to the front windows, peering out most of the morning as we watched the coroner's car, ambulances, and police cars come and go. Our laughing, frivolous mood at breakfast had been replaced by somber reflection on the cruelty of life.

That day ended. In bed, I stared at the ceiling. I lay there, unable to get the vision of her lifeless, fixed eyes out of my mind. I woke up tired, not knowing when I had drifted off to sleep.

The restless days that followed caused me to reflect on life. It was hard and short and then over. I wondered if there might be a possibility of life after death. It was strange for me to even consider the possibility. I had stared death in the face for the first time, and it had unnerved me.

My second strange meeting happened just three days later. After work, I was heading toward the lakefront on Elysian Fields. I had just come to a stop at the light on Gentilly Boulevard. I stopped probably a little too close to the back of a large truck. A bicyclist whizzed by me on my right. He disappeared from my view as he shot forward on the right side of the truck in front of me. I thought for just a split second, *That dude's going way too fast into this corner.* No sooner had I had that thought than I heard a terrible screech and thud that shook my pickup. I couldn't see what had happened. I strained to see around the truck.

That second I noticed through my passenger-side glass a dark figure with hat and goatee walking toward the corner from the right. He disappeared from sight on the right side of the large truck in front of me just as the cyclist had. I was frozen for a moment. *He couldn't be the same man, could he?* I'd seen only the side of his face for a moment before the turned-up collar concealed it. I sat there for what felt like an eternity, wrestling with creepy fear. In reality, the time must have been just seconds. I jumped out of my truck and ran along the left side of the long truck, more anxious to solve the mystery than concern over the accident.

Other drivers were getting out of their vehicles. I whirled around the front of the truck. The shock of seeing the cyclist's crumpled, twisted body at the base of a telephone pole made me forget about the stranger. It was obvious the cyclist had been killed on contact. I averted my gaze from the horror and searched for the stranger. He wasn't there. He'd disappeared again with no sign of ever having been there. I asked the truck driver if he'd seen the man in the hat and long overcoat. He said that the accident had happened right in front of him but that he hadn't seen anyone with that description.

For the second time in three days I had seen death up close. It wasn't the same as seeing death in the movies. I could watch movies all day long and never be affected. This was different. There was no cold detachment to hide in. The vivid picture in my mind of a real person being horribly broken and the mangled bicycle haunted my thoughts.

Had he been a father, a husband? Had he had great dreams and aspirations? I felt a deep sorrow at the loss of life, the kind of sorrow that penetrates your very soul. I didn't know either of the victims, but I still felt a connection to them. It was as if in a larger sense we're all in this together. We were all somehow connected by the fact we would all meet the same fate in one way or another. One day, we would all meet the grim reaper.

The following week, I had appointments for estimates in Chalmette and Algiers. After my first appointment in Chalmette, I took the ferry boat at the end of Paris Road. I enjoyed the slow ride and the peace of the rolling waters of the Mississippi. I sat in my truck, enjoying a slightly warmer day, as the worst of the cold snap was letting up. My window was cracked slightly as we pulled away from the dock. The swoosh of the water and the hum of the engines on the ferry made me feel I could nap all day. I closed my eyes, enjoying the moment. After a minute or two, I half-heartedly opened my eyes. I noticed a man in a long, dark coat standing at the railing. I wasn't looking at him directly; I sort of noticed him out of the corner of my eye. My thoughts drifted to the oddity of a heavy coat in relatively warm weather. I suddenly felt that sick feeling and snapped to attention to look directly at him. *Oh my gosh! It's him! Or at least I think it's him.* My thoughts were racing. His back was to me, but the hat, black coat, and turned-up collar were unmistakable. In spite of my fear, I was determined to find out who he was. This time, he was not going to get away. I refused to take my eyes off him while I fumbled for the door handle. I dared not even blink in case he was an apparition. I slowly got out of the truck and made my way to him.

"Excuse me, sir, can I talk to you?"

He stood there. No response.

I made my way a little closer and slightly to the side, hoping to catch a glimpse of his face. "Sir, can I talk to you?"

Still no response.

I took two more steps to the side and saw the goatee. A shot of adrenaline made me feel shaky. My knees almost buckled as he finally spoke while staring off to the other side. "What do you want to talk about?"

"Who are you?"

"It's not important."

"Yes it is! You just took off when that lady died and left us to explain what happened to the police."

He said nothing.

"Why did you leave?"

"There was no reason for me to stay."

"What's your name?"

"I've had many names."

"What is that supposed to mean? Hey, were you on Elysian Fields Boulevard last week?"

"Why do you want to know?"

"I saw you there at the cyclist's accident!"

"I have no power but what is given to me. You are the one who got away, but the law is absolute. You can't escape me forever. I will come for you." He turned. He looked at me. For a moment, his dark eyes seemed to turn completely black.

"You ... What? ... I ... you ... What did you say? What are you talking about?"

Just then, a jolt nearly knocked me off my feet. The ferry had hard-landed at the dock. The ramps were lowering. Horns began to honk in preparation for disembarkation. I ran back to my truck and jumped in. People hated stragglers who held up disembarking. I looked back to find what car the stranger had gone to. I didn't see where he had gone. The engines were running, and the attendants were waving us off, but no one was moving. Horns started beeping. Several attendants ran up to the front and began pushing one of the cars to the side. Cars started moving around the stalled vehicle. It was finally my turn, and I was glad to get off the ferry. I slowly drove my truck around the stalled car and the crowd of attendants when I heard one of them through my cracked window. "The man's dead! It must have been a heart attack."

I looked into the car and saw a slumped, white-haired figure in the driver's seat. I almost hit the guardrail. The black-coated man was creepy for sure. I looked at all the cars that got off but never saw him in any of them. I thought my mind was playing tricks on me. I had always considered myself a logical guy with feet planted firmly in reality. There had to be a logical explanation for all the bizarre things that had been happening to me. I was just a regular guy, a carpenter; what had I done to deserve all this?

The next day, I met Jon and the crew at the job and told them about my encounter with the black-coated weirdo. Jon and the others listened intently. When I told them about the dead man, Carl jumped up and said, "You're scaring me, man!" The others laughed and called him a wimp.

Jon didn't seem to be himself the rest of that day. He was more intense and serious in demeanor. He told us that he had made a decision and that he needed to talk to us. We all calmed down and gave him our full attention.

"Guys, we've worked together for quite some time, and I've had a great time with you. I find myself at a crossroads in life, and I've had to make some decisions. I've decided to enroll at the Baptist Seminary."

We all looked at each other, looked at Jon, and started to laugh.

"What's so funny?"

The idea of the commensurate jokester, the devilish prankster, the king of comedy becoming a preacher was the most absurd thing we'd ever heard. We waited impatiently for the punch line. We laughed all the harder knowing we were being set up. Juan responded, "Okay, okay, I'll bite," barely able to contain his laughter.

Carl chimed in, "Do they let heathens into that place?"

Oscar added, "You already know how to fleece the sheep. Ha, ha, ha!" One after the other, they threw out one-liners like skilled boxers jabbing their prey.

"Do you have to supply your own snakes, or do they give them to you? Ha, ha, ha!"

"You'll be the best snake charmer ever! Hee, hee, hee!"

"Can I help take up the offering? Ha, ha!"

"Hallelujah, sister!" HA, HA!"

"Amen! Preach it, brother! HA, HA, HA!"

We all began to settle down so we could hear the punch line. Jon sat there, looking at us straight faced. We were almost giddy with anticipation. Carl spoke as the rest of us chuckled, trying to think of snappy comebacks. "Come on, come on, what's the catch?"

"No catch! I'm serious!"

More thunderous laughing. "You're good, really good!" Juan's declaration caused us all to ponder the inevitable punch line. "Weeeellllllllll?"

"Well what? I've met with the registrar, and my church and pastor have given me recommendations. I'll be starting summer classes in June."

"You're serious?" It suddenly began to dawn on us that he was for real, that there was no joke. "I don't understand, Jon. Why do you want to be a preacher?" I was confused. We had a great team, and we were making good money. "Why would anyone want to be around a bunch of religious people?"

"It has nothing to do with religion or religious people. I've wrestled with this calling for a long time. I feel called of God to serve Him."

"I know you go to church, Jon, but you're not religious. You're just like us!"

As the words rolled off my lips, I knew that wasn't true. Jon never went out drinking with us. As I thought about it, I realized I'd never heard him cuss other than when those pigeons had flown at us. It's funny that I'd never noticed it before. Even when he hit his thumb with a hammer, he never cussed; the rest of us cussed like drunken sailors and never thought a thing about it. Jon would stand looking at us with a Cheshire cat grin. I always thought of it as his silent approval of our ranting. In that moment, I realized it was not approval but acceptance of who we were. He'd never condemned me or made me feel like a great sinner. He'd been a friend to me in more ways than I had recognized.

I realized he had never told an off-color joke. Even when he told his ethnic jokes, it was always in the presence of the intended ethnic victim. It was hard to explain. It was as if he were a member of that ethnic group or race and was poking fun at himself. His deep empathy and love for everybody made him the furthest thing from a racist. We were a mixed bag of Mexican, Black, Honduran, white, and possibly Jewish or Semitic. He never condemned us or made us feel we were less than him.

"Enoch, God loves us all the same. Each one of us is special to Him. You're right that I'm just like you in that I hurt, bleed, and have great ups and great downs like everyone else. The only difference is that I trust Him even though His ways don't always make sense to me. I believe in Him and His ways."

We all tried to absorb what he said. I was a little angry. God, if He was there, had taken away my family, my childhood, and now maybe my best friend. I thought the last thing Jon needed was to have a bunch of religious types messing with his head. I had encountered people from that seminary on the streets of the French Quarter. I listened a few times to their ranting about repenting and burning in hell and all that stuff, but I never felt comfortable enough to stick around. I thought they were weird, strange, odd. I thought it even more odd that Jon would find comfort around that bunch.

I started drinking a little more than usual over the next few weeks. Things were going to change in the summer, and I didn't like change. Jon had been what had kept me going through all the weirdness of my life. I told myself that it would be okay, that Jon was just going to be part time for a while. Maybe this was just a passing phase he had to go through.

It was a Thursday night. I was sitting in a bar. My usual routine was to go to various bars in the evenings and drink beer until it was time to go home. I went for the music and friends. Most of the people in the bars were more like well-known acquaintances than friends. We saw each other so often that it felt like friendship. We had a common purpose—to drink, laugh, dance, and have companionship in a lonely world.

It's odd that I never allowed any women into my life on any sustained basis. I was always nervous and uncomfortable that they might discover the bizarre happenings that plagued my life. It didn't seem fair to thrust all that on innocent people who had no part in my burden and didn't deserve to share it. The whole bar scene was a façade, but it filled my time and kept my mind on frivolous things. Even though Jon had never sat and drank with me, I felt he was somehow always with me. His humorous jokes would come back to my mind when things got too hairy, and my heaviness would lift almost immediately.

As I left the bar to walk up Bourbon Street, I passed a homeless person with a hat on the ground and a small, torn cardboard sign that read, "Please help!" My thoughts raced back to the tragedy of the poor, homeless woman who had died in our presence. I felt the sorrow even through my beer buzz and reached for my wallet. I studied the unfortunate soul's unshaven, pale, drawn face. He sat on the hard sidewalk, seemingly too embarrassed to look up. His overcoat had several holes, and his mismatched socks puddled on his oversized brown shoes, revealing a little skin under the soiled, blue pants. His long, salt-and-pepper hair had thinned enough that I could see his scalp. The indented ring in his hair suggested he usually wore the hat that doubled as an offering basket. I wondered how a person could ever come to that state of being. I'd never given people like him a second thought; I was hardened to their plights in times past, thinking they somehow deserved what they had gotten. I thought they were lazy or unwilling to work.

I'd developed a bad attitude toward vagrants as a result of several attempts to help them. People often stood at interstate ramps with signs that read, "Will work for food." One day, I waited for the light to change at an exit ramp when one approached my truck. "Hey, pal, can you spare a little change?" I thought I'd test his need. "Jump in the truck and I'll give you some work and feed you." His quick response was, "No thanks. I just need a little cash to help me out." I tried my new approach several more times but always with the same result. I felt it was all a con; the bums didn't want to work at all. I thought they were all drug addicts or winos who were looking for their next fix or drink. I used to tease my friends that I had bought a "Will Work For Food" franchise. I'd go into long explanations of the intricacies of negotiations on which territories and ramps were open for this exciting, new, lucrative field.

All the laughing at their expense somehow felt cruel to me in the light of the death of that cold, lonely, homeless woman. Once, I had been stranded in the cold on a highway for just a few hours and was miserable. I couldn't imagine what it would be like to freeze to death, no roof over your head or bed to sleep in. To die with no one in the world to mourn your passing.

I pulled a twenty out and dropped it in his hat. I turned.

"Thank you, Enoch! I will soon visit you!"

"What did you say? Do you know me?" I spun to see who had spoken. The man was looking at the sidewalk. I glanced around for anyone else who could have spoken, but no one was within a block of us.

"Excuse me, what did you say? Do you know me?"

The man looked up. "What?"

"I asked, do you know me? How do you know my name?"

"No ... I don't know you ... I didn't say anything!"

He grabbed his hat and jammed it on his head, twenty and all, and got up. "Leave me alone, mister. I ain't done nothin'."

He walked slowly away. I sobered up almost immediately, trying to focus on what had just happened. *Am I hearing things?* My thoughts raced to the many strange occurrences in my life. *What's wrong with you Enoch? Jeez, now I'm talking to myself!* I started to chuckle as I remembered something someone said to me once. "You're not nuts if you talk to yourself as long as you don't start answering yourself!" Once again, a moment of humor had helped me cope with another odd moment. I wondered if we were God's big joke; maybe we made Him laugh with all our craziness. I wondered if God had a sense of humor. If He did, maybe He wasn't so bad after all. If there was a God, I could only hope He had a sense of humor.

I had to be the biggest joke of all to God. Maybe He was up there somewhere having a great time while He watched me squirm. It was all very funny to Him, I was sure. I imagined a heavenly scene in which the angels asked permission to come up with some new way of harassing me. One would suggest I needed a good scare, so another would suggest a chimney should fall on my head. At the last minute, another angel would blow my plywood around to save me. After all, why ruin a perfectly good patsy? Don't kill off the little Jewish kid; he's way too much fun. I could see the angels walking off, laughing about what new mischief they could cause the next day. That was my view of God. Is it any wonder I was agnostic?

I guess I struggled with the same questions everybody did. If God was so good, then why ...? You just had to fill in the blank. God was all about regulations and laws and fear. I wondered how anyone could truly be religious. I couldn't believe Jon wanted to follow rules and regulations of religion. He was too smart to buy into all that, but he seemed to believe in his faith deeply. I didn't understand all that faith stuff. How can you have faith in something with no evidence? I could trust in what I could see, but how could I trust in what I couldn't see? You might as well believe in fairies or the Jolly Green Giant. At least they had cartoons you could see.

Jon had told me he would pray for me and ask God to limit the bizarre stuff happening around me. I figured that couldn't hurt, and I always appreciated his heart no matter how misguided he was.

CHAPTER 5

Who Am I?

It was April 1997, and the air was full of spring smells and wonderful cool breezes that caressed the face. I loved that time of year. The cold was over but the heat of summer hadn't arrived. I felt good for a change, not having experienced any strange happenings for some months. Maybe the weird stuff was a thing of the past. I wasn't having troubling dreams, nothing was moving on its own, clocks and compasses were behaving normally, and I had a sense of well-being. It was odd for me to feel that way. It was as if all the strangeness was behind me. Maybe I could get on with a normal life.

I thought maybe I could settle down and raise a family. I was getting tired of apartment living and dreamed of having my own place. I never needed much in the way of things besides a few tools, a truck, and basic furnishings. Even the memories of the attic incident were fading. Not that they were *not* still vivid if I thought about them; it was just that I chose not to think about them. I tried to believe it was like a dream ... not real ... just a weird sort of misinterpreted event, something that could have been logically interpreted in several ways. After all, it made sense that the armoire legs had broken as a result of the door damaging them. Maybe it wasn't an altar but just an old coffee table with a few oddities on it. I could find logical reasons and other possible interpretations of the scene—no mystery, nothing supernatural to be concerned with.

I could explain it all, except for my name on the wall. That was a problem. Even though the first word was incomplete, the second two were too coincidental. E ... ch Kingu Galah was as vivid as ever. I had often carefully framed the first word spacing in my mind. There was just the right spacing for two letters. Eltch, Esach, Etich, Eboch, Ealch ... I had sat many an hour trying to find alternative words to fit the missing part of that name. Kingu Galah was unmistakable. I could find no rational explanation for the spelling of my second and last name. It was like a mystery I had to resolve if I were ever to live a normal life. Kingu. Very strange. I was mad at the police or whomever had left me with the stupid name. Who just accepts a note left on a blanket? Galah was okay, I guess, though no last name with that spelling ever appeared in any phone book. I hated my name, but I'd been branded with it just the same. Why had my name been written on a wall long before I'd been born? That's it! My mother must have known Mr. Bellisaire's family. Maybe I had overlooked the obvious. Maybe I was named after the person whose name was on that wall.

It was the eureka moment I'd long waited for. I sat in my truck, basking in my newfound knowledge. The mystery was solved; logic has prevailed. If I could solve this, I could solve all the other things as well. A huge weight had been lifted off me. Things were going to get better; I was going to be just fine. All I needed to do was verify my hypothesis.

I turned my thoughts to the possibility that Mr. Bellisaire could be connected to my family in some way. I was trying not to think about the implications of crazy cultists being in my family; religious people were bad enough, but satanists had to be a whole lot worse. What people in their right minds would want to worship the Devil if there even was one? The thought struck me, *What if my people are wackos?* That was sobering. I wasn't sure if it was a good idea to investigate, but I had to know in spite of what I might find.

I procrastinated for several weeks about following through with my investigation. I'd found Bellisaire's phone number but hadn't worked up the courage to call. I told myself I just didn't have the time. In truth, I kept trying to find courage in a bottle in the company of my drinking buddies.

Damon Blackstone, one such buddy, was an interesting character. He wore all black before Goth was the style. In acknowledgement of his wardrobe, I called him "Johnny Cash" or "Cash." Cash had ten to fifteen chains around his neck and rings on every finger, even his thumbs. His long, jet-black hair and silver-tipped cowboy boots made him look like a confused combination of horror and western. I liked him, though, because I could tell him anything over a glass of beer and he'd listen. He'd always say, "I believe you, man." It didn't matter how outlandish my story was; I could tell Damon about things I could never tell anyone else.

I'd call him once in a while, but he seemed to always show up at the same bars I did. Like circuit riders traveling from place to place, we'd land for a while and visit with friends and move on. Like a scene from *Cheers,* everybody knew your names. We weren't known by our real names of course but by the nicknames the patrons gave us. Damon was Cash, (I'd given him that!), and I was Hammer, probably because I was a carpenter. There were also Chuckles, Skinny, and Two Shoes; someone had just started calling him Two Shoes, and it had stuck.

The names were as endless as the characters themselves. The tourists gave us endless entertainment. They thought they could do anything they wanted because of the reputation of The Big Easy. They were the drunk ones; the locals knew better. We'd jokingly place bets on how long it would take for an obnoxious or foolish drunk to get snatched by the cops. It gave us endless hours of entertainment watching the antics of the tourists. We tolerated them for the most part unless they took all the seats. I'd feel indignant if I didn't have a seat in any of my bars!

I spotted Damon in one of my normal haunts. "Hey Cash! How you doing?" "Good, Hammer, how 'bout you?" It was our usual greeting. I took a seat next to him and began to talk about my plight. "Cash, do you remember me telling you about the attic above that gay bar on North Rampart? I told you about the weird stuff in the attic and what looked like my name, right?"

"Yeah, I remember. Pretty bizarre."

"Well, I think I figured something out."

"What's that?"

"I think I might be related to the owners of that property, or at least maybe they know my people."

"How do you figure that?"

"I don't think it was coincidence that my name was on that wall."

"How did it get there then?"

"I think I must have been named after the person whose name is on that wall. It could be a lead to my family."

"That sounds logical. I think you should check it out."

"Thanks, Cash. By the way, I appreciate that you never called me nuts."

"Are you kidding me, Hammer? I live in the bizarre! Look at the way I dress!"

We both laughed. I genuinely liked his willingness to poke fun at himself.

"Nothing happens by accident," he said. "Someday I'll tell you some of the bizarre stuff I've seen that'll make you feel completely normal. You know we're all just pawns in a game of fate and we have no say in the outcome. It was fate that caused us to meet, and its fate that's causing me to drink this beer! I don't have any say in it."

I laughed as he turned up his glass.

"Cash, I'm going to do it. I'm going to call Bellisaire. Hey, I want to hear about your weird stuff sometime. It'll definitely make me feel better."

The next day was Saturday, and I slept in, recovering from the night before. After some coffee and a fruit bar, I was awake enough to make the call. I figured I had nothing to lose. I dialed the number. "Hello, Mr. Bellisaire?"

"Yes, this is Mr. Bellisaire. Who's this?"

"This is Enoch Galah, the contractor who looked at your property in November a few years ago. I'm sorry to bother you, sir, but I need to ask you a question about something I saw in your attic."

"In my attic? All that work was finished a long time ago, son. I had another contractor take care of it."

"Yes sir, I understand, but that's not why I'm calling. Sir, I was orphaned as a baby and left on the steps of Cabrini High School, and my name was pinned to a blanket."

"You know, son, I think I remember that. That was back in the fifties. It was in the papers. Are you saying you were that baby?"

"Yes sir, I am. My question has to do with something I saw in your attic. It could give me a clue as to who my real family is. This is going to sound weird, sir, but when we were looking for leaks in the attic, we saw a lot of strange writings on the walls, real cryptic stuff. My name was written on the wall, and I wondered if you knew anyone with my name."

"You say your name was written on the wall?"

"Yes sir. It's the first clue I've ever seen that could point me to my real family, my real mother."

"I see, son. The construction company told me about the birds. I can understand why you didn't want to take that job. They told me there was a lot of graffiti on the walls. I had them clean all that crap out of there. It was probably just a coincidence."

"I thought the same thing except that my name is too unique for it to just be coincidence."

"Tell me your name again, son."

"My full name is Enoch Kingu Galah!"

"Let's see ... Gala ... Gala. I think I've heard that name before. Or maybe I'm thinking of a party event or something."

"No sir, Galah with an *h*, not *gala* like a party, It's spelled g-a-l-a-h."

"Galah. That's an odd spelling, son. Let me see ... No ... No, I don't believe I've ever heard that name. Sorry I can't help you."

"I'm sorry to take your time, sir, but this is real important to me. I'm just trying to find my family."

"I understand, son, but I just don't have any answers for you."

"Could I just ask you one last question?"

"Okay, but be quick, son. I'm meeting an old friend for lunch. I have few friends left, and at my age, I can't waste time."

"Is it possible someone from your family might know my name?"

"I doubt it, son. My great-great-granddaddy lived in that space. He was a bit of an eccentric nut from what I understand. He died when I was a baby. My granddaddy, my daddy, and me were all only children. I never grew up having any cousins or aunts and uncles from my father's or my mother's side of the family. Come to think of it, my grandmother was an only child too. Well anyway, my daddy said his parents never allowed him to go around his crazy grandfather. My great-great-grandmother died in that house under unusual circumstances. Some thought the old coot killed his wife, but it could never be proven. After his mother died, my granddaddy ran away from that house and never went back. My daddy inherited the property but never set foot in it because he said it was haunted. I don't know why I'm telling you all this, son.

"Anyway, all those generations have long been dead. Even my daddy has been dead for close to twenty years. You and your momma, whoever she is, would be way too young to have any connection to my great-great-grandfather. I'm eighty-four, and I'm not aware of anyone ever going into the attic before you and your partner did. I doubt anyone had been in there for seventy years or better. I don't know why your name would be on the wall, son, but I wish you the best of luck. I hope you find what you're looking for."

After the call, I felt no closer to solving the mystery of my life. Instead of answers, I was left with more questions. Another dead end! The only lead I had turned out to be a dud. I had a new found desire to find out who I was.

I thought about all sorts of ways to try to find out who I was and where I was from. I hired detective agencies three times but to no avail.

I even considered psychics or mediums. I never actually consulted one because Jon said it was an abomination to God to talk to people like that. I didn't believe in that stuff anyway, but when you're desperate, you'll consider anything no matter how bizarre. I had convinced myself that there was no such thing as the supernatural. Religion and the supernatural were merely the fears and imaginations of needy people.

My skepticism was going to be dealt a big blow in the days ahead. I had to hold on to the rational world as my anchor. The thought that there was any supernatural element in that attic was too frightening to consider. The mere thought that the Devil was real and had followers was very disquieting. The idea of going down that road would give me a panic attack. It was safer and more peaceful to search for reason and logic than consider the possibility of something else. The idea that a devil worshipper had looked into the future and had put a curse on me was ridiculous, but I had no answer to any of it any way you cut it.

Damon was sympathetic to my frustration. He told me about an old woman who could help me. He was very vague about her credentials. He just smiled and said she was an expert in hidden mysteries. "I'll set up a meeting next Saturday at her place. She's very hard to get in to see." I wondered about what it was going to cost. "Cash, I've spent a fortune on private eyes. I've had it with all of them! They're all worthless!" Damon surprised me. "There's no cost to you. I'm covering this." Wow! I hadn't expected that. Ol' Cash was a great drinking buddy, but I'd never done anything with him outside a bar. Truth is, I couldn't see myself hanging out with him in any context that didn't involve drinking. A bar was a safe place to mingle with characters you'd never be friends with outside a bar. Cash was not the kind of guy you would take home to meet your family if you had one. I mean, really—how do you introduce your everyday friends to a character like Damon? With his strange, black clothes, silver chains, rings, and cowboy boots, he was a sight to behold. In the bar, you were all the same—just sojourners in the journey of life enjoying a cold beer and a little company along the way. I had to think carefully about if I wanted to be with him in another venue, but I wanted answers about my family. My need to know outweighed my discomfort. I agreed.

But I wondered about Damon's motives. What was he after? You don't just do that for someone you barely know. I didn't even know this man, but I'd told him things I'd never told another living soul. In the bar, it was fine, but outside, I was uncomfortable with gaining any intimate knowledge of my life. His strange appearance spoke of an eccentric personality. He was definitely a character who fit into New Orleans's bizarre elite.

"Cash, why do you want to do this for me?"

"Hammer, this woman is an associate of mine. I've told her about you. She's anxious to meet you. Once you meet her, you'll understand."

"I can't have you paying someone to help me. That wouldn't be right, as much as I appreciate it."

"Chill, dude. She isn't charging me a thing. I told you she was an associate of mine. I'm just covering the ride to her place."

"An associate, huh? I don't think you ever told me what you do."

"I'm a recruiter of sorts."

"Certainly not for the military, unless they've relaxed their dress code."

"Ha! Nope. My boss looks for specialized talent in a number of fields all over the world. He sends me in ahead of an offer to cultivate a relationship with the talent. This lady was recruited by my boss. She's an asset of the organization. She works for us."

"Sounds interesting. It must be day work because you're always in the bar at night. Do you get good pay?"

"The best! I have a life of leisure when I'm not working. If my boss wasn't so demanding, I could retire right now. The benefits are out of this world."

"Retire! You can't be more than thirty-five!"

"Wrong. I'm forty-seven. Another benefit of working for my boss."

I pondered the legitimacy of his statement. I'd thought he was younger than me. I was thirty-eight and was already seeing a lot of gray on my head. It was hard to know if what he was saying was true. I wondered if he was pulling my leg. How can working for someone make you look younger? I'd never send this guy to represent my company. I had been to a seminar one time at which a corporate recruiter spoke. He was dressed in a suit and tie and was completely professional in every aspect. Cash was nothing like him; Cash would scare any normal person.

"Hammer, I'll pick you up at your place on Saturday morning."

"You don't know where I live."

"I know where you live."

"I've never told you where I live."

"It's my job to know things like that."

"But I just moved two weeks ago to a townhouse near UNO. Nobody, not even my buddy Jon, knows where I live."

"I know where you live. I'll pick you up at ten Saturday morning."

I didn't go to any bars that week. I still had some unpacking to do. I was curious if Cash was going to show up. I purposely didn't tell him where I lived. I was hoping he was full of crap.

When Saturday rolled around, I got up about nine, made a pot of coffee, and jumped into the shower while it was brewing. I wondered if he was going to come or if I was getting ready for no reason.

I was dressed and ready by 9:15. I paced by the front window, wishing time would hurry up. It was all very mysterious, but I didn't care. I was looking for answers. I alternated between the couch and chair and repeatedly picked up the paper. I'd read a sentence or two and look out the window. At one point, I read an entire column and realized I didn't have a clue as to what I'd just read.

Time just dragged on until it was finally 9:59. I knew it! He wasn't coming! At 10:00 sharp, a car pulled into my driveway. It appeared to be a dark-gray or black car that looked brand new. It had one of those grilles that made it look like a Rolls Royce. The door opened, and Cash emerged. His silver-toed boots glistened in the morning sun. I ran to the door and rushed out, not wanting him to see my sparsely furnished townhouse. I felt a newfound respect for this black-clad figure. He must have something going on to drive a car like that. I bounded out the door and told him to get back in his car. I ran around to the passenger side and opened the door.

"You ready, Hammer?"

"I'm ready!"

I looked around the car. I'd never before seen a car like his let alone sat in one. The soft, white leather was outlined with dark-gray cording that matched the carpet. The beautiful wood on the dash continued in the center console, and the passenger seat had an armrest on the left. I'd never experienced such luxury.

"What kind of car is this?"

"It's a Bentley Turbo R. Do you like it?"

"This is unbelievable! I'm gonna have to start calling you Mr. Blackstone."

"Ha, ha! Cash is just fine!"

"Yeah, but I didn't know you had cash."

"All part of the perks of the job."

"I've known you for over a year and never knew anything about all this. Why didn't you ever tell me you were a bigwig?"

"I'm just a recruiter. I got this New Orleans assignment over a year ago."

"That's about the time I met you. Who are you recruiting?"

"I can't tell you that, but he's a big fish."

"You mean you've been trying to recruit this guy for a year and a half? Did he reject your offer?"

"No. We just haven't made him an offer yet."

"Hold the bus, Gus. That doesn't make any sense! Why would you spend all this time and money and not make the guy an offer?"

"It doesn't work that way, Hammer. The game changers take time and require finesse. You can't rush these things."

We pulled into a parking garage in the quarter, and Cash and I got out. I kept looking back at the car as if it were going to disappear. It was a surreal experience. It made me feel important somehow.

As I walked with Cash, I wondered why this guy had taken an interest in me. I was just a nobody, and he was used to dealing with people way above my pay grade. You certainly can't own a car like that and be a nobody. I'd always thought Cash was an embarrassment, but I felt proud to be walking with him.

We traveled up Bourbon to a shop area and entered one. I saw the usual voodoo paraphernalia and various porcelain masks. The shop also sold crystals, posters, books, and all the normal tourist crap you could find in a hundred shops in the quarter.

"Wait here. I'm going to see if it's okay to go up."

Damon disappeared down a hallway behind some old beads from the seventies. I looked at some of the spines of the books on the shelves. Some were about the history of New Orleans and old plantation homes, and I saw a voodoo cookbook. I had to laugh at that. I mean, really! Zombies eat only brains, right? Maybe there were recipes for fried brains, or maybe sautéed brains, brains étouffée, cream of brain soup, or maybe brains jambalaya. I chuckled at the thought of gourmet zombies and thought it would make a funny spoof on the typical zombie movie.

"She's ready to see you, Hammer."

The words distracted me from my musings. "Okay, let's go."

We went down the narrow hallway and climbed dimly lit stairs. We walked toward the front of the building through another hall that was a little larger and had some light coming in from a window at the front. We went through an old door into a very dark, dingy apartment that reminded me of a shotgun house. The living room was at the front, and you had to pass through a bedroom to get to the kitchen. I followed Cash toward the kitchen. This dingy old place didn't jibe with the thought of a high-powered asset of some huge corporation. If she was so important, why did she live in such a dump? We walked through a door. There she was.

She looked to be in her eighties or even older. She was black. Her grayish hair stuck out from under a patterned red and white scarf. Her eyes were completely white. She was blind. Her gums were receding, but it looked like she had all her teeth. She was thin; her clothes sagged on her body. Her old dress and sweater looked as though they were worn every day for years. This woman couldn't be any help to me unless she knew Bellisaire's great-great-grandfather.

"Miss Sadie, this is Hammer," Damon said. "I'm going to leave you two to talk while I go up front. Hammer, come and get me when you're done."

"Hello, young man. Would you like a cup of coffee?"

"No ma'am, I ... I'm not sure why Damon brought me here."

"I asked him to." She was up, pouring herself a cup of coffee as though she weren't blind.

"Cash ... I mean Damon, said he told you all about me."

"Not really, young man, I told him all about you."

"You told him all about me? Do you know who I am?"

"Of course I do, dear boy." Her voice was matter of fact, almost indignant.

"How do you know me?" I wondered if she knew Bellisaire.

"I saw you in the basket under the arch."

"Were you at the school, ma'am? Did you know my mother? Did you see her? I ... I mean ... before you were blind?"

"Boy, what are you talking about? I've been blind since birth! I don't mean I saw you with my eyes. I saw you in my mind. I've been following you your whole life, boy. Like when Mrs. Blackburn made you stand with your nose on the wall because you didn't pass the peas."

I felt a shot of adrenaline, and fear, go through me like a freight train. My head started spinning with the full weight of all the unexplained incidents of my life. I couldn't breathe. *She couldn't know that!* I wanted to run away, but I was frozen.

"I know you're afraid, boy, but it's okay. Are you sure you don't want a nice cup of coffee? It'll make you feel better."

"N ... no, ma'am. I ... I ..." I could hear my heart pounding as though my ears had become stethoscopes. The room was closing in around me. All my logic was failing me. *How could she know about an incident from my childhood? This is impossible! I believe in science and logic. How could this be happening?*

"Relax, boy. Now take a deep breath and I'll explain. Don't fret, child. I won't bite your head off over a piece of cheese."

I was unable to talk, but the thought of an explanation gave me just enough hope to hold on to reality. Maybe she knew Mrs. Blackburn or the Wellingtons. Maybe the kids had told the priest, and he'd told the Wellingtons, and the Wellingtons had told this woman. I started to breathe a little easier. There might be an explanation to all this yet.

"Y ... Y ... Yes ma'am," was the only response I could muster.

"You see, boy, I'm a seer. That's my special talent ... It's what I do. It's why the boss recruited me. Do you understand?" She spoke slowly and deliberately in a calm, reassuring voice.

"N ... No ma'am."

"Alright, son. Let me explain it another way. You see, we're all interconnected with each other. Nothing happens by accident. You were found on the seventh hour of the seventh day of the seventh month. That was not a coincidence. It's like threads running through time and space and connecting each person and event to all others. I can feel the vibrations of those threads and interpret them. That's how I see things in my mind. Do you understand now, son?"

"I just came to find out about my family. I don't understand any of this."

"That's alright. In time, you will understand. You will know your purpose and why you were put on earth. You are going to have to choose which side you're on, where your loyalties lie, you know, who you believe. You got to choose, son. That's called free will."

"Ma'am, I don't know how you know this stuff about me, and I don't understand what you're talking about. I just want to know where I come from."

"You're an old soul, boy. You have been alive longer than me. Do you know what that means?"

"No ma'am."

"It means you're a paradox. You should be dead but you're alive. You can't be alive, but you are. It's like the laws of the universe have been suspended. It's like being eternal and temporal at the same time. It doesn't fit. It's an anomaly, and yet here you are. Do you know what a paradox is, son?"

"I think it means when two things are true but are contradictory. Logic can't reconcile the contradiction. Is that right, ma'am?"

"That's right, son. *You* are the paradox. You shouldn't be, yet here you are. That's why clocks, lightbulbs, and compasses sometimes go haywire when you're around. You throw things out of balance."

I'd wondered how many of my stories Cash had told the old woman. I'd never told him about the compass or the clock or for that matter anything about my childhood. Where had she gotten her information?

"Child, there was a special event in the heavens on your birthday in 1959. Venus occulted the star Regulus."

"What, ma'am? I don't believe in all that occult stuff!"

"No child! That just means to overshadow or to obscure, you know, like an eclipse."

"I don't know what that means, ma'am. What does that have to do with me?"

"That was the dawn of the age of the female, son. Don't you see? Venus overshadowed the brightest stars in Leo the lion. The brightest of Leo was overshadowed by the goddess of sensuality. Nothing happens by accident, boy. It began the time when the female will overshadow the male. Her feminine wiles will control the stronger. The female will be empowered in this age like never before. It's all a part of the plan. Women will become strong like men, and men will become weak like women. It's a role reversal, son. It will be a time of great confusion for the male. Men will prefer men and women will prefer women. Man won't know who he is or what he's supposed to do. Many will become effeminate. Others will know they must lead but will forget how. Women will be exalted and preferred above men, and they will be portrayed as stronger and smarter than men. Women will lose all modesty, and men will lust after them with great carnal desire. This is important, son, so listen up! It means it all has to change to usher in the great day, the end of the world."

"What? The end of the world? What the heck does that mean? Lady, I don't know anything about all that. I just want to find my *family!* Do you or do you not know anything about my family? That's all I want to know."

"I understand, son. My master knew your father, boy."

"My father? Who is he? Why did he abandon me? Please ... Please ... I ... I just want to know."

"Slow down, son. Your daddy didn't abandon you. You were taken away."

"What? Who took me away? Why? Where's my father?"

"I didn't want to tell you this, son, but it was my master's father who conspired to take you away from your daddy."

"Your master?"

"That's right, son. We all have a master whether we admit it or not. My master had a big fallin' out with his father over you. I'm surprised they're still on talking terms."

"Do you mean your boss? Are you talking about Damon's boss?"

"No, son. The boss answers to my master."

"I want to talk to your master now!"

"Yes, yes, child. He wants to talk to you as well, but not just yet. He didn't want you to think he had anything to do with your abduction. He'll let you know when he's ready. He's been mad at his daddy for a very long time. Not just about you, child, but about a lot of things. His father never wanted him to reach his full potential. You know, wouldn't let him be who he wanted to be. Held him back, that sort of thing."

"When can I meet him?"

"Don't worry, child. It'll be soon. Everything has a season."

"Where does he live? I need to see him now!"

Sadie chuckled under her breath. "You are an anxious one, aren't you? Like tearing clothes off a Barbie doll to see what's underneath, you just can't wait. You never could. I don't know where my master lives. Way up north somewhere I've been told. He's all over the world all the time. You don't contact him—he contacts you. Son, I'm tired now. That's enough for today. I have to rest a spell. You go on and get Damon up front. He's been waiting patiently for you. Don't worry, child. We'll talk again. I promise."

"Ma'am? Ma'am? I have more questions! Hello? Miss Sadie? ..." She was fast asleep.

In just a matter of seconds I heard a slight hint of a snore. I sat there staring at her for a minute before I slowly stood up from the chair. I paused another moment, considering how it was possible that a sweet, old, blind, black woman could possibly know the things she knew. I quietly opened the kitchen door so as not to wake her and made my way to the front room, where Damon was sitting. "Cash, she fell asleep."

Damon looked at me. "Well, what did she say?"

I stopped at the door, feeling this wasn't the place to start a long dialogue. "Dude, I'm not really sure. I'll tell you about it in the car. Let's go."

When we finally settled into the car, Damon was anxious to hear all about our talk. "So what did she say, Hammer?"

"For one thing, she said your boss's boss knows my real parents. Why didn't you tell me?"

"Whoa, Hammer! I didn't know anything about that."

"How could you not know?"

"I swear to God, Hammer, I'm on a need-to-know basis. If the boss knows your parents, he sure didn't tell me. He must have figured I didn't need to know."

"WHO IS YOUR BOSS! And who is Miss Sadie's master?! She said your boss answers to her master."

"Hammer, you're putting me in a tough spot here. I'm not allowed to say anything about my boss. It's a part of my contract, believe me. Bad stuff will happen if I violate my contract. You don't cross the boss, understand? Nobody crosses the boss! I don't have a clue who he answers to."

We sat in silence. I was fuming! Who was this mysterious guy? How did he know my parents? Had his father kidnapped me from my parents and left me on the steps of that orphanage? I wanted answers, but I kept getting more questions.

"Look, Hammer, I'm not trying to be mean. It's just that I can't talk about it. I'm not your enemy here. I'm just trying to help. What else did Miss Sadie say?"

"I'm sorry, Cash. I didn't mean to snap at you. Your boss or his boss is so freakin' frustrating."

"Yeah., tell me about it! He's a stickler for details."

"Miss Sadie knew stuff about my life that nobody could know."

"She's something alright. The boss says she's a princess in his world. She can read a person faster and better than any sighted person could ever hope to. That's her talent, man, that's why the boss recruited her. What else did she say?"

"She said some cryptic stuff about Venus eclipsing Leo and women being empowered and overshadowing men."

"Wow, that's interesting. Have you noticed how women are the heroes in the movies now? It's like they can beat up ten men with a single blow. They're smarter and faster, and with one sexy look, they can cause men to fall on their knees full of desire and ready to worship at their feet. Ha! Like that could ever happen in real life."

"Now that you mention it, I think you're right! I'm playing a video game. The hero is a woman who kicks butt while looking for old artifacts. I was talking to my buddy Jon the other day, and he told me a woman got prayer taken out of school in the sixties. She was an atheist or something. That's something, how a woman could have the power to change a law like that."

"Atheism is the stupidest thing I've ever heard, Hammer. I mean, really? To think this all just happened with no purpose? It's absurd! What do you believe, Hammer?"

"I'm not sure what to believe. I've kinda always been agnostic. I don't know if there is a God or not. I've always found comfort in logic. To me, the world has to make sense. All the religious stuff is confusing. It contradicts itself. How could anybody know what to believe with all those opinions? But today, I'm not so sure. There has to be something beyond all this. Miss Sadie doesn't fit into any logic. She's beyond my experience. She scares me. I still want to hold onto my logic, you know. Knowledge has always helped me cope."

"I'm with you a hundred percent, Hammer. My boss says 'Knowledge is power and is the ultimate truth in the universe.' He says to know is the greatest thing in life and is above everything. Sorry, Hammer. I didn't mean to bring up my boss again. I'm a true believer, though. Everything is according to a plan, but all that's way above my pay grade. Well, what else did Miss Sadie say?"

"I don't know, man. Something about paradoxes. I already told you about Leo getting eclipsed by Venus or something and the end of the world, but I didn't understand any of it. One thing I did understand is that your boss's master's father took me away from my parents ... I got *that* part real clear. So listen up. I want you to contact your boss or whatever you have to do to get me a meeting. I want to meet his boss."

"I'll try, Hammer. I can't promise anything, so don't get mad at me if it doesn't work out. My only contact is with my boss. I always knew someone was above him, but I don't know who he is. All I know is that he's powerful beyond anything you could imagine."

We arrived at my little townhouse. I wanted to press Cash a little more, but I felt it wasn't right to keep pushing. I had to trust he would set up an appointment with his mysterious boss.

I didn't get much time with Jon anymore. He'd graduated from his preacher school and was preparing to go as a missionary somewhere in New England. The thought of a Southern boy going up among all those Yankees was delightful. I wondered if Northern folks knew what they were in for with Jon coming their way. I knew he would terrorize those poor people. Maybe they would send him back if they couldn't handle him. I could at least hope he'd come back.

I wished I could have talked to him that day. I began to feel that maybe I was wrong about a lot of things. It was as if some spiritual journey was beckoning me. Over the years, I'd wondered if there was anything more. Do we live and die and that's it? Or is there a grand design in all this? Damon didn't seem religious, but even he believed in a higher plan.

His boss believed in knowledge. If you know the answer to a thing, it's no longer a mystery. I remembered watching a children's magic show at the foster home. The magician stuffed a handkerchief in his hand and it disappeared. Later, I saw the elastic string and a little sack with the handkerchief edge hanging out. It had pulled up his sleeve. I might have believed in magic if I didn't know how the trick had been done. Knowledge solved the mystery! Miss Sadie had to have an explanation. The mystery could be solved with the right information. I was not willing to say any religious thing was false but rather just not yet explained. Miss Sadie along with many of my experiences proved to me that there are phenomena beyond our current understanding. With the right information we should be able to figure it out.

CHAPTER 6

Visitations: It Can't Be!

Over the next few months, there was no meeting with Damon's boss. When I would see Damon at the bar, he'd say his boss hadn't contacted him yet. I was getting very tired of the bar scene and went less frequently. The old crew had drifted into other jobs and situations, and Jon had left to be a missionary. I always thought missionaries went to other countries. Jon told me our country needed God's work as much as anywhere else in the world. He was a home missionary!

I called him on occasion just to see how he was doing. In his usual mischievous style, he would tell me about some new trick he was perpetrating on the poor Yankees. "Did you know you can freeze a man's boots to a steel plate by pouring coffee on them in the winter?" I saw visions of some poor construction worker being stalked from behind by Jon, a stealthy leopard creeping toward prey and preparing for attack. At just the right moment, before the victim was aware, a little coffee around the shoe, and then, in just a moment ... the shoe was frozen solid to a steel beam! I imagined workers trying to move or step away only to realize they couldn't move. Perhaps they'd step out of their shoe leaving socks and all. I could see them hopping around in the snow in their bare feet amid a chorus of ouch, oooo, eeee! Poor, poor Yankees; they were in for a ride. They really didn't know what they were in for with Jon.

He'd always encouraged me to seek answers in the Bible, but I didn't like to read religious literature. Logic couldn't grapple with the crazy things that had happened to me over the years, but like most people, I longed for answers in life but did little to find them.

In a reflective mood one day, I decided to look up Rabbi Levy. I hadn't talked to him in years. I knew he was getting up in years and I had neglected him for a long time. He was always kind to me and told me many times that I must Jewish. I think he tolerated me because of it. Maybe I was Jewish, maybe I wasn't. As long as the mysterious boss was gone, I had no fresh leads to pursue. I thought Rabbi Levy might have the perspective I needed.

The Wellingtons had moved out of their house a long time ago. I never had an attachment to the house even though I'd lived there for a number of years. I liked Rabbi Levy next door; I felt more connected to him than to the Wellingtons. The Wellingtons were good people for the most part; my problem with them came from the religious stuff. I always felt condemned no matter what I did. If I didn't want to eat, I would be told about all the starving orphans in the world. If I didn't turn down my bed just right, God wasn't happy with me. Many times, I was told I'd be thrown in hell over this or that. I felt like an outsider. There was only discipline and more discipline and all in the name of God. I guess I formulated my opinions about God from all that. I didn't ever know love from them. Mr. Wellington never spoke. He would come home from work and preside over the dinner table and then send us all up to bed. We were not allowed to speak at the dinner table. In those days, children were to be seen, not heard.

I never felt happy in my childhood. The Wellingtons would tell me Jesus loved me but if I didn't trust Him I'd burn in hell. We were given descriptions of burning alive forever and worms that would eat you; that gave me many nightmares. I believed it all when I was a kid, but I stopped being afraid of burning in hell when I got a little older. It's funny how you believe anything adults tell you when you're a kid. The innocence of a child should never be taken advantage of. The problem for me was that they talked all about the love of God but never had any love in them. They constantly talked bad about other people's religion and said they were all going to hell. I'm not talking about just Jews and Muslims but also most members of Christian denominations that weren't their particular brand. I guess I developed a closed mind to all they said because it was different from what they did.

I guess I'd call them hypocrites. Not in the sense that they were out doing all manner of sin but rather more subtle stuff. I heard Mrs. Wellington on more than one occasion chew out a lady up one side and down the other and then see her in church and smile as if nothing had happened. She would assassinate others' characters with gossip but be all lovey-dovey to their faces. I never understood that.

I guess I shouldn't think ill of them. After all, they did house and feed and clothe me. Well, they got paid by the state to do so. They really played up the poor orphan bit when it came to getting donations from various charities. They would have us wear old clothes and shoes to make us more pitiful so donations would be larger. I think they made a pretty good living off us poor orphans.

Rabbi Levy was a different story. He had always been kind to me. I stayed out of the kitchen after the cheese incident and let him bring snacks to me. I felt I needed some answers from a religious perspective. I decided to contact him. The experience with Miss Sadie made me question my beliefs. It's funny to think that an agnostic had beliefs. I believed in logic, not superstition. Knowledge was the answer to all of life's mysteries. I believed knowledge would set me free. Perhaps I would find out how Miss Sadie seemed to know so much about my childhood. Her boss must have told her about me. I bet he'd been following me since his boss's father kidnapped me. It had to be! He felt guilty over what his father had done and told Miss Sadie everything about me. He'd probably had people watching me all my life.

Maybe there was no mystery to Miss Sadie; maybe she was just an old woman who was being used by a man behind the scenes. It made sense to me that he wouldn't want to meet me. If my father had done some unspeakable thing to someone, I might have felt the same way. He was probably ashamed of what had happened and was trying to make amends. I wondered if his father was still alive. If I met his father, what would I say or do? Would I want to wreak vengeance on him? Kill him? I didn't know how I'd react. All the other stuff was just my nerves, just coincidence. I wanted to know for sure what was going on. I thought in the spirit of searching for truth I'd cover all bases, including the religious base. If for nothing else, it could aid in the process of elimination.

I hated how I wavered back and forth from logic to some other explanation; from the natural to the supernatural. I felt like a yo-yo. Miss Sadie was a mystery. If she could read threads or whatever she did, there had to be a logical explanation for that. Maybe it was some kind of electrical aura thing. It *had* to be based on science. They could actually read brain waves. It's common knowledge that blind people develop higher senses of hearing, smell, and touch as compensation for the missing sense, so maybe Miss Sadie had an overdeveloped part of her brain that could somehow pick up and interpret signals from other people's brains.

It was on a Saturday that I pulled up to Rabbi Levy's house. I made my way up the driveway. "I'm around back, Enoch. Come to the back porch!" I turned the corner and was shocked to find a very old-looking gentleman. The man with a full black beard and hair and thick black glasses had been replaced by a bald man with a white, thinning beard and wire-rimmed glasses. I almost didn't believe it was him, but his voice was exactly the same as I remembered.

"Hello, Enoch. It has been too many years."

"Yes, Rabbi, it has."

"You've grown older, son. I see a bit of gray on the sides."

"You're one to talk, sir!" I felt that instant connection to him.

"I was glad you called, son. I have wanted to talk to you for a long time. Stay here just a minute. I'll get us a nice glass of tea. You just rock in that chair and I'll be right back."

I felt comfortable. The old porch was just as I remembered. The old rocking chairs and vinyl wicker couch were a little worse for the wear but still comfortable. The old, brown cushions had been replaced by some with a bright floral pattern. The wicker coffee table had books and trays and coasters just as if it hadn't changed in twenty years. Being nosy, I scanned the latest reading material on the table. A large book was open with the pages face down. I picked up the book and turned it over and began to study the page.

"Oh my gosh! Rabbi Levy!" I threw the book on the floor and backed up.

"What is it, son? I'm coming, I'm coming!" Rabbi Levy came out the screen door backward with two glasses of iced tea. "Enoch, pick up that book you dropped. I got it out when you called." He arranged the glasses on two coasters. "I want you to take a look at the page with the clip on it." I slowly picked it up off the floor. The book opened to the page I had just seen.

"I've seen those symbols before. What are they? What do they mean?"

"I told you many years ago about the importance of identity. Do you remember?"

"Yes sir. You told me I was Jewish because of my first and last names. You said my last name meant 'to reveal' or something like that in Hebrew."

"Do you remember anything else?"

"Yes sir. You said my first name was from the Jewish Bible, but I don't remember if it means anything, and my middle name means 'king.'"

"Well, that wasn't exactly right. In Hebrew, Enoch means 'dedicated'. It comes from the Hebrew verb *hanak*. It's also used in Hanukkah, the Feast of Dedication. Do you remember now?"

"I think ... No ... I don't think I remember that. But what does that have to do with these symbols?"

"That book in your hand is ancient cuneiform, the oldest form of written language on the earth; it predates all others. It's ancient Sumerian."

"Rabbi, I saw these symbols on an old plaster wall several years ago."

"Where? At a museum?"

"No sir, in a building on North Rampart."

"That's a very odd thing. Are you sure the symbols looked like these?"

"Yes sir, exactly like that! Except that above it were a bunch of those feminine symbols of a circle with a cross under it and a word ina ... ni ... inan. Wait a minute. It's spelled i-n-a-n-n-a. I remember it because I made an off-color joke to my partner about it."

"Really?"

"You know, like 'I'd sure like to get in Anna.' Yeah, I know. That's the same look Jon gave me. I felt embarrassed after I said it." I felt the same embarrassment as I caught his disapproving glare.

"Hmmm, that is very strange indeed. We'll look that up in a minute. Before I get distracted again, I want to show you something in the book. Look at the words and their translations. Go down to the *k*'s. Do you notice anything?" I focused my eyes on the words and their definitions. Right there in the middle of the *k* section was the word *Kingu*. "OH LORD! It's my middle name."

"Read what it means, Enoch."

"It means 'great emissary'."

"That's right, Enoch. Your whole name means Dedicated Great Emissary of Revelation. You've been dedicated by God to be a great emissary of His revelation. It's your identity, son. It's who you are!"

He had a big grin on his face as if some great cosmic joke was being played on me. I felt uncomfortable with the implications of the meaning. "Rabbi, I'm scared."

"There is nothing to be afraid of, Enoch. It just means you have the hand of God on your life. It's a good thing. You have a destiny to fulfill, and God will accomplish it in His own time."

"That's not what I'm afraid of, sir. The attic I told you about had some words in it that ... I ... I ... don't know what to think. I don't know what to do."

"What is it, Enoch? What's troubling you, son? You can tell me."

"Rabbi, it read, 'The emissary must die.' It was right above my ... my name."

"Hold up, son. Did you say your name was on the walls?"

"Yes, sir. I think it was written in blood." That old, familiar fear was back as though it had never left.

"Son, someone was just playing a practical joke on you. I wouldn't get too concerned about it." His words were reassuring and calming even though I knew it was not the truth. "It is very odd, though. If God has called you to be His emissary, you will have an enemy."

"Who's that, sir?"

"That would be the dark one. He opposes God in all things and seeks to stop His will from being accomplished."

I sat with the rabbi for an hour, retelling the story of the attic. I described in detail what I'd seen and all about the conversation with Mr. Bellisaire. I told him every word I saw on the wall that was in English. After I had exhausted the whole surreal scene, I paused to get Rabbi Levy's response.

"I see why you are concerned, Enoch. I have never heard of anything like this. You said the attic had been locked for seventy years or so. I can't explain it son. I will tell you this, though. The ways of God are above the ways of man, His thoughts are higher than ours, and He moves in mysterious ways. We all have a purpose to fulfill, a destiny if you will, and God has planned it all. Nothing escapes His notice, and He is never taken by surprise. I am sure in due time He will reveal what it all means. One thing is for sure—whoever wrote those things on those walls must have been very disturbed indeed. He did not follow the one true God."

As the rabbi was speaking, I glanced at the book in my lap. I happened to notice the *i*'s above the *k*'s, and my eyes landed on Inanna. "Rabbi! I found Inanna! It says she was the goddess of sexuality and war. She made bloodthirsty calls for violence in the underworld. She was also known as Ishtar and Aphrodite, and in the Roman period, she was known as Venus!"

"Yes, son, many false gods were worshipped by ancient people. We as Jews believe in the one true God. The Law of Moses and the Talmud are quite clear on this. We do not consult the stars but put our faith in the one true God and His law."

I had been so captivated by the new revelations of my name that I had completely forgotten why I had decided to visit the rabbi. I'd been on a mission to get answers about Miss Sadie and I needed a religious perspective on recent events.

"Sir, I almost forgot why I came today. I don't want to wear out my welcome, but I need to ask you a question."

"Yes, Enoch, it has been quite an afternoon, but go ahead and ask your question."

"I met an old, blind woman who told me things about my life she couldn't have known. Is there a way for people to have secret knowledge, I mean, from a religious perspective?"

"Tell me a little more about it, son."

"Well, she's been blind her whole life, but she described incidents in my life as though she'd been there. She even knew about the cheese I put in the wrong sink in your kitchen. How could someone know about things like that?"

"That is a difficult one, Enoch. In the Holy Scriptures, there were witches and mediums who consulted the dead. Such ones seemed to have secret knowledge. King Saul consulted the Witch of Endor to get answers by consulting the dead. Saul was killed soon after for his disobedience to God."

"Yeah, my friend Jon told me it was an abomination to God to consult a medium."

"That's right, son. We must find our answers only from God."

"I don't want to give you the impression that she talked to the dead or anything—she just freaked me out. She was a nice old lady. I just want to know if it's possible ... I mean, can a person have a special gift or talent that can't be explained by science?"

"There are many stories in the Scriptures of the supernatural. Samson had supernatural strength. Elijah called down fire from heaven and burned up the sacrifice that had been doused in water. Daniel's friends were cast into the fiery furnace and were unharmed. I believe in the supernatural even though I have never seen it."

"Yes sir, I know about all those stories from when I was a kid. They're just stories that teach a religious perspective. They're just myths to inspire fear ... Oh, I'm sorry, Mr. Aaron. I didn't mean to imply that your faith ... I'm sorry. You know I struggle with the whole faith and God thing. I didn't mean to offend you, sir." I felt embarrassment at my unguarded words.

"No offense taken, Enoch. You will find your faith someday. And by the way, thank you."

"For what, sir?"

"For calling me Mr. Aaron! It's the first time today you have called me by my first name. I liked it."

As I left Rabbi Levy's house, I wondered about the possibility of the supernatural. What if Miss Sadie's gift had come from a supernatural place? The idea of the supernatural was difficult at best to even consider. We were pounded with the supernatural in movies, but in real life, it was hard to accept.

After tossing and turning that night until after 2:00 a.m., I finally drifted off to sleep. In a way that I could not describe, I was in the presence of a being clothed in white with a brilliant light emanating from his upper body. He spoke to me in a calm, rich voice. "Enoch ... Enoch, I have come to visit with you." I knew it was a dream, but it seemed real. I remembered the light people from my childhood nightmares; they had always calmed me down. But this felt different; it was like I was awake and thinking clearly in the middle of a dream. I had never had a dream like that. In all my past dreams, I had no control over what happened. It was very strange to feel fully awake while sleeping.

"Who are you?" I asked. I couldn't see the one who was talking to me.

"I am your advocate. I have come to tell you of what must shortly come to pass. You will teach the world of Me, and I will show you My ways. I have been established from everlasting, from the beginning, before there was ever an earth. When there were no depths, I was brought forth. When there were no fountains abounding with water, before the mountains were settled, before the hills, I was brought forth; while as yet nothing had been made, not the earth or the fields, or the primeval dust of the world. When the heavens were prepared, I was there. When the circle on the face of the deep was drawn and the clouds were established, I was there. When the sea was assigned its limit, so that the waters would not transgress His command, when He marked out the foundations of the earth, then I was beside Him as a master craftsman; and I was daily His delight, rejoicing always before Him, rejoicing in His inhabited world, and My delight was with the sons of men. Now listen to Me. Blessed are those who keep My ways. Hear instruction and be wise, and do not disdain it. Blessed is the man who listens to Me. For whoever finds Me finds life."

I woke up in a sweat, trying to determine what had just happened. I looked at the digital clock—3:00 a.m. exactly. I didn't realize what an impact the meeting with Rabbi Levy had had on me. My imagination was taking over. I sat there wondering if I needed psychiatric help.

I'd never been able to have consciousness in the midst of a dream. I wasn't sure what to make of it. It seemed like my life was spiraling out of control. I didn't know what to believe. It was beginning to dawn on me that I could be influenced by some sort of suggestibility. The strange dream felt familiar somehow. It was as if I had heard those words somewhere before, but I couldn't quite put my finger on them.

It was very strange to have a dream that was a kickback to my childhood. When I was a child, the light people scared away the monsters. As an adult, I had no need for some light-clad savior to pull me back from the clutches of death. Those were childhood nightmares brought on by child abuse and insecurity. I'd had no need to fear sleep for many years.

I didn't think about the dream the next day. We were in the thick of a renovation on Prytania Street, and I had to deal with problems all day. The architect had redesigned the cabinet layout in the kitchen after we had installed the cabinets. The owner's wife didn't like the layout because of insufficient counter space. She was giving us a hard time about who was going to pay for the changes. I'd already paid for the cabinets, but through no fault of mine, she thought we should have anticipated her future whims. She said, "You shouldn't have put those cabinets in yet!" She had the plans for seven months before we got the contract. Her husband knew she was in the wrong, but he just let her terrorize us.

I'd had similar experiences too many times. A wife wouldn't like what she had chosen so would look for someone to blame for her bad choices. One time, a man's wife screamed at the architect because he'd designed a pool at her request. I was in some of the meetings in which she carefully laid out all that she wanted. He carefully sketched it all out and got signed plans and documents. When it was built, she said it was the ugliest pool she'd ever seen. Her husband had to pay to tear it out and start over.

I was glad the architect was taking the heat rather than me. It's not that I blamed women in general; I just wished they had more common sense. I couldn't stand the weakness of some of these men. They just kept taking it and letting the women get anything they wanted. They'd just say, "Whatever she wants."

Once in a while, the men would cause the stress. Usually, the passive-aggressive wife would work them over at night, and the husband would have to be the "bad guy" the next day. You could always tell who was pulling the strings. To me, it seemed like Miss Sadie's words had a ring of truth. I loved it when a husband wouldn't allow emotions to rule over a jobsite. That sure made jobs go easier. It was as if these women couldn't help themselves. Once emotions got involved, there was trouble on the horizon.

On the flip side, I hated men who controlled their wives. I was embarrassed for all men when I'd see a man belittle or degrade his wife. As much as I felt like slapping the manipulating, controlling women, I felt like punching the controlling, terrorizing men as well. I felt brokenhearted for any poor woman in such a lonely, terrible prison. I'd seen such women withdraw into self-made prisons. Like whipped puppy dogs, abused women seemed to be but empty shells. I probably identified with them because of my own abuse as a child. To live in fear of constant retribution for saying or doing the wrong thing was a horror no one should experience.

In short, I saw the extremes in the American family in my work. I often wondered if there were any truly balanced marriages. If they were out there, they had to be rare. It's probably one of the reasons why I never got married.

I saw Damon at the bar that night. I had to relieve the stress of the day in spite of the lack of sleep from the night before. I wanted to talk to him anyway. I hadn't seen him in a few weeks and wanted to catch up. I also wanted to ask about Miss Sadie.

"Hey! Johnny Cash!"

"Yo, Hammer! Long time no see."

"Let me buy you a beer, Cash."

"No, let me buy you a beer. I have good news. My boss has contacted me and he says he's going to set up a meeting in the near future."

"Are you serious? That's great! There's been a lot of strange stuff going on, and I hope he'll have some answers." It was a relief to have the mystery man contact his recruiter. I've never heard of a business with so little contact between employee and boss. How do you conduct business like that? It wasn't my business; I figured it took all types in life.

"Oh yeah, he'll have all the answers you'll ever need."

"I wanted to ask you about Miss Sadie. How's she doing? She said she'd talk to me again."

"Miss Sadie hasn't been out of that apartment in thirty-nine years from what I understand."

"You're kidding me! Who takes care of her? How does she get food and medicine?"

"The woman who runs the shop downstairs takes care of her. It was all part of her contract."

"What exactly does she do for your boss? She seems a little old to be of much value. If it's true she hasn't left her apartment in thirty-nine years, how does she earn her pay? How old is she anyway?"

"I was told she was born in 1889."

"What? That's impossible. That would mean she was what, a hundred and eight?"

"Yeah, I know. Pretty incredible, isn't it? As far as her pay and what she does, I don't have a clue."

"The incredible seems normal lately. How does your boss get hold of her?"

"You got me! She can't read, and she doesn't have a phone. I was told to go see her."

"Cash, I gotta ask, did you tell her anything about me? You said you told her about me."

"No ... not really, Hammer. I'll try to tell you what happened. I was cultivating my relationship with my assignment when my boss called. He told me he wanted me to go to a shop and meet an old woman who lived on the second floor. I was told to do whatever she wanted me to do. When I got to the shop, I was to say to the shop lady, 'The boss sent me.' When I got to the shop, I did what I was told, and the lady behind the register took me up to Miss Sadie's apartment.

"I told her I'd been told by the boss to come and see her. She actually asked me about the man called Hammer. I told her I knew a man whose nickname was Hammer. She told me she wanted to meet you and to bring you to her. That's all I said to her. I went downstairs and talked to the lady there for a long time. She told me all about Miss Sadie. She's as much a mystery to me as to you."

I sat there a minute thinking about what he'd said. There was so much intrigue and mystery to these people. They seemed like nice people but were odd to the extreme. I felt both comfortable and nervous around them.

"Cash, do you think the big boss's father is still alive? Do you think he could take me to my father?"

"Need-to-know basis, remember? The boss is involved in big-time international stuff. Do you think he'd let me know about his personal life or introduce me to his boss? I've never even met the man. I'm just a pawn, a recruiter."

"I found out some disturbing information yesterday. You know the female sign; the circle with the cross under it? I'll show you." I drew the symbol on a bar napkin. "You know the sign for Venus?"

"Yes, I guess I did. Why do you ask?"

"It's something Miss Sadie said. She said that on the day I was found, Venus eclipsed Leo. I don't read all that astrology crap, so I couldn't tell you about any of it, but the Venus signs were in that attic I told you about. One was above a word I found out was a goddess of ancient Sumeria. Well, I went to see my old neighbor yesterday, and he showed me a book that had my middle name in it. It's ancient Sumerian, and it means 'great emissary'."

"That's kinda cool."

"No... it's not! The attic walls I told you about said, 'The emissary must die'."

"Wow, Hammer. I don't think you ever told me that. That's kind of disturbing."

"Tell me about it. I just don't know what to think about it. It seems my whole life changed since that day. It's like some cosmic force is out to get me. My buddy Jon told me all that stuff was satanic. Do you believe there is a real Satan?"

"Sure I do, but I think he's gotten a bad rap."

"A bad rap? What do you mean? Isn't he supposed to be the ultimate evil?"

"That's ignorance. He sets people free!"

"Free from what?"

"Tyranny, man, God's tyranny!"

"You're saying God's a tyrant?"

"The worst kind. He makes up laws that no one can ever follow just so He can crush them. Satan was a name God gave him. His real name means 'bright' or 'morning star'. He was one of God's sons. The way I hear it, God was jealous of his beauty when the other angels started to follow him. This isn't common knowledge, but God didn't want any of the angels to talk to him. I've read a lot about this stuff. Think about it. God put the Tree of Knowledge in the garden and told Adam and Eve not to eat its fruit. Satan taught the angels about free will and the inalienable right they had to reach their fullest potential. You know, man, he wanted them to have freedom to explore other philosophies, other options. He just wanted to do good! God wanted to keep him and all the rest of creation ignorant. He wanted all the power for Himself. He wanted all the angels to follow Him blindly in complete ignorance. Satan just told his brethren to seek knowledge as the enlightenment of freedom. The serpent was a friend of Satan and told them about the knowledge in the tree. He sort of encouraged them in civil disobedience."

"I don't know all that much about the Devil. When I was a kid, I heard the Devil was evil. Wait a minute. I thought the tree would kill them. Wasn't God trying to protect them?"

"Protect them? You kidding me? Who do you think poisoned the tree? God made the tree, not Satan. God killed those innocent kids. The Devil has always gotten a bum rap."

"Cash, I never knew you believed in all that stuff. Are you like a Satan worshipper or something?"

"I'm a true believer in freedom. I think the Devil's an interesting guy. God has done nothing but try to kill us off through floods, famines, pestilence, and who knows what. Why? Because we can't line up like ducks in a row and be perfect in every way. I would rather be free to do what I want to do. Have you ever tried to follow all God's rules? Have you ever known anyone who followed God who was happy?"

"No, not really, except Jon. Jon's a pretty happy guy, and he's all up in that religious stuff. I like Jon. Rabbi Levy is a good guy too even though he's a little over the top on rules."

"Sounds like a couple of good guys, but they're exceptions to the rule. I don't have anything against religious people. They're just trying to please a God who can't be pleased."

"Yeah, you're right. Most religious people I've known were pretty hypocritical. Of course, I don't know that many religious people. You know what bugs me is all the TV preachers. Every time I turn on the TV, one of those characters is telling you to send him money. I can't stand that! Talk about a money-making racket."

"There you have it!" His words made a kind of sense to me, but they didn't feel right. I'd never heard anybody say the Devil was a good guy. He seemed to have some sort of belief system as weird as it was. People have all kinds of beliefs. Who knows if there's any truth in any of them? I understood what he was saying. If God was a God of love, why did He let so much evil take place? Why did He kill so many people in the past, and why have so many people been killed in His name? If Cash was right, God was at the heart of the pain and evil in the world. Religion was too confusing to me; it was easier to believe that we just evolved from a primordial soup. It's all a natural process; there's no purpose or meaning to life. In any case, I still enjoyed talking about God and politics over a good beer.

I thought a lot about Cash on the way home that night. He was an odd duck. He was madder at God than I was, if there was a God. I often caught myself talking about God as if He were real. I'd laugh at myself and remind myself that science was the truth I believed in.

The pillow felt extra good that night. I thought about what was planned for the next day as I drifted off to sleep.

"Enoch? Enoch? I have come to visit with you."

"Who are you?"

"You know who I am."

"No I don't. I think I remember you from my childhood, but I don't know who you are."

"I have been with you always, and you have been with Me." The voice felt familiar, safe.

"What do you want from me?"

"You will be My witness. You were chosen for this purpose."

"What have I witnessed?"

"You will testify of what you have seen and heard."

"I haven't seen or heard anything! I don't know what you're talking about! Please help me understand."

"I am Wisdom, and I will teach you what you have forgotten. I will send you before Me, and you will tell the world to prepare. The time of woes has begun. The end is at hand."

I was wide awake and upright in bed. I looked at the clock. It was 3:00 a.m. exactly again.. *Another dream! I'm an idiot for talking about all that religious stuff before going to bed. Am I ever going to learn? I should know myself by now. Why do I do this to myself every time? Did I seriously imagine some great spirit of wisdom was talking to me?* For a moment, I wondered if it might actually be something from the spirit realm. It couldn't be. Could someone be visited by a spirit? I wondered if people of antiquity had strange dreams. Maybe writers of the Bible were sincere but just didn't know about the capacity of the mind to dream. Perhaps they had similar dreams and thought they had been visited by God. We're all so suggestible. It's no wonder man seeks the reason for his existence. It's also understandable to contemplate the end of our existence.

Miss Sadie had talked about the end of time or the end of the world. I wondered why everybody was so caught up with the end of the world. The earth had been around a long time, and the sun still had a long time before it would burn out. As long as we didn't get hit by an asteroid or something, we should do just fine. All that end-of-the-world stuff was meant to sell lots of movie tickets. The religious end-of-the-world perspective was to keep people in line. I figured churches used fear of God just to bring in revenue.

CHAPTER 7

Why Me?

Over the next few weeks, I waited for the fateful call from Damon. My mind was constantly consumed with the thought of meeting the "boss." I imagined all manner of scenarios of how the boss had been my benefactor all along. Why was he so aloof? I couldn't blame him for what his boss's father had done; it wouldn't be right to hold him responsible for the sins of his boss's father. I felt like the big boss was in a tough spot too. On the one hand, he didn't agree with what his father had done, and on the other, he was still his daddy. If I knew my father, I would protect him too. It's just human to protect your family no matter what they've done. I totally understood why he wouldn't let anyone talk about him. He was afraid of revenge, retribution for something he had nothing to do with. I felt a kind of empathy with the mysterious boss; I could identify with his plight and fear.

I wanted to reconnect with Miss Sadie. I went looking for Damon at all the local haunts. He was usually in the first place I went. We always seemed to end up together. It was uncanny how he'd be there at just the right time when I needed company. But this time, there was no Damon anywhere. I ended up drinking by myself that Friday night. *Where the heck is Cash?* I sat there wondering if something had happened to him. He was always at the bar. It was strange to be in a sea of people and yet feel completely alone. I stayed in the bar for three hours, constantly looking at the door and hoping Cash would walk in. At about midnight, I realized I'd been nursing one beer for over an hour. I got into bed around 12:40 and drifted off to sleep.

I suddenly found myself in a large space filled with light. I knew it was just another dream. It was almost comforting. I was wondering what my imagination would come up with next. Imagine that! While dreaming, I was wondering what my mind would come up with next. It was as if my consciousness was curious about my subconscious. I had perfect cognitive reasoning skills while in a dream. I knew it was a dream, and yet I could think like I was awake. I wondered if my imagination would produce the man clothed in light or something else.

"Enoch, I am here."

"Hello, imagination! I was just thinking about you."

"You have always delighted Me, Enoch. When I formed you in your mother's womb, I gave you a questioning mind. It has always been good for us to reason together."

"What do you want to be called tonight? Wisdom, or something else?" It was funny to be having a conversation with yourself in the middle of a dream. I'd lost it for sure. I was talking to my imagination, and it was talking back. I stopped for a minute to think about whether it counted when you were asleep. I guess if you're asleep, anything goes.

"You're not crazy, Enoch."

"Sure, you would say that! After all, you're my imagination."

He laughed at my comment. "I am more than your imagination. I am that I am. As the seed has life in itself, so do I have life in Me."

"Wait a minute. What? What are you talking about?"

"In Me is the life. And through Me were all things made that were made." I wondered where my subconscious would come up with such cryptic, egocentric stuff. Maybe I was remembering stuff from church when I was a kid. I decided to test my subconscious by asking for information I couldn't possibly know.

"Okay, Mr. Wisdom, tell me something I couldn't possibly know. This way I'll know if you're more than my imagination." I'd called my subconscious "Mr. Wisdom." I laughed as I thought of a cartoon character from my childhood. "Mr. Wizard! Mr. Wizard! Help me!" The wizard would rescue the wayward apprentice turtle from his trouble by saying something like "Trizzle, drizzle, trazzle, drone, time for this one to come home!" The apprentice would be caught in a spiral vortex and end up back safe in the wizard's presence. I felt like that little turtle. I was musing over the clarity of my thoughts in the midst of a dream when I was distracted by His voice.

"I will tell you something you could not possibly know by asking you a question."

"Okay, I'm game. What do you want to ask me?"

"In your childhood, have you heard of the lamb that takes away the sin of the world?"

"Yeah, I guess so."

"You knew a lamb was used as a sin offering. Can you tell Me why the sin sacrifice for the common man has to be a female lamb?"

"A religious question? You serious? I don't have a clue about religion. Rabbi Levy never told me about sacrifices."

"You know more than you think! You have been with Me several millennia or a few days depending on the perspective. A day is as a thousand years, and a thousand years are as a day."

It amused me that I could talk in my dream and have thoughts about what I'd just said. Where in the world did my imagination come up with this stuff? I was amazed at my subconscious.

"Well, I'm beginning to enjoy this! I remember something from my childhood. Jesus is the lamb who takes away the sin of the world. Right? No. Jesus was male ... No, that doesn't fit." It dawned on me. Ah, yes. Proof positive. I was remembering preaching from my childhood. I didn't think I had been paying attention back then, but my subconscious had apparently picked up more than I was aware of. Wow! My dreams were fantastic. I wondered if everybody dreamed like this.

Knock, knock, knock, knock, knock.

"Alright, Mr. Wisdom. Where's the door? I hear it but I don't see it."

Knock, knock, knock, knock, knock.

My eyes opened. I realized someone was knocking on my front door. It was 10:00 a.m. I grabbed my pants and hopped to the door while trying to put them on.

Knock, knock, knock, knock, knock.

"Wait a minute. I'm coming, I'm coming."

As I got downstairs, I saw a long, black car outside. Cash! I hurried to the door and flung it open. "Hey, Johnny, what are you doing here?"

"I'm here to take you to see Miss Sadie."

I thought for a minute. I hadn't told anyone why I'd been looking for Cash.

"How did you know I wanted to talk to Miss Sadie?"

"It's my job to know things like that."

"You're a strange one, Cash."

"Go ahead and get ready. I'll wait."

I ran upstairs as Cash found a seat. After brushing my teeth and combing my hair, I looked for a shirt. With a gratuitous sniff of the shirt and underarms and a brief slicking of deodorant, I slid into a pullover and was ready.

"Let's go, Cash." I didn't care how Cash had figured it out. I was glad to be going to see her.

We arrived at the door of the shop. Even though I had passed the shop many times since that first meeting, I never had the courage to go in alone, uninvited. It wasn't the fact that it was a voodoo shop; that touristy stuff never bothered me. It was a respect issue. Miss Sadie was like a wise, old sage, and you don't just barge in on a wise old sage, do you?

Up the stairs and through the door we went. I looked more closely at the first room. The old patterned wallpaper was peeling in places and was dark yellow, almost burnt orange in color. The original color had so faded with age that there was no color left, just outlines of patterns in between stripes about every sixteen inches or so. It looked like aged paper I occasionally saw in some of the renovations we had done, usually in unused, hidden spaces such as attics. I thought it didn't matter that much to a blind person. I don't think I would care either if I were blind.

Damon knocked on the kitchen door. "Miss Sadie? Enoch's here." Damon smiled and went up front.

"Come on in, dear boy. I have hot chocolate on the menu today. Would you like a cup?"

"Hi, Miss Sadie. No, I don't think so, but thank you. I've wanted to talk to you for the longest time."

She opened a packet of instant hot chocolate and poured it in a cup. She retrieved a tea kettle from the stove, poured water into the cup, and stirred it.

"I know, but everything has a season, son. The timing for everything has to be just right. Like this cocoa. If it's too hot, it'll burn you, but if it's too cool, it's not very good."

"Mr. Blackstone told me you were over a hundred. Is that true?"

"Time has no meaning for me, son. I exist to serve, to help the cause of universal freedom, that's what my master calls it. I've got to move on soon and join my master."

"You're leaving? How long are you going to stay with your master friend?"

"The master is going to send his second in command to pick me up. I'll spend the rest of my time with him. He and I have much to do in preparation. He'll be coming for me tomorrow, son. That's why I wanted to talk to you today."

"Ma'am, can I meet him please? What's his name?"

"My boss calls him Morté. It's sort of an inside joke. Anyway, you've already met him."

"I've met him? When? I don't remember meeting any one named Morty."

"You mean Morté."

"Mo ... where ... tay! I can't speak Cajun! I'm just going to call him Morty. You say I've met him?"

"Sure, son. You met him on the boat. Don't you remember?"

"Are you talking about that dude with the goatee, hat, and coat?"

"I've never actually met him or seen his face, not even in my mind's eye. I've been told nobody ever sees his face unless he has business with you."

"If it's the same guy, I've seen his face, Miss Sadie. He's real pale, like he's never been in the sun, and his face is drawn and thin. He has the darkest-brown eyes I've ever seen, almost black, and he has a thin, black goatee. How did you know I met him on the ferry?"

"I told you, son, it's the vibrations of the threads of time, places, people, and such. Don't you remember, boy? It's my special talent. He's coming for me tomorrow at ten in the morning. I have to prepare. I must look my best."

"Miss Sadie, do you think it's wise at your age to go off with a perfect stranger? And this Morty fellow is real strange. I think your blindness has caused some sort of overcompensation process in your brain. Everyone has brain waves that can be measured, and we actually generate electricity to some degree. I think you're able to read or maybe feel that energy because of your condition. Someday, science will catch up with this phenomenon and explain it."

"He, he, he! You're a pistol, boy! Don't you believe in anything?"

"Of course I do. I believe in the power of the mind. Science answers all the questions if given the right information. Miss Sadie, you have a unique gift. It's rare, but I'm sure it's explainable. In the future, people will be able to move things with their minds. All kinds of research is going on right now to develop the technology. I realize you're ahead of the curve, and I'm grateful. I get why your boss sought you out. It's a pretty extraordinary talent you have."

I could see how this skill or ability could be used in business; what I would pay to have such a skill. Miss Sadie's boss had to be pretty sharp to find people like her. It was probably how he'd gotten all his wealth and power.

"Miss Sadie, I'd like to see if you have any answers to a couple of questions. I want to tap into your special talent if you don't mind. I understand why you can't tell me who the boss is, so I'm not going to ask you about him. He's under the one you call master and probably doesn't have any say in this. You seem to know a lot about my life, and I think you can read my memories or something. Well, anyway, as you know, I want to find my real family. Can you tell me anything about them?"

"Only what I'm allowed to, son. I can tell you your father's name was Jared."

"Jared Galah, Wow. Are you sure?" She nodded. "What was my mother's name?" I felt a sense of relief. If she was right, I had a lead to pursue.

"I don't know, son. I haven't been told." She took another sip of her hot chocolate.

"Can you tell me where my father lives?"

"Child, he's not even from this country. I wouldn't know how you could get in touch with him. That's beyond my gift. I think he's been long dead!"

"I appreciate it, Miss Sadie. A name is more than I had before. It's a starting place. I suspected he was a foreigner because of my name. I can't thank you enough for your help. If he's dead, there should be a record somewhere."

"That's quite alright, son. I'm glad to help."

"I want to ask you another question. It doesn't have anything to do with my family or your boss or his boss. It has to do with a strange dream I had and something you said. First of all, I want you to know I respect your religious views. I mean ... you know ... your astrology thing and women taking over the world."

"He, he, he! Child, you sure do twist things around. That's your imagination at work."

"Yes ma'am, that's what I want to talk to you about, my imagination. I've been having some strange dreams lately, and I wondered ... since you can read minds and all ... if you could help me figure out a mystery in my mind. It has to do with sacrifice."

"Go on, boy."

"I think I had some memory from my religious upbringing. Well, anyway, I was talking to myself in my dream ... don't ask! ... and I think my subconscious wants me to figure out something about women. I asked myself ... well, my subconscious or whatever asked this question. Why did the Jewish sin sacrifice have to be a female lamb?"

"I see light, boy. It's blocking my way! I don't know what it means. I will tell you this. I've been told that all life starts out as female. All human embryos start out female and then change into male with the right seed from the father. Does that help you, son?"

"Yeah, maybe a little, I actually read an article on that recently. I had no idea you kept up with genetics. You're full of surprises, Miss Sadie."

"There will be a new understanding of the feminine, son. You were born to bring this understanding. The feminine will have true equality with the masculine. The master was born perfect in beauty. He was covered in precious jewels, and he was full of wisdom. All was well until his father became jealous of him."

"Beautiful, huh? Kind of sounds like a woman. He's not like a transvestite, is he? I don't mean to be offensive, Miss Sadie. I just got a weird picture of him in my mind."

"No, son, he's not a transvestite, but he is the most beautiful being I have ever seen in my mind. He came to me long ago when I created juju against my enemies. He is the god of my ancestors. He was pleased with me and told me he would send a man to take care of me. He sent me Damon's boss. My master told me Damon's boss would be revealed one day as master of the world. He would be the most powerful man who has ever lived. He would solve all crime and create a system in which all would have security."

"He sounds like a great man. I doubt anyone could ever straighten out this crazy world. I didn't mean that crack about the transvestite. I'm just saying men don't typically adorn themselves with lots of jewels. Except Cash, maybe. He's an exception to the rule."

"Child, you are impossible. I understand why my boss's enemy wants you." She chuckled under her breath at my words.

"Miss Sadie, do you have any family? Have you told them about your going away? Do you have any children?"

"No, son. No one wants an old blind lady. That's why I made strong juju to get my gift. It gave me power to see even though I was blind. I learned my juju from my daddy. My daddy learned his juju from my granddaddy. Granddaddy was a slave and was tortured by his owners. My daddy was released from slavery as a very small boy. My granddaddy was a full-grown man when he was released after the South lost the war. My granddaddy taught my daddy the ways of the old religion. My granddaddy took vengeance on his former owners and called a great plague of yellow death on New Orleans to kill his former owners. My daddy learned his ways and called another plague when I was very young, but for a different reason."

"What reason would that be?"

"Archbishop Placide Louis Chappelle confronted my daddy about the old ways. He told my daddy he would burn in hell if he didn't turn to the true faith. My daddy made strong juju to kill him with yellow fever. His juju left me barren, and my granddaddy's juju made me blind. My daddy was born with a bad heart and died shortly after he killed the archbishop. He paid the price for my granddaddy's juju. That's how it works, boy. When strong juju is used, the descendants pay the price. My family was cursed because of it. My daddy should not have killed Archbishop Chappelle. It brought great evil on my family, and they all died except me."

"Oh, Miss Sadie, Archbishop Chappelle died from yellow fever. Your blindness wasn't caused by your granddaddy, and the yellow fever epidemic had nothing to do with your daddy or granddaddy. Mosquitoes caused it! Have you been living with the false guilt of that your whole life? That breaks my heart, Miss Sadie. You shouldn't feel responsible for something you had nothing to do with. Don't blame your family for those disasters. It had nothing to do with your old religion or your family."

"There are things in this world, boy, that are beyond your puny science. You are narrow minded in your thinking and approach to life, son. You're as closed minded as any religion ever was. Now, I want to tell you why I sent for you." She grabbed my hand. "Listen up. There is a test coming, and you will have to choose which side you are on. I want to warn you that the enemy of my master will try to get you to reject his help. He has been your benefactor all these years. His enemy will try to get you to hate him, but you must not listen! If you follow our enemy, you will die. He works for my master's daddy, and he will try to get you to work for him. But he has a mind to kill you, boy. He'll tell you my boss and master are evil. Don't listen! Do you understand me, boy? We're going to win the final battle. Our enemy cannot defeat us for we are too many and we're growing every day. My master has assured me that I will rule with him and that all I desire will be mine. Our enemy will enslave you and take away your freedom. If you follow my master, you can be your own god. He will give you ultimate freedom."

Her demeanor and voice changed. She was stern, almost angry. I was taken aback by her straightforward manner.

"Okay, Miss Sadie! Relax. It's okay. I'll be alright. I can spot a phony a mile away. I'm not going to die for a long time. Besides, a simple carpenter doesn't demand all that attention. I want to thank you for the lead on my father's name. I'm looking forward to meeting your boss, whoever he is. I hope he'll take good care of you. You're the real deal, Miss Sadie. I don't know how you do it, but I'm very glad I met you.

"Don't worry. I won't let anyone con me about your boss. I think I understand why he did things the way he did. Thank you so much for your time. I wish you were going to stay in town a while longer. I'd love to spend more time with you. I also want you to know I don't look down on your religion. If you think your god is going to win some big war, that's fine with me. I believe in 'each to his own.' I have an appointment this afternoon, but I'll try to check in on you later."

"It was good to spend time with you. Enoch, I know you'll make the best decision. You must trust in knowledge, son. It is that path that leads to enlightenment. My master will win, and you need to choose our side. You go on with Damon now. He's been awful patient."

I thanked her for her leads and interesting conversation. I wasn't sure what she was trying to tell me. I got Damon. We left. After we made our way back to his car, he was curious why I'd wanted to see her. Miss Sadie was a little scary, but she was also sweet and kind.

"Okay, Hammer. What did she say?"

"She says your boss and his boss have an enemy!"

"I suppose so. He has a lot of enemies, including his father."

"I wonder why she'd call your boss's boss her master. If I came from a slave family, I'd never want to call anyone 'master'."

"Well, Hammer, Miss Sadie walks in a power I can't even begin to understand. The shopkeeper told me she got her power from her master. She dedicated herself to her master, and he rewarded her with her ability."

"How can a man give someone an ability like that?"

"Who said he was a man?"

"Miss Sadie said her master was still on talking terms with his father."

"His father has a lot of power. It's a delicate balance. I understand they're still talking, but I think he mostly argues with his father. You can't go directly at someone with that kind of power. It's a family thing. I'm not privy to all the stuff that goes on between them. I trust my boss, though. He says his boss is poised for a takeover of the whole organization. He just has to get enough people on his side to make his move. Somewhere over a third of the organization has already come over to his side. He knows he doesn't have enough forces in place for a hostile takeover, but he's working on it."

"Wow. All that corporate stuff is beyond my puny brain. Miss Sadie told me last time I saw her that his father had held him back and that was why he was so mad. Listen, I don't want you to get in trouble if you can't talk about it."

"Nah. He doesn't care about this stuff. I just can't talk about certain things before their time. It's like a corporation giving research to the competition. I suppose you could do it, but it's sure stupid.

"Anyway, his father used to be real lovey-dovey, but then he started to change when his son started to become as powerful as him. Well, that's not exactly right. He's not as powerful yet, but he's learning constantly. Once he knows how his father got his power, he'll be ready for a coup. All the key players have to be in place first—you know, the game changers."

"You said that before. I can't imagine that world. It's enough for me to strap on a tool belt and put up some crown molding. I can't even keep on top of four or five guys. The minute I turn my back, somebody screws up something. Hey, did you know Miss Sadie is leaving tomorrow?"

"No I didn't. Where in the world would she be going at her age?"

"She said the big boss's second in command is coming to get her tomorrow morning at ten. She also says I've met him. His name is Morty."

"You've met Morté? Wow!"

"Miss Sadie says I have, but I don't know for sure. The guy I met I've actually seen three times. If it's the same guy, and I do mean *if*, I don't know why he'd be walking around New Orleans all the time."

"If this is true, it's a big deal! No one's ever seen Morté and lived to tell about it."

"You're funny, Cash! My whole crew saw him when we were doing a renovation uptown."

"Did any of them see his face?"

"No. They were all focused on this poor, homeless person who had frozen to death. It was the saddest thing I'd ever seen. I looked right at him, though. I'm the only one who saw his face. He was about six two, and he had—"

"Stop! I don't want to know!"

"Okay, okay! Geez, Cash, I don't know what the big deal is."

"Sorry, Hammer. I didn't mean to snap at you. I've never seen Morté, thank the gods, but from what I know, he scares the life out of me!"

"The guy I met was pretty weird. I tried to get his name, but he said he had a lot of aliases and something about me getting away from the law or something. I think he had me confused with somebody else. Now that you mention it, he was scary. I think I disturbed the guy. It took a while for him to even acknowledge me. It was like I was an annoyance to him or something. Anyway, I talked to him only for a minute, and I didn't get any helpful information from him."

"But you saw his face! That doesn't happen!"

"Relax. It's probably not even the same guy. What would a high-powered exec be doing walking around everywhere? Those kinds of guys have chauffeurs and limousines."

"You saw his face, though. You saw his face ... That just doesn't ..." Cash drifted off in thought. I listened to him mumble for a few minutes. He had a strange look on his face. He didn't look like he was going to snap out of it.

"Earth to Cash! Earth to Cash!"

"Sorry, Hammer. I'm just totally surprised by all that."

"I think I know how I can find out if he's the same dude."

"What're you planning, Hammer?"

"I don't want to tell you. I'll just say I have a way to prove it one way or the other."

"It's probably better if I don't know."

"Change of subject for a minute, Cash."

"Okay. What do you want to talk about?"

"This morning, you woke me up from a very strange dream."

"Sorry about that. It was a little early for a Saturday morning."

"No, no, it's all good. I wanted to see Miss Sadie anyway. But about the dream ... Do you know anything about animal sacrifice?"

"Animal sacrifice? What are you talking about?"

"I think my brain is trying to work through some kind of puzzle. It has something to do with Miss Sadie ... something she said. Well anyway, the whole female eclipsing the male thing is showing up in my dreams."

"She really got you going, didn't she? She has a way of doing that."

"I'm not so eager to dismiss her talent. I think she has some kind of ability. Like extrasensory perception or something."

"You? I can't believe my ears. The skeptic believes in something supernatural. Wow! Somebody call the president! We need to have a parade or throw a party or something."

"Hold your horses. I didn't say it was supernatural. I think it has something to do with her blindness. Her brain probably has developed some ability to access other brain waves. You know they're experimenting with devices that can move things by thought."

"You're too much, Hammer. You just can't believe the obvious, can you?"

"Sure I can. It's obvious that science hasn't figured it out yet. It's just a matter of time."

"You're going to like the boss. You and he think a lot alike."

"Well anyway, back to my question. Do you know anything about animal sacrifice?"

"That's all religion. It's just like God to kill a bunch of innocent animals. What kind of a God would do that? What did all those little innocent animals ever do to God. It's barbaric!"

"Yes, I kinda see your point. You don't like God much, do you?"

"Eh, he's just a big killjoy, you know."

"Anyway, back to my question. Do you know why in Jewish tradition the sacrificial lamb for the sin of the common people had to be female?"

"Hammer, in all my days, I've never met anybody who can come up with stranger questions than you can. I don't have a clue unless females are less aggressive or gentler or something. Of course, the black widow's an exception to that rule. I don't have a clue. You'd have to ask a Jewish scholar, I guess."

After Damon dropped me off, I prepared to go on the appointment in the afternoon. I hated Saturday appointments, but some people had no other time to meet. Through the day, I hatched a plan to catch the stranger called Morty. There were several shops and cafés across the street from Miss Sadie's place. I figured I'd get to the café at 9:30 for coffee and wait to catch the famous Mr. Morty. I was curious to know if he was the man I had met.

Around 4:30 that afternoon, I called Rabbi Levy about the animal sacrifice question. He told me there were many different sacrifices and offerings for various sins. There were male and female offerings and even grain offerings. The animals were the wealth of that period, and one would give up his wealth as a show of love for God. I listened to everything he said. After all, he was the expert. At least he verified that the lamb sin offering of the common man did have to be female. He read the passage over the phone.

"Here it is, Enoch. I'll read it from a passage in Leviticus chapter four, verses twenty-seven to thirty-five."

> If anyone of the common people sins unintentionally by doing *something against* any of the commandments of the LORD *in anything* which ought not to be done, and is guilty, or if his sin

> which he has committed comes to his knowledge, then he shall bring as his offering a kid of the goats, a female without blemish, for his sin which he has committed ... If he brings a lamb as his sin offering, he shall bring a female without blemish. Then he shall lay his hand on the head of the sin offering, and kill it as a sin offering at the place where they kill the burnt offering.
> The priest shall take *some* of the blood of the sin offering with his finger, put *it* on the horns of the altar of burnt offering, and pour all *the remaining* blood at the base of the altar. He shall remove all its fat, as the fat of the lamb is removed from the sacrifice of the peace offering. Then the priest shall burn it on the altar, according to the offerings made by fire to the LORD. So the priest shall make atonement for his sin that he has committed, and it shall be forgiven him.

"What has gotten you interested in the sacrifices for sin, Enoch?"

"Well, sir, it's a puzzle I'm working on. It may have something to do with my childhood memories or maybe something an old woman said to me. I guess I'm just curious about it."

He couldn't remember a time when we had discussed the animal sacrifices of the Old Testament. I didn't know how I would know that. I couldn't think of why that little factoid had stuck in by brain after so many years. It was like a mystery driving my thoughts. There had to be a reason I'd remember it.

In the end, Rabbi Levy was no help solving the riddle. Maybe there was no mystery to solve. Perhaps I'd once again been given over to suggestibility. Miss Sadie's astrology thing had probably just caught me off guard. If the symbols in the attic hadn't been there, I would've never made the connection.

It was difficult to swallow that a series of random events could have such an impact on my subconscious. I didn't know what Miss Sadie's religious beliefs were. All I knew is that it was an African religion called juju. I thought she also believed in astrology because of some of the things she'd said. I never had a chance to ask her what she believed in. It seemed everybody believed in something. I enjoyed getting all perspectives, especially over a cold glass of beer. I've met all kinds of people with differing beliefs; some believed in crystals while others believed in aliens. I've heard of Hinduism, Buddhism, and a bunch more isms as well as a hundred Christian denominations. I believed in science, so I guessed others had a right to believe whatever they wanted no matter how bizarre. The only ones I thought were too nuts were the triangle people. Every Mardi Gras, I'd see a few of them wearing pyramids on their heads. They were trying to channel some energy from the stars or something. Each to his own, I guess. Maybe some of them had met Miss Sadie and had gone off the deep end. If you were unstable, you definitely didn't need to hang around Miss Sadie. Her special talent would mess with you on your best day.

I wondered what it would be like to take her to a nut house and leave her there with the patients for a while. I could imagine the pandemonium that would ensue. Who knows, maybe Miss Sadie was the reason some of those people were in there. Well, not Miss Sadie actually, but maybe someone like her.

Miss Sadie made me glad I wasn't superstitious. With the crazy things that had happened in my life, including that clock and compass, a superstitious person would have gone nuts, but I was sure of rational explanations for all of it.

Jon used to tell me that I was very religious, that my religion was knowledge, and that it took as much faith to believe in science as it did to believe in God. Science and religion were nothing alike. Science looked for a rational, reasoned approach to life. It's based on empirical evidence, while religion is based on myth. How do you believe in something with absolutely no proof? To me, the whole argument was ridiculous. Knowledge is the way to understanding, not fables. If I actually believed for a minute there were supernatural causes to all the strange things in my life, I would've gone insane. It was safer to believe in a rational world governed by laws of physics. If I was religious in my pursuit of truth, then so be it.

I usually went out to see friends on Saturday nights, but that night I stayed home and played video games. I didn't want to oversleep on Sunday. I had a date with a certain dark-clad character named Morty.

"Enoch, I am here."

"I'm sleeping. Leave me alone."

"I want to talk to you."

"You're just a figment of my imagination. I'm tired tonight. Come back and bother me tomorrow night."

"Don't worry, My friend. You will wake up refreshed and ready for the day."

"I can't believe I'm talking to myself again. Okay, what do you want?"

"You have not yet solved My riddle!"

"Of course, you would know that. You're my subconscious! I asked Rabbi Levy, and he didn't know. I can't believe I'm doing this again! I'm so suggestible!"

"I am real, Enoch. In time, you will believe Me. You will be My witness and tell the world of Me."

"Ha! No no no. That's unbelievable. I have the most arrogant subconscious on the planet. Do I have a need to be important or something? Why would I feel I was important enough to tell the whole world anything? I'm just a carpenter. I do renovation work!"

"I also am a carpenter, and I have always used the insignificant things of the world to confound the wisdom of men."

"You are my alter ego, right? Like a superego! You must be my supercarpentry subconscious on steroids." After saying that to my superego, I thought how amazing the human mind is. It was as if I were awake. I was amazed at this new form of dreaming.

"I want you to continue to look for the answer to My riddle. By My riddle you will know I have come to visit you."

"I don't know why my mind is fixated on this whole male-female thing. It has nothing to do with real life."

"In the riddle is the answer to the hidden mystery of Wisdom from before the foundation of the world. You are to reveal this mystery, and then you will testify of Me! You shall be My witness."

Wow! I must be losing it! I don't even make sense to myself. I thought about it for a few minutes. My subconscious was trying to tell me something. I didn't know if I should just dismiss it or pursue it. What do you say to someone? "Hey buddy! Do you know why a lamb has to be a female lamb before it's killed in some sacrifice? My superego subconscious wants to know!" I'd be laughed out of New Orleans. Thanks a bunch, Mr. Subconscious!

The alarm rang at 8:00 a.m. I jumped out of bed with an extra spring in my step. I didn't need coffee. I was ready to find out about the elusive second in command. If I could talk with him, I might get a better handle on the great mystery boss. I took a shower that bright, cheery Sunday, and the morning air was cool and relaxing. I was going to have breakfast at the café on the corner across the street from Miss Sadie's. I was too anxious to stay home, so I decided to go earlier than my first plan. I drove to the quarter and found a parking spot along Royal. I felt good about getting to the café a little earlier. I wanted to be sure I didn't miss Morty.

I ate eggs, bacon, and beignets. The coffee and chicory tasted extra good that morning. In spite of the distraction of my food, I rarely looked away from the front door of Miss Sadie's shop. I would glance down only for a second or so to make sure I wasn't stabbing a napkin with my fork. I'd get nervous whenever cars rolled down the street because they'd obscure the door for a couple of seconds. Even though I could see both ways for a good distance, I was still uneasy at each passing.

The streets were not very active for the French Quarter. Mornings were recovery time. At about 9:59 a.m., a truck stopped and blocked my view. I got up from the table and moved to look at the door. As the door came into view, I noticed a dark-clad, hatted man with a goatee stepping into the door. Him!

I ran to the cash register to pay my bill. A little old lady was in front of me. I hadn't thought about the time it would take to pay the bill. I fidgeted, huffing like a child who needed to go potty. It had no effect on the lady; she slowly counted out the exact change after returning to her purse several times. I threw a ten down. "Keep the change." I headed for the door.

I ran across the street and down the block to the store. I burst into the shop with a little too much gusto. The door slammed against the wall, clanging the bell.

"Hello, ma'am. I'm Enoch. Do you remember me from the other day?" I had not actually spoken to the woman, but she had acknowledged me on both my previous visits. She was a black woman in her sixties.

"Yes, I remember you."

"Where did the man go? The one who came in a few minutes ago?"

"No one's come in except you. I just unlocked the door."

"I saw him from across the street. He must have slipped by you. He's here to pick up Miss Sadie. I have to see him."

"No sir, I don't think so. I would've seen anyone coming in."

"I know, ma'am, but this guy has a way of slipping by unnoticed. Can we go check on Miss Sadie?"

"I suppose. Let me lock the door first and we'll go up to check on her. Nobody ever comes in on Sundays anyway until lunchtime." She locked the door and pulled down the shade. "Come on. Let's go up to see her. She was getting dressed just before I came down to open up. Must be something big going on today. She never puts on her best dress. I'm sure she'd like to see you."

We went up to the apartment. She opened the door. "Wait here while I go see if she's finished getting dressed." She disappeared into the bedroom while I waited.

"Aaaaeeeeee!" A blood-curdling scream came from the bedroom. I ran to the room and jerked open the door. I saw Miss Sadie lying on the bed in a beautiful dress from the thirties or forties. Her hands were clasped and folded over her stomach. Her eyes were closed. Her assistant was sniffling. "She's dead!"

"How do you know she's dead?"

"I felt her pulse!" She collapsed, sobbing, on the bed.

I checked Miss Sadie's pulse. I could find no trace of one. There was no breath or any sign of life in her. Today was the day she was to leave on her new adventure. If Morty had been here, there was no sign of him. I was hoping to meet him, but if he'd found her like this, no wonder he took off. It was strange that every time he was around, someone had just died. I couldn't believe she was gone. She was one of the most interesting people I'd ever met. I was going to miss her. I didn't know how she had made it that long. I had known only one other person in my life who had gotten over a hundred. I wasn't sure if she actually was. When I was a kid, I was told by the housemother about a woman in the main building who was supposed to be over a hundred. I never actually went into any old folks' home after I left the orphanage. It was quite an accomplishment to live that long. The amazing part was that she'd been so spry for her age.

I stayed with Miss Sadie's assistant for the rest of morning. Her name was Mildred, and she had been helping Sadie for over thirty years. She sobbed uncontrollably as I called the police. Mildred was in no shape to deal with things like that. I couldn't imagine what it was like to lose a friend of thirty years.

Until Miss Sadie, I had only heard about people with special gifts. I'd seen a lot of TV shows and science fiction movies that portrayed people like her. But to come in contact with someone like her was incredible. I thought often about getting her tested at a lab. She had a gift that needed to be understood, but I doubt she would have put up with electrodes stuck to her head. I was no scientist, so I couldn't have begun to tell her where to get tested. I was just a carpenter who liked to have a sensible world. I was going to miss her. She was the real deal.

As I lay on my pillow that night, I wondered if Miss Sadie was in some energy universe, a heaven if you will. Science says that energy is neither created nor destroyed, that it just changes form. Maybe she'd gone to a higher consciousness.

Did I just say there was an afterlife? The events of the day were making me explore that possibility of an afterlife. If I create brainwaves every day, maybe that energy remains after my body ceases to function. Perhaps there's a residue of whom you are after this life, some form of energy not yet measurable by science. I think if I had been a true scientist, I would have had to consider the plausibility of such a theory. We aren't able to measure such energy with existing instruments, but perhaps someday the technology will be available. Brain waves are electrical, but what does electrical brain energy turn into? If energy just changes form, is one form of energy a spirit? Could all the religions be right about the possibility of a soul? It's interesting how the death of someone you know can cause you to consider such things.

"Hello, Enoch."

"It's you again?" I realized I must have drifted off to sleep while thinking about Miss Sadie.

"I enjoy our talks, Enoch."

"Well, I might as well go with it. I guess if you're going to be held captive by your subconscious, you don't have a choice. I mean, you can't escape yourself, right? Wherever you go, there you are!" I chuckled at my comment, and my subconscious character laughed as well.

"You make Me laugh, Enoch! I enjoy your fellowship."

"What great mystery do we have tonight? I don't have anything to do except maybe sleep."

"Did you wake up refreshed today?"

"I hadn't thought about it before, but yeah, I did."

"I told you that you would be refreshed and ready for the day."

"That's kinda strange now that you mention it. Anyway, I'm curious as to what my imagination will come up with next. You *do* understand, Mr. Wisdom, that I'm just going with the flow. Well, go ahead, give me some great mystery no one knows the answer to."

"I understand, Enoch. You want a new mystery? You have not yet solved My first puzzle."

"I'm working on it! I still have to call my friend Jon about it. He's real religious, and he might know the answer. Come on, now. You have to admit it was cryptic. I'm sure if you come up with another mystery, I'll be able to answer it."

"So very wise, are you? Very well, I will give you a second mystery. Why was Eve and all women cursed specifically with pain in childbearing?"

"That's an easy one! If I had a grapefruit pass through my butt, I'd scream too!"

"I suppose you would. The mystery is not in the mechanics of the pain but what the pain represents."

"Okay, okay, I get it! You're asking what's the reason for the curse in the first place, right? I got this one! Because she sinned against God, right?"

"She did disobey God, but that is not the mystery. This mystery reflects wisdom."

"Man, these religious questions are tough. Let me think about it for a second. Let me see. Uh, the pain represents God's anger, right?"

"No, Enoch, it represents His love."

"His love? How can pain represent love?"

"That is precisely the mystery I want you to solve."

"Why don't you ask me a science question instead of all these religious questions? You know I don't know much about religion."

"Science and all knowledge fall short of God. Science cannot solve this simple mystery. Only through revelation can you know the secrets of life."

"Science will answer all questions very soon, I hope."

"Science falls infinitely short, Enoch. Consider the value of pi. Mathematics is the highest form of science and represents the knowledge of man, but the ratio of the circumference to the diameter cannot be measured. If you are so wise, tell me why pi always falls short of a finite answer. It cannot be calculated precisely."

"Wow. Finally a science question. It's about time. Okay, the ratio of the diameter to the circumference is about three-point-one-four-one-five and so on. Science calls it an irrational constant. They've calculated it out to over five or maybe seven trillion or so digits with no repeatable pattern. Okay, okay, give me just a second. I'll figure it out. Ummm, let's see. We know a circle exists and the diameter exists but pi can't be calculated precisely. Hmmm ... Now that I think about it, you might be right. The number falls infinitely short of an answer. Huh. I never thought about it like that before. Okay, I'll give that one to you, but science is constant. Everything is governed by the laws of physics!"

"Are you so sure and wise in your own eyes? Is everything as constant as you believe?"

"Yes, everything makes sense in science. Mathematics is theoretical, so maybe that's not the best choice for a question. Try another question. Make it a science outside math."

"Very well, Enoch. First, tell Me about positive and negative charges."

"Easy one, Mr. Wisdom. Like charges repel one another, and opposite charges attract."

"Is that a law of physics, Enoch?"

"An absolute law that's constant! Much science in physics is based on this immutable principle. It's a constant that does not change. How do you like them apples?"

"Then answer Me this, O wise one. How is it that the positive-charged protons in the nucleus of an atom do not repel themselves? If like repels like, what force holds the positive charges together? Tell Me!"

"Wow. Good question. I believe it's called the unknown nucleic force. I get it. Another scientific anomaly, right?"

"Enoch, by My power are all things held together. I am the unknown nucleic force."

I thought for a minute about my subconscious and was troubled. Could I be so arrogant as to believe the universe revolved around me? Maybe I was disturbed beyond my understanding. I suppose we all live as if the universe revolves around us, but to actually say it to yourself had to be a new level of crazy.

"Enoch, I did not say by your power. I said by My power!"

"Oh, you read my mind now! Of course you do. you're my subconscious! I wonder if psychiatrists can fix this? Maybe I have a chemical imbalance. Why me?"

"I have chosen you to be My emissary. You will believe soon. I will visit you again. Rest for now."

The alarm rang at 6:00, and I jumped out of bed, pumped for the day. I was ready for work in fifteen minutes and flew out the door. As I drove to work, I pondered the dream I'd had the night before. It was as if the clarity of the dream had not dissipated one bit. Most of the dreams I ever had were vague, and most of the time, I couldn't remember what they were even about. These dreams, however, were different. Every time I woke up, I could remember every detail. I remembered a few nightmares from childhood, but these were different. I still felt my subconscious was trying to get me to understand something, but I didn't know what. I was sure it was my own mind, but it seemed like the thoughts of somebody else. Maybe everybody has dreams like this. I wasn't sure. Probably nobody would talk about it if anyone did. How would you explain a dream in which your subconscious believes it's the reason the universe is held together? No thanks. If they didn't talk about such dreams, I was sure not going to either.

Through the day, I continued to ask myself, *Why me? I'm just a normal guy. I don't have any huge aspirations for greatness.* I was just trying to make a decent living and enjoy some friends, drink a few beers, and play some video games. I wasn't trying to change the world or think of myself as important. I just wanted to relax and have some fun after I'd put in a good day's work. That was the perfect life for me. No worries—that was my philosophy. Then again, I wondered why my mind was playing tricks on me.

I thought about calling Jon, but I had to prepare myself for that. I had to figure out how to tell him about my dreams in such a way that he wouldn't think I was crazy. I loved Rabbi Levy, but he couldn't help me solve the riddle my mind had conceived. Maybe Jon could help me even though he was a Christian. I thought of how to phrase it in such a way that would make it a philosophical discussion rather than a question from my subconscious. I finally formed a way to ask the question. I called him.

"Hello."

"Hello. Is Jon home? This is Enoch Galah calling."

"Just a minute ... Dad? Enoch's on the phone."

"Hey Enoch! What's up, ol' friend?"

"Hey Jon, how's life treating you?"

"I've been busy. I'm not working construction anymore. The ministry's supporting me full time."

"That's great, Jon. I'm glad to hear it. Those poor Yankee construction workers probably had enough of you anyway."

"Yeah. Unfortunately, I had to quit before I could finish my evil plan. *Mwahahaha!*"

"You haven't changed a bit, Jon. Anyway, the reason I'm calling is to ask you a religious question."

"Really?"

"It's kind of a technical religious question. You know about my old neighbor Rabbi Levy, right?"

"Yeah, from when you were a kid."

"Well, he told me that the lamb in the Old Testament, you know, the sin offering for the common man, had to be female. Do you know why the lamb had to be female?"

"A female lamb? Really? I'd never picked up on that before. In the New Testament, John the Baptist said Jesus was the Lamb of God who took away the sin of the world. As far as I know, I've never heard a single lecture about that. I never knew the sin sacrifice for man had to be a female lamb. That's a good question. I'll ask some of my old professors. Why do you ask?"

"Something from my childhood, I guess. So do you know anything about the sacrifice of lambs in general?"

"Yes, I know the lamb for the Passover sacrifice had to be male. That had to do with the deliverance of Israel out of Egypt by the hand of God through Moses. In Jewish tradition, the lamb was sacrificed as an offering to God. The blood of the lamb was put on the doorposts and the lintel of the house so the angel of death would not kill the firstborn of the Hebrews. The word *Passover* comes from the angel of death passing over any house with the sign of the blood. Say Enoch, this is pretty in-depth stuff for you. I'm very surprised you have a curiosity about spiritual things."

"Jon, I didn't say I was curious about spiritual things. It's more like a puzzle I'm trying to solve. Why did the Passover lamb have to be male?"

"I'm not done yet. Let me finish explaining. In the Christian tradition, the Passover lamb represents the Messiah, who is male. We believe the Messiah will come back at the end of days and we won't see death. Communion for the Christian is the same thing as eating the Passover lamb is for Jews."

"You know, Jon, that might help a little. I remember a little about that since I was in an Episcopal foster home. I'm probably Jewish, though. I haven't embraced any religion per se. Rabbi Levy told me that the Jews rejected Jesus as the Messiah because He didn't set up the messianic kingdom on earth. Also, Jesus said His followers would not die, but they all did."

"Jesus did say, 'Some of you standing here will not see death,' but I think He was misunderstood. I believe He meant His followers would not see the angel of death but would be changed in a moment and be in the presence of God. Everyone must die. According to God's law, the wages of sin is death."

"Jon, that could be helpful. I need to study this stuff to understand it, I guess. Just one more question if you don't mind."

"Anything for you, Enoch. I've been praying God would give you a thirst for spiritual things."

"I still have a pretty good thirst for beer! I'm just kidding you, Jon. Do you know why God cursed Eve with pain in childbirth?"

"Sure. Because she ate the forbidden fruit."

"I'm not even religious and I could've told you that. What I mean is, why that specific curse and not some other?"

"Man, you're coming up with some wild questions. What's gotten into you? For a nonreligious guy, you're asking the tough questions a scholar might ask. They love those unanswerable questions. I'll tell you this. There must be a reason, because God doesn't do anything by accident. I don't have a clue about that specific curse. Just remember, with some questions, you just have to trust God by faith."

"That's the problem, Jon. You want me to accept something on faith with absolutely no proof. This is all just speculative religious philosophy. I enjoy it over a beer, but it isn't empirical evidence. None of it can be proven. If you could prove God exists, I'd believe in Him."

"Enoch, the Bible says in Romans, 'For since the creation of the world His invisible attributes are clearly seen, being understood by the things that are made, even His eternal power and Godhead, so that they are without excuse.'"

"I don't understand that."

"It means we can understand God and see the proof of His existence by observing His creation."

"You mean like why the nucleus of an atom doesn't blow itself apart?"

"Yeah, I guess so. All I can say, Enoch, is that there's more to life than what science can measure. You don't realize it, but it takes as much faith to believe in science as it does to believe in God. A true scientist would accept the possibility that God exists. We all place our trust in something."

"I suppose you're right on some level. I appreciate your help. If I have any more questions, can I call you back?"

"Always, my friend. I'll continue to pray that God will open your mind."

Over the next two weeks, I waited to hear from Damon. I had a lot of work going on, and every night I went home exhausted. My alter ego didn't visit me in my dreams, and I hadn't thought about the questions much. If I had dreams during that time, I had no memory of them. Life seemed a little more normal. My thoughts were once again focused on work and on finding my family.

I thought Damon might have a lead I could follow. I went to a bar on Bourbon Street to find him. I hadn't talked to him since Sadie's death. Morty had disappeared again without a trace. It seemed like every time he showed up, somebody died. I often wondered what the odds of that were. I still wanted to find him.

As I made my way to the bar that night, the familiar Cash was tipping one up. I took a seat to his left. It suddenly dawned on me that almost every time I went into a bar and saw Cash, at least one of the seats next to him was unoccupied. It's how we'd first met. He bought me a beer, and we've been drinking buddies ever since. I wonder if he scared people out of sitting next to him.

"Hey Hammer, how ya' doing tonight?" His partial smile was comforting to me for some odd reason. It was a strained smile that portrayed sadness rather than happiness, "I'm good, Cash. I guess you heard about Miss Sadie." I felt the same sadness I perceived in Damon. I felt loneliness as the words came out of my mouth. It was strange to feel such empathy for someone you'd met only twice. I was sad her talent would go into history never having been understood or tested by science. I'm sure they would have gone through the same elimination process I had and would have concluded she was for real. That would have motivated them to find answers. It was sad to know she was gone with no one but a select few to know she'd ever existed.

I ordered a beer. We sat for a minute in an impromptu moment of silence out of respect for a great presence who had passed.

"She was something, Hammer."

I nodded, but I couldn't answer. What could be said? I firmly believed in her ... finally. I had frequently wondered how she'd known the details of my life. I decided after much consideration that she could not have known them through conventional means; there were no connections between her and my various unguarded moments. She'd spoken truthfully. She could feel the vibrations or touch the subconscious of another person. She hadn't been out of her apartment since before I was found. She couldn't have known about the Barbie doll and yet she did.

"Cash, I was connected to her in some strange way. I'm going to miss her."

"I know, Enoch." He called me by my real name. It was more intimate ... personal ... heartfelt. We were connecting in a way that was beyond the usual surface bravado. For the first time I felt a *real* connection with Damon. One old, blind, black woman had bound us in a way I would never have expected. I held up my glass. "To Miss Sadie, one of a kind."

Damon responded, "Hear hear! By the way, Hammer, I have another lady I want you to meet."

"I hope she's not old. I don't want to see another person die. I've seen too many lately."

"Nah. She's in her forties. She's like an expert in all things feminine."

"Really? Interesting you should say that. I have some questions on the subject of the feminine. It might be some mother fixation. Probably because I never knew my mother."

"What questions?"

"I don't know how to put it. They're general-knowledge questions, how evolution caused there to be two genders. If all embryos start out female and then about half become male, why was there a need for the male? Why's there more genetic material in the female? Why would a lesser genetic sample have dominance over the greater? The male genetic chromosome is missing a segment. It's like it's incomplete. Think about it—a woman can bring a child into being and sustain its life through her body, but men can't."

"Whoa, Hammer, I'm sorry I asked. I think you're secretly a frustrated mad scientist or something."

"I'm no scientist. I'm just puzzled over women I guess. I've never understood them."

"Amen to that."

"I love the ladies, but they don't think like us. They're smart, intelligent, and great multitaskers, but they're driven by their emotions. Their emotions are like the wind—no one knows where it's coming from or where it goes. All you have to do is say the wrong thing and the wind of emotion will blow you down."

"What I don't get, Hammer, is how the supposed weaker sex has so much power. We do anything they want us to. I've seen friends crumble at the first sign of a tear from a woman."

"That's the truth. I've never had any long-term relationships with women because I don't understand them. I get too frustrated with their emotions."

"Nobody understands a woman but a woman."

"Ain't it the truth, brother! Tell me about your ladyfriend. Is she a feminist who hates men or something?"

"No. She's like a spiritual advisor who helps women find their true inner selves. You know, their authentic feminine self or something like that."

"No offense, Cash, but I don't know if I can deal with another religious nutcase."

"She's not like that. She has real insight into stuff like that. I thought of her after you told me about what Miss Sadie said, you know, about the age of the female and all that."

"I appreciate it, Cash, but I'm not sure I'd elevated Miss Sadie's comments to the level of something I needed to pursue. I just figured it was her religion or horoscopes or something. On the other hand, I think some things she said have had an effect on me. I've been dreaming about some feminine questions."

"I dream about women all the time." His sly grin had a sexual overtone.

"Not those kind of dreams, Cash, you sick puppy." We laughed. "I guess I'll go see her out of respect for Miss Sadie. Hey Damon, I forgot why I came looking for you tonight. Have you heard anything from the boss about a meeting?"

"He's been real tied up in Afghanistan and Iraq lately, setting up some big events or something. I know he'll get to you. You just have to be patient."

"Patience, huh? Not one of my strong suits. Even Miss Sadie picked up on that. The other reason I came to find you tonight was to ask if you could get me a meeting with Morty."

"Morté? Are you kidding? You don't see him unless he has business with *you*! I don't think you understand, Hammer. He's the boss's hatchet man! You don't want to see him, you don't want to know him, you don't even want to know he exists!"

"Calm down, Damon. Sadie told me your boss or his boss was sending Morty to pick her up."

"And what *happened* to Miss Sadie?"

"She died before he could pick her up."

"You're as thick as coagulated blood, man. You look like a balloon but you're made of lead. You should be soaring in the clouds but you're rolling around on the ground. To be gifted with so much logic and reasoning, you sure can't grasp the obvious right in front of your nose. You can't see the forest for the trees. You're as dense as a hammer!" He started to laugh at his joke.

"Now that's getting personal! What's the big mystery here anyway?" I chuckled along with him.

"Yeah, you're right. I'm sure my boss wouldn't want me to *hammer* you down that way anyway."

We laughed for a few more moments and finally settled down.

"You're too much, Cash, but your boss is a very mysterious guy. I've been curious. Has he bagged his quarry yet? Have you made an offer to the big fish? Has he gone to work for your company yet?"

"It's getting close. I'm not allowed to say when, but it should come any time now."

"I appreciate you helping me out on the whole feminine thing. When do we meet the mystic lady?"

"Saturday."

"Don't tell me, you'll be at my place at ten sharp."

"You got it."

CHAPTER 8

A Feminine Perspective

Cash pulled into the driveway at 10:00 on the dot. We headed uptown to a house on Annunciation. As we drove, Damon told me this woman was a leader in feminine mysticism. He also informed me she was another corporate asset. She had a special insight into the divine feminine. It sounded like a bunch of hog slop to me, but I was game if for no other reason than to honor Miss Sadie's memory. I guess my skepticism was in its usual high state of alert. I thought I would query the poor gal and easily reject her point of view. I didn't like to talk to religious fruitcakes on their own turf. It was uncomfortable to even be going to see her. This was not like Miss Sadie's meeting; I had had a purpose with Miss Sadie—I'd been trying to find my family. This was more like a curiosity about some imagined mother fixation. I felt this trip was going to end up being a waste of time. Philosophical discussions were better suited to drinking beer in a good bar.

We arrived uptown at a pleasant house that looked like a double shotgun. It was well manicured with a typical porch with an older, white balustrade. The house was white with a gable roof that bridged both sides of the former double. Damon rang the bell. We entered.

I was not expecting the woman I saw. She was from India, I think; she had a somewhat thick accent. She was dressed in a long, yellow dress. Part of it somehow came over the top of her head like a scarf. The dot in the middle of her forehead mesmerized me like a hypnotic eye. I hadn't ever met a woman like this up close. Her visage and presence were foreign, exotic, not at all like the everyday people I was used to. I felt a presence around her that gave me an odd sexual energy. She had no appeal to me, and I didn't desire her even though she was attractive. It was more of a general feeling of desire or lust in general. It was as if common sense and normal thinking were suspended for a time. I felt an influence that could have made a whole group fall into some sort of negative sexual energy. I immediately felt I was in the presence of evil. But it made no sense. It felt addictive, but I knew it wasn't in me but was emanating from this woman. I felt like running from this controlling, manipulative, enslaving presence.

I decided to take control of the feeling through a reasoning process. If Miss Sadie could pick up thought waves, maybe this woman could generate some type of thought waves that rendered men incapable of rational thought. Once I got hold of myself, I guarded my mind from her influence. I wondered if this was what made some people addicted to sex or porn. It was nothing the woman was doing or how she was dressed; she seemed perfectly gracious and chaste. There was no visible hint of sexuality in the room or anything that would warrant such feelings. I felt it was evil because I thought a weaker mind might have given in to it. I was sure such feeling was at the root of rape and uncontrollable urges to take what's not yours. I had never felt such a thing, and I never wanted to feel it again.

"Kavita, thank you for seeing us today. My friend Enoch seeks your wisdom. I'll just wait in the car."

I panicked when he said "wait in the car." "Cash, don't leave. I'm not comfortable being here alone." I was almost embarrassed as the words slipped out of my mouth. I'd just suggested that this woman couldn't be trusted in my presence, that I'd perhaps entered into the presence of feminine evil. I hoped she hadn't perceived the deeper insult in my comment.

"Yeah, sure, Hammer, if it's okay with Kavita."

She nodded, smiling.

"Miss Kavita, this is no big deal. I was just wrestling with some thoughts about the feminine perspective. Mr. Blackstone here took it upon himself to invite me to see you. I'm a bit of a skeptic on spiritual things. I thought you ought to know that before we talked. Well, I think I have a void in my life from not having a mother. Lately, it's caused some pretty strange dreams about the female aspects of life. Also, a woman who recently passed away told me this was the age of the feminine. So would you mind if I ask you a few questions?"

She hesitated for a moment with her eyes closed. She opened her eyes and said, "I will consult Shakti. Please give me a moment to meditate."

She closed her eyes again as if she were praying or meditating. In a moment, she opened her eyes. “Shakti has granted your request.”

“I’m sorry, ma’am ... Shakti?”

“Shakti is the Great Divine Mother. She is the source of all creative energy.”

“I see. Well, here’s my first question. Do you think women will take over the world?” I didn’t even know why I had asked that question. It felt superficial, stupid. It was like an insult to someone who already thought the feminine was God.

“Women have the divine essence. The female is the energy of the heart of love. The sacred feminine is the unity that is in all things together. It has been important for the feminine to break out of the masculine, for the feminine must be exalted to her rightful place. She has always been the creative divine.”

She seemed to go back to her meditation for a moment. It sounded like the typical feminist perspective. She was probably in a group of feminists who were very mad at men for all the oppression of the past. I didn’t agree or disagree with that; if she wanted to think women were gods, who was I to rain on her parade?

“I guess that would be a yes then, ma’am. That wasn’t the question I needed answered the most. Do you know why the woman suffers such pain in childbirth?”

“The birthing is a ritual of the soul, a union with a woman’s divine, creative power. Through yoga and meditation, the transformation of the divine is complete through the bringing forth of life. The joy of the divine feminine is to create.”

“Yes, ma’am, I appreciate all that, but it doesn’t answer my question. Is there another reason pain is involved in childbirth? I mean, if Shakti is god, why would she curse herself with pain? Why would she curse all women with pain? If I were the divine essence, I think I’d avoid pain like the plague. I mean, where’s the joy in all that pain?”

“I don’t understand. The divine essence is ... the pain. I don’t know. I must consult Shakti.”

“Cash, I don’t think she knows,” I whispered with exaggerated lip movements.

“I am sorry. Shakti is silent on this question.”

“I guess she would be. I don’t mean any disrespect, ma’am, but I think Miss Shakti has a lot of explaining to do to a whole lot of women. By the way, I don’t suppose you believe in animal sacrifice, do you?”

She shook her head.

"I didn't think so. You can't help me on any other questions, ma'am. We'll find our own way out. Thank you for your time. Let's go, Cash."

Cash and I got back into the car. I was a little miffed at his misguided attempt to help me search for answers to my questions. I wasn't about to jump down his throat because I knew he was just being a friend. "Cash, did you feel any strange energy in there?"

"Yeah, but I don't want to say anything."

"C'mon! Spill the beans, man."

"Nah. It doesn't make any sense."

"Try me."

"Alright, alright, Hammer. I felt some weird sex vibe."

"I knew it wasn't just me."

"You too, Hammer? Seriously?"

"It was scary. I don't know what to make of all this, Cash. Do you think I made her mad with that Shakti crack?"

"Yeah, you probably did. Now her god is going to torment her real good."

"Yep, you're probably right. Or at least her brain is going to twist around a little for a while trying to figure out why a female god would curse females with excruciating pain. If there is a God, He must be male because we have no such problem! Listen, Cash, I appreciate your trying to help, but I don't want to meet any more of your strange fellow employees. I don't know what that lady could do for your boss, and I sure don't see any special talent in her. Now Miss Sadie had real talent. Why did your boss put her to work?"

"Well, she was hired for her teaching abilities. She can have women eating out of her hand and soaking in every word she says. She empowers women to find their inner strength. Most of the women who come to her end up divorcing their husbands to be free from the tyranny of their oppression or some such thing. She's good at her job. That is, until you came along. If the women who come to her ever heard what you said to her, they'd abandon her in a heartbeat. My boss would have no more use for her."

"I see. It's a money-making feminist scam, right?"

"They do make money, but that's not why she does it. She's a true believer, at least until today. I think she's questioning everything right now. Did you see the look on her face?"

"Yeah I did. That hit her like a ton of bricks. I didn't mean to dash her beliefs. If something's true, it's going to make sense. I guess it never occurred to any of the women that a female god would have the power to give them birth with no pain. If she couldn't, she's not a true god, right?"

"True dat."

Damon dropped me off. I sat on my couch, pondering the events of the morning. My real issues in life revolved around my deep sense of loss over my parents. I had learned to live with it, but it was always in the back of my mind. The loss of a mother was devastating. No mother would be willing to give up her child unless it was in the child's best interest. A mother would give up her child only if she couldn't take care of it. A mother's love is self-sacrificing; even the courts recognize that. It's universally recognized that women will sacrifice all for the sake of their children. I wasn't angry at my mother; she must have had a good reason.

The funny thing is, I always liked and respected women. I felt that women were more sensible when it came to things like war and violence. I heard many a conversation about the feminine perspective, and I agreed with much of it. I've heard it said, "If women ruled the world, there would be no wars." I felt there was profound truth in that. No woman wanted her son to go to war. Some of the mothers I knew wouldn't even let their boys have play guns because they didn't want them to learn the ways of war. I didn't get it when they were given dolls to play with. Not that I didn't have a doll. His name was GI Joe, and he was the most abused doll in the world. He'd been shot and stabbed, his carcass had been torn apart, and he'd fallen off pretend mountains for the sheer pleasure of his shattered death below. When I was a kid, I couldn't wait to get a gun or a bow and arrow. My first guns were a set of six shooters in holsters. I killed many a pretend Indian and saved many a damsel in distress.

When I got a little older I got an M-16 play rifle that made sounds like a real gun. We would play army with the neighborhood kids. We chose up teams and decided who was going to be the good guys and who would be the commies. We played war for hours on end, never tiring of pretending to shoot the bad guys dead.

We wrestled and play-fought with swords and fists and in general wanted to destroy the forces of evil. We never had any girls join in on our war games. They weren't interested. They would much rather play with their dolls, feeding and clothing them and generally nurturing and holding them. They didn't make sense to us guys. We wanted to be the heroes and change the world by destroying all oppressors and every evil thing that lurked in the shadows. The girls were content to play mommy and Suzy Homemaker.

The nature of the two genders was radically different. Their basic outlooks on life were too different to be attributed to learned behavior alone. I was taught to think it was environmental. In my personal experience, we were as different as night and day; we didn't think the same, dress the same, or act the same.

As I got older, many things began to change. I noticed the words of Miss Sadie becoming more truthful all the time. Men and women in many ways were morphing into each other. I'd never condemned people who weren't like me. Several of my childhood friends turned out gay. I never had a thought that way; it seemed unnatural to me somehow. Some of the guys were tough as nails as kids but later, they were almost indistinguishable from some women I knew. Some of the women, on the other hand, dressed and looked like men. I always felt uncomfortable around some of the people, but I still felt they had freedom of choice. Each to his own. Nevertheless, changes were happening in the world.

There was some truth in Miss Sadie's words. Her observation about the changing reality in the world was more on target than I wanted to admit. The feminine was gaining power all the time. But what did that mean? Maybe Miss Sadie was tapped into some cosmic brain that gave her special insight. I didn't believe in astrology, but I did feel Miss Sadie was on to something.

The feminine perspective did feel more loving and nurturing. The masculine perspective was more warlike and violent. Our DNA dictated how we were. It was way more than some learned behavior; it was genetic. My subconscious was trying to tell me something. I wondered if it represented some greater truth. Perhaps I was just missing a mother I'd never had. One thing's for sure—Miss Sadie connected it with the end of the world; that was a sobering thought. How in the world could she think I had some role to play in the end of the world?

I didn't believe in all that religious hype. Jon used to tell me the world was coming to an end very soon and Jesus was coming back. He told me about the great woes and terrors that were coming. He talked about the mark of the beast and that nobody would be able to buy or sell without the 666 mark. Those myths had no bearing on reality; there was no way such a thing could happen. If any of it were true, we would have to see it coming a mile away. I must admit, it made for great stories and even great movies.

The idea of painting a 666 on your head was utterly ridiculous. I mean really, could you see ladies letting the government paint a number on their foreheads, a sacred makeup zone?! You don't mess with a lady's makeup. I think World War III would definitely happen over that. My part was simple—eat, drink beer, and be merry. After all, I was just a carpenter.

CHAPTER 9

The Call

It was a Thursday afternoon when I got a very strange call from Jon. He was unusually cryptic; he said God had a message for me. I couldn't talk at the time, so I told him I'd call him back. I was in the middle of floating some drywall we had hung the day before. I always hated to get calls when I was in the middle of a messy job. I usually had globs of joint compound all over my hands and various parts of my anatomy.

I never knew why I was stupid enough to do the same thing over and over. I always thought the ring of a phone was somehow more important than the inconvenience of mud all over the side of my face. I was afraid to miss an important call that might lead to a new job. No matter how much I tried to resist the call, I still gave in to the obnoxious ring tone.

The noise of the construction site could drown out the best ring tones. You had to find the loudest one and then boost it as loud as possible. If you forgot to turn the volume down at night, you could cause a person to spill a beer; that wasn't a very good way to treat your drinking buddies, but it was fun to see a person jump due to the loudest, most obnoxious sound he or she had ever heard.

The phone could be silent all day, but the minute you had mud all over your hands, it wouldn't stop ringing until your hands were clean. The guys always said it was karma. What did I ever do to the construction gods to cause me such affliction?

After work, I wondered why Jon had called during the workday. I was curious what supposed revelation from God he'd have. I didn't want to call him that night; I wasn't in the mood for religious stuff. Life was much easier when I wasn't distracted by thoughts of the divine feminine or the end of the world. The possibility of some undetectable spiritual reality has always unnerved me. Every time I talked about spiritual matters, it caused me to search for a logical explanation. It seemed that my subconscious was my greatest adversary. I could give a possible reason for almost any scenario except the questions my own mind came up with.

I'd never thought about the fact that the atom should not be able to maintain its nucleus but does. It's a scientific impossibility, but still, an unknown force holds it together. There are paradoxes in science, especially math. That doesn't prove there's a God, right? I often thought about Miss Sadie's words about me being a paradox. What in the world had she meant by that? I shouldn't have been, but I was? If she hadn't told me such secret knowledge about my life, I would have completely dismissed her words as the ranting of an old, crazy woman. According to her, I threw things out of balance. What could I make out of that? It was too mind-boggling to consider. It's probably what caused me to think the world revolved around me or at least the superego of my dreams. She certainly had a way of sparking your imagination. I'm grateful she expanded my mind. I had a greater respect for the unknown and possibility thinking.

I always loved Jon, so I had to call him out of respect and love. If it had been anybody else that day on any subject of religion, I would have blown him or her off. Not Jon, though. His smiling face and humor had been there at some of the worst times of my life. His humor anchored me in reality. I think I would've gone nuts when those strange things scared me out of my mind. He was there when I'd needed him. He kept fear at bay. I would've been swallowed up in torments and terrors if he hadn't been there. It seemed odd that one huge anchor in my life was not a scientist or a humanist but a devoutly religious guy. Rabbi Levy was a great anchor in my life as well. They both had a type of stability. They knew who they were and what they believed. Even though their faiths were different, they were more alike than they'd ever admit. I finally quit procrastinating and made the call.

"Hey Jon, I'm sorry I couldn't take your call today. I had joint compound all over my hands."

"I understand that! Have you ever noticed as soon as your hands are in something nasty the phone starts to ring?"

"Tell me about it."

"I called, Enoch, because I had a dream last night I felt was from God."

"You know, Jon, dreams are just your imagination run amuck."

"No, this one was different. I'd never had one like this before. Do you mind if I tell you about it?"

"No man, I got time. I was just going to nuke a pot pie and watch some TV."

"Well, I was in a dark place, and I felt an evil presence chasing me like it was going to swallow me. I ran into a brightly lit room, and there was a presence in the room. I can't describe the presence, but it was like a person clothed in light, and he spoke to me."

"Stop right there, Jon! Did you say a person clothed in light?"

"Yes. Why do you ask?"

"I've had similar dreams my whole life! Wow! That's a pretty big coincidence. You got my attention now. Keep going."

"Well, like I said, I went into the room, and I heard a voice speak to me. 'Do not worry. I will not allow them to hurt you.' I tried to look at the person who said this, but his face was too bright. I felt peace, and I knew it was the Lord."

"This is weird, Jon. That is exactly what happened in one of my dreams as a child. I must have told you about it. You're probably remembering what I told you."

"What? Enoch, in all the years I've known you, you never told me a single dream of yours, not once!"

"Noooo ... I had to! You couldn't have come up with this on your own, Jon. I'm convinced dreams come from suggestions from everyday life we don't always remember. A little comment here, a little suggestion there, and your subconscious picks up on it. It's called REM sleep. It's when the neurons firing off in the brain are very similar to when you're awake. That's why the dreams are remembered so vividly during that phase of sleep. They've proven that phase of sleep is necessary for the brain. I guess it's a kind of valve that releases pressure or something. Now the terror is a parasomnia sleep disorder called *pavor nocturnes*. It's all very scientific."

"Sounds like you've studied it."

"I like to know what make us tick. The mind is such a mystery and has such potential. I'm interested in solving the mystery. I've met some people with some powerful abilities in the mind. A lady I knew could pick up on people's brainwaves. It was amazing! I'd never have believed it if I hadn't seen it with my own eyes. I know that sounds crazy, but I swear to God it's the truth."

"I don't doubt the supernatural."

"I didn't say it was supernatural. It's an anomaly for sure but not supernatural. Here's the thing. She was blind, and I think her brain developed some sort of mechanism to compensate for her blindness. It's common knowledge that other senses are heightened when one sense is deprived."

"You're always looking for a natural explanation to everything. You keep trying to fit a round peg into a square hole. Sometimes, Enoch, it just doesn't fit. Anyway, let me tell you about the rest of the dream."

"Okay, but I'm pretty sure I must have told you about my dream. I may not remember it, but we must have talked about it."

"Well, I'm not going to argue about it, but I am sure you have never told me about any dreams of yours. That'll be a debate for another day. Well anyway, back to the dream. The voice that came from the light said He had visited you and wanted me to call you to tell you a few things. I know this sounds nuts, but He said He had a plan for your life and you were going to fulfill a great mystery. He said you have been dedicated to be His emissary. He also said at the end of three and a half years, when you've completed your work, you will die."

"Stop, stop, Jon, I have to cut you off. Maybe you're just remembering the words on the wall from that attic on North Rampart. Don't you remember? 'The emissary must die'? Ooooo ... very scary. The boogeyman is going to get me." I chuckled at the thought. "Seriously, Jon, just because my middle name means 'emissary' doesn't mean I'm going to die."

"What? Your middle name means *emissary*? You never told me that!"

"Yeah, I must have. Maybe when we were working together or something."

"I've been gone from New Orleans a good while now. You definitely told me your last name meant 'to reveal' or maybe 'revelation' in Hebrew. You said your middle name meant you were a king."

"Yeah. Now that I think about it, you might be right. I forgot I just found out recently what 'Kingu' means. Are you sure I haven't told you this? I guess it was a long time after you left."

"Really? Tell me how you found out."

"Rabbi Levy told me. He had a book of ancient Sumerian, and he showed me a translation of the word *kingu*. It means 'great emissary'. It was a little disappointing. I kind of liked the idea of being a king."

"I didn't know that. I would have definitely remembered that! That's further testimony this dream was from God. The Bible says in the book of Joel that in the last days He will cause people to have dreams. Wait a minute. Let me read it to you. I looked this up after I had this dream. It's found in Joel, chapter two, verses twenty-seven through thirty. It reads:

> I am the LORD your God And there is no other. My people shall never be put to shame. And it shall come to pass afterward that I will pour out My Spirit on all flesh; Your sons and your daughters shall prophesy, Your old men shall dream dreams, Your young men shall see visions. And also on My menservants and on My maidservants I will pour out My Spirit in those days. And I will show wonders in the heavens and in the earth: Blood and fire and pillars of smoke.

The Bible tells us that God's spirit will pour out on us and we will have dreams from His Spirit."

"Jon, you did say old men! It's obvious it's talking about you because you're older than me." I always took every chance I had to poke fun at Jon.

"I'm glad you haven't lost your sense of humor. Now stop interrupting me. I'll never get through this dream if you keep interjecting. Anyway, the spirit in the dream said He'd given you a mystery to solve but you wouldn't be able to solve it on your own. You'd finally ask Him to solve it, and He would tell you what it meant. Does this make any sense to you?"

"That's very freaky, Jon. I'm not sure I can accept the premise that there's some sort of a God out there. I have a lot of unexplained riddles. I think you must be remembering something I told you." I secretly wondered if other people might have had a little touch of Miss Sadie's talent. Maybe we could tap into the thoughts of others in a dream state.

"The Spirit in my dream said you'd reject what I'm saying. God has closed your eyes and has veiled His ways to you for now. He has many things to say to you, but you cannot receive them yet. He's protecting you through a hidden veil of wisdom. I'm supposed to tell you this even though you won't believe it. You are to be a great emissary of His revelation. He's dedicated you for that reason. You'll travel the world in the last days and reveal a deeper knowledge of Him to the world. You'll open a dialogue among His people and will answer questions that have long bothered the seed of Abraham. I know this sounds weird, but that's what I was supposed to tell you."

"Jon, it's not like you to get all mystical on me. I'll think about what you said. I'm sure there's a rational explanation for it. I thought you didn't believe in all that mystical charismatic Christianity stuff. You told me the Bible was the only revelation of God we could depend on. You said Baptists believe there's no more revelation since the Bible was canonized. Is that the right word? You also said other Christian groups believed in continuing revelation but you didn't. You said we've been told everything in the Bible and we had to accept it all on faith, right? So now you're saying something that isn't in the Bible is from God. Do you get the contradiction there? That's one of the problems I have with the Bible—it's full of contradiction. And all you Christians have different ideas about everything."

"Yes, I did say that, Enoch, but I didn't mean it to sound so dogmatic. I do believe in continuing revelation. For instance, my call to serve God is not found in the Bible. I was speaking in more-general terms. I'm afraid I've held the party line on some things, but I'm reassessing my understanding about how God speaks to us. There have been dreams all through the Bible. Joseph dreamed he'd be elevated above his brothers, and he was. Abraham and others had dreams from God as well. It's just that I've never had a dream like this. It was like I was awake while I was dreaming. I could remember every word in the dream. I can't explain it, but I know it was from God. I have to be obedient to what I was told. You've been called by God to serve Him and to live for Him."

"Uh, excuse me, Jon, did you say *live* for Him? I could've sworn you told me I was going to die when He was done with me. Jon, if your God is going to kill me when I'm done working for Him, why would I want to work for Him? Catch my drift? I'm lacking in my motivational level here. I mean, who wants to work for someone who wants to kill him? If you're trying to get me to convert to Christianity, you're doing a poor job of it."

"No, Enoch, I'm not trying to get you to convert. No man comes to God unless he's first drawn by God. Only God's Spirit can open up our eyes and mind to Him. I wish you were a Christian. I think God has big plans for you. My telling you about the dream has less to do with you than with me."

"How's that?"

"It is about my obedience, not about your acceptance. I had to overcome a lot of second guessing of myself to call you. I've told you in the past I didn't believe in things like dreams. That kind of thing goes on in charismatic Christian circles. I knew you'd call me on my words. I knew I'd have to eat some crow. I had to overcome all my fear of sounding like an idiot to call you. I always thought people who said God spoke to them directly were a little unbalanced because I've always believed the Bible was enough. Now I feel I've been visited by the Spirit of God."

"Jon, that happens to me all the time. It's just your subconscious releasing some steam. You know, REM sleep is like a pressure valve. It's a vital part of sleep, and if you're deprived of it, you'll go nuts. The way I see it, Jon, is that you're perfectly normal ... in a very nutty way."

"I'll keep praying for you, Enoch. I don't think it's just some random coincidence. I feel it's important. Oh, I almost forgot one other thing. The Spirit in my dream said, 'There is much pain in love.' Do you know what that means?"

"That's the first strange thing you've said. That kind of scares me a little. You make me wonder if maybe there is a God. I've been wrestling with that. Remember when I asked you why Eve was cursed with pain in childbirth?"

"I remember. As a matter of fact, I may have some insight into that. In the Christian tradition, the pain of the cross was actually a great act of God's love. Jesus died as a substitute for you and me. He suffered pain so you and I wouldn't have to. We'd be reconciled to God through His blood."

"Jon, that argument doesn't make sense. Why would God kill His kid for something He didn't do? It's illogical. You don't kill an innocent person and let the guilty go free. That isn't love, that's insanity. I sort of understand your point of view, but it's a huge leap over logic to get to that understanding. I can't believe something unless it makes sense to me. I can't just put my brain on hold and accept something on faith."

"The impossible is possible with God. He reconciles the paradoxes of life."

"Now you're just messing with me. You know I've been studying paradoxes. You sure know how to push my buttons. Your comic genius is legendary, you know."

"No, I'm not messing with you. It's just that Christianity has a lot of paradoxes that are hard to understand."

"Such as?"

"We believe God is one but in three separate personalities, Father, Son, and Holy Spirit."

"Rabbi Levy says there's only one God. His view makes more sense."

"Then why does the Jewish Bible say, 'Let us make man in our image and after our likeness'? I know it's hard to understand. All the early church members were Jews, and they believed in Jesus as their Messiah. They accepted Him as God's Son, which made Him divine."

"Yeah, I know all that. Jon, you know I love you man, but this religious stuff makes my head hurt. I like philosophy as much as the next guy, but just not too much at one time. We could sit here all day and not get anywhere. But I want you to know I appreciate your attitude and I'm glad you called me. Some of the things in your dream do give me pause. Some of the things you described were spot on with some of my dreams. Probably everybody has similar dreams but just don't talk about it. One thing's for sure, Jon—whether you're telling a good joke or trying to figure out the mysteries of life, it's always good to talk to you."

"Well, thanks for that, Enoch. I hope you know the feeling's mutual. I'll continue to pray for you."

I truly meant what I'd said to him. It was always good to talk to Jon. He had some strange ideas about life and God, but I still thought he was one of the best things to happen to me. I knew he cared about me, and he'd always been a true friend. I always respected him regardless of his religious beliefs. I knew he had a good heart and wanted only the best for me. He never pushed his views on me. He always let me ask questions about his views. He respected me. He believed deeply in his faith and would express it, but I never felt condemnation from him. The Wellingtons had made me feel I was going to burn in hell for every infraction, but Jon was never that way. He was a lot of fun and kept me in stitches most of the time. I was glad he trusted me enough to tell me what was on his mind as misguided as I thought it was.

Something he said continued to trouble me for a few weeks. The idea that God had called me to some big task or event was a theme that hit me several more times. I carefully considered Jon's dreams along with my own and some things Miss Sadie had said. Every time I thought about a construction worker changing the world in some way, I'd laugh. Still, it gave rise to my imagination. What if I were a secret agent sent from a being of immense intelligence that wanted to get a message to the world just before an invasion? Beam me up, Scotty. That's the stuff of science fiction, a posthypnotic suggestion being released by a precise sequence of words to usher in the master plan of alien conquerors! Actually, if I were a writer, those would be some pretty cool ideas for a movie, but it's probably been done before anyway.

If you think about it, changing the world is a big concept. The world changes all by its self with no help. I don't deny that some people have had great influence because of something they did. Alexander the Great had a profound impact on the world of his day. In our time, Hitler may have had the worst impact on the world. Many people died as the result of that man's madness. I had no such lofty ideas. I didn't want to change anything, except maybe a full glass of beer into an empty glass of beer. I wondered if that made me a pessimist. I was never a glass-half-empty guy. I wanted the glass empty so I could fill it again. I must have been in a category of my own when it came to pessimism.

The following Saturday, I was enjoying some beignets and coffee at Café Du Monde when one of my bar buddies was looking for a table. I waved Two Shoes over to the table. The only thing I knew about Two Shoes was that his first name was Rick. I'd played pool and tipped a number of beers with Two Shoes but had never gotten to know him. Most of the guys from the bar were just fun people to hang around with. We'd idle away hours listening to music or playing pool. The only one from the bars I had any kind of relationship with was Damon.

As Two Shoes made his way to the table, I wondered about his life outside the bar. Perhaps he was interesting in some way I hadn't picked up on. I guess it's odd to have so many "friends" and not know anything about them. I never talked about people's hopes and dreams or how they felt about life; our conversations were always more surface than that. We had lengthy discussions about the boldness of the flavors of various beers, the depths of color, and the judicious use of hops. You'd think we were connoisseurs of fine wines rather than just a bunch of beer guzzlers. We could talk forever about great quarterbacks and who we thought was the best and why.

It was easy for us to be lighthearted and fun; we never wanted to scratch below the surface of a person's life in case something vile lurked there. It was better not to know. We all liked the façades we lived in. I felt most of my friends would never understand the crazy things I'd seen. It was far easier to play the part of the happy-go-lucky Hammer, a typical guy wading through the waters of life. The mask I wore was a happy face, and my beer-drinking buddies wore similar masks.

"Hey Hammer, thanks for saving me a chair."

Two Shoes sat in the seat next to me. In an unusual surge of curiosity I wanted to have a deeper connection to people that day. It just happened that Two Shoes had come along when I was feeling the need to be more than superficial. As I smiled at him, I wondered who he really was. Did he have a family? Did he have great goals for himself? Perhaps he had an interesting story that would give me a connection to the deeper things of life. In any case, I was feeling the need for something more intimate, a type of empathy that transcended the mundane. I wanted to know and to feel something that was real. I wanted to ask him about the deep realities of his life but couldn't think of how to do that. The characters we'd created for each other were void of depth and meaning. How do you forage into unknown territory? I could think of no good starting point to explore the true man sitting at my table, so I thought of his nickname and felt it might lead to a deeper connection.

"Hey, Two Shoes! How're you doing today? This ain't the bar!"

"Yeah, you're right! You know, Hammer, you shouldn't have just beer running through your veins, you have to mix it up a little with coffee. It's a principle of the balance of life, you know, like yin and yang. Everything has to be in balance. The coffee counteracts the beer. They cancel each other out, which allows you to drink more beer. Are you getting this, Hammer? Pay attention! This is deep stuff, you know, the meaning-of-life type stuff."

His humorous anecdote reminded me of why I liked the guys in the bar. They had a way of looking at life though the bottom of a beer glass. They were for the most part all good-natured guys. We'd laugh and joke and carry on for hours entertaining each other while dispensing frothy suds into the bottomless pits we called stomachs.

"Yeah I got it, Two Shoes. Beer makes the world go 'round. The more beer, the faster it spins—the faster it spins, the more you fall down! Is that what you mean?"

We both laughed at each other's comments. Two Shoes was a funny, clever guy. It was hard to keep up with him when it came to witty comments. I always felt insufficient in the area of wit. I'd been in the presence of masters of the art, and Jon was the chief among them, but Jon's absence had left a hole in my soul that used to be filled with his daily jokes and companionship. I missed him. Maybe I should say I missed a spiritual connection of sorts with him. Perhaps I was feeling his loss that day. Any time I talked to Jon at that time, it was more real, less fun.

"Two Shoes, I've always wanted to ask you why everyone calls you Two Shoes. What's the story?"

"Well, a few years back when Mardi Gras was going on, I decided not to dress up in a costume. Instead, I found the most outrageous shoes you could imagine and wore them with regular clothes. They were bright turquoise, but I wasn't satisfied with how they looked. So, in order to kick it up a notch, I hot-glued jewels all over the shoes. They were the godawfullest, most obnoxious things you'd ever seen. Well, when I went to the bar, I found a table and sat down and hid my shoes. Everyone was wondering why I hadn't put on a costume or a mask. I slowly got up from the table and began to do a little soft-shoe shuffle everybody could see. When everyone saw the shoes, they started laughing and insulting my precious shoes. It was a lot of fun. Well, anyways, Chuckles started laughing so hard he couldn't catch his breath. Skinny screamed, 'One shoe could kill a man with laughter, let alone two.' So the word spread far and wide of the evil plot to kill men through the power of 'two shoes.' Ever since then, I've been known as Two Shoes."

"That's hilarious. I finally know the infamous secret of the slayer of men, the dastardly power of Two Shoes."

"You know where Chuckles's name came from?"

"Oh yeah, he's the laughingest guy I've ever known. He could chuckle at anything. He could find something funny about any situation."

"We've had a lot of fun in the bar over the years."

"Yes we have, Two Shoes. I'm going to call you Rick today. I want to know about Rick the man rather than Two Shoes the legend. Tell me something about yourself."

"This is new, Hammer. You know, I wonder about the guys all the time. It's like we hang out all the time but never know anything personal about each other."

"That's exactly what I was thinking."

"What can I tell you about myself? Let's see. I'm married, believe it or not."

"That's news! I've never seen your wife."

"We have an understanding. She spends all my money, and I get to hang with the guys at the bar."

"Do you have any kids?"

"Two boys, eighteen and twenty-one, both in college. The younger one is making his way through school teaching martial arts while the older one is finishing up a degree in engineering."

"Wow, Two Shoes domesticated—who would've thunk it? Oh. Sorry. Today you're Rick. What else?"

"I'm Catholic."

"You? No, I don't believe that. I would've never figured you for a religious guy."

"I'm at Mass every Saturday night. Why do you think I always come in late on Saturday?"

"Do you believe all that stuff, or is it a family tradition or something?"

"God moves in mysterious ways, Hammer. For a lot of years, I just went through the motions—you know, doing my duty for God and country, but lately, it's been different."

"In what way?"

"I'm not sure. I was sitting in Mass a little ways back, listening to the priest's message when I felt a touch from God. It was like God was telling me I had a purpose and things were going to soon change in my life. I never felt anything like that. Anyway, a little after that, I started having strange dreams. I went to my priest and told him about a few of them. Here's the funny thing. I've been a Catholic all my life but never felt God was real. All of a sudden I started thinking I was feeling the presence of God. I didn't know what to make of it. The priest said God had touched me and I needed to respond to that touch."

"Wait a minute, wait a minute! Go back to the dreams. What do you mean you started having strange dreams?"

"Well, this is going to sound strange, but I started having dreams about the end of the world. In my dreams, God was calling me to trust in Him and prepare for His coming."

"I can understand the impact of a dream. I've had a few strange ones lately myself. You know your subconscious can come up with some wild stuff when you're asleep."

"What was your strange dream, Hammer?"

"Well, I've had this recurring dream since childhood. I see and hear a man who's too bright to look at. He tells me things like I've been called to do some big job. I think it's my unconscious id battling with my superego in some huge Freudian war."

"Did you say 'called,' Hammer?"

"Yeah. Why?"

"That's weird. I had a dream about you! I saw you in a long, white beard, and you were speaking to people, and they were falling on their faces and weeping and crying. The next thing in the dream was a voice that said, 'My emissary will testify of Me to the world.' It was weird.

Even with the beard, I knew it was you. You're not planning on growing a beard anytime soon, are you?"

"No sir, not me! But that emissary thing is a little strange. Have you been talking to Cash?"

"No. Why do you ask?"

"Well, I may have told him my middle name means 'great emissary.' The way I see it, the two of you are conspiring to set me up for a good joke."

"Are you serious? Your name really means 'emissary'? Are you kidding me?"

"I didn't say 'emissary', I said, 'great emissary'. There's nothing average about me. I'm the greatest, and I have the superego to prove it!" I started to laugh at my preposterous statements, but Rick wasn't laughing.

"Hammer, that's too weird. It freaks me out! I didn't know that. I think God has a call on your life."

"I don't believe in God, but I do believe in the power of a well-timed joke. Don't worry. I'll figure out what you guys are up to."

"Seriously, Hammer, we're not playing a joke on you. Everything I told you was the truth."

"Right, Rick. I can wait for the punch line later. I get it. The cosmos is calling me to do the will of God. Nothing could be simpler, right? I'm good with it! I'm going to be God's emissary. God always picks carpenters, right? I mean, Jesus was a carpenter, so it's open season on carpenters. The carpenters' local has a sign above the door that reads, 'Only called of God may enter.' I'm way ahead of you."

"Hammer, I wouldn't joke around with stuff like this."

"I'm not making fun of your beliefs, Rick. I'm laughing at the absurdity of God calling an agnostic to work for Him."

"Yeah, that would be kind of funny. You don't even go to church. I see your point, Hammer."

After we parted company, I felt it had been time well spent. I had a little deeper connection to someone I saw fairly regularly. It seemed that the dream theme was picking up momentum. I had to wonder if my friends were pulling together for a massive joke on me, though; you never knew with those guys. It was like Jon was pulling strings behind the scenes. He'd somehow gotten hold of some of my drinking buddies to pull the best joke ever. Jon was the only one I knew with the sophistication to pull off something like that. His Mexican car joke convinced me there was never a better prankster than Jon. His dream sequence and feigned concern was all a part of his master plan. It couldn't be coincidence that Rick had had the same dream as Jon.

This had Jon's fingerprints all over it. I mean really, Two Shoes had had the same dream? I was almost delighted imagining when the punch line was going to come. Two Shoes was a great jokester, but no one could compare to Jon. I knew he was reaching down from up North with a plot that would make the best TV mystery blush with respect; I thought that much about his ability to pull a fast one. He deserved my respect. As I thought about it, he had called me with his dream. He must have known my imagination would take over and I'd fall into his evil clutches. His talent and comic genius was truly beyond mortal men. He was a god among comedians. I often wondered why he chose a life of religion when he could have been one of the greatest comedians of all time. To me it was like he had missed his true calling.

For the time being, I couldn't let on that I knew I'd been set up. I even wondered if Jon had set up the attic scene—. Could he have done it? I wondered if he had gone on that job before I did and set up the whole thing; the writing on the walls, the armoire rigged to fall over at just the right moment, and my name on the wall. Could he have done all that? Why would he wait so many years to deliver the punch line?

I hadn't really considered that I might have been set up from the start. One thing he couldn't have faked was all those birds that had been in that attic for years. Still, as difficult as it was to set up, it might have been possible. It's a tough one to figure out for sure; all that just to pull off a joke about me being called of God? Maybe I was just grasping at straws. The likelihood of all this being a setup just didn't jibe with the facts. Nobody could have set all that up.

CHAPTER 10

The Meeting

I got a call from Damon toward the end of 1998. He told me that the boss had contacted him and that he'd contact him in two years to explain everything to me. I had for the most part forgotten about the big boss. If it had been a practical joke, I was no longer in the mood to play along. No one ever told me what was going on. Fortunately, my work was a distraction that I needed. We were working on turning the old Pitney Bowes Building into an architect's office. There's nothing more challenging than working for a whole group of architects on their building.

I saw the gang at the bars on occasion, but with my heavy workload, I had less time to hang out. Damon told me the boss would talk to me on Sunday at 3:00 on November 26, 2000, two years from then. By then, I felt this was all baloney, so I didn't pay it much mind. I had a life; I was tired of being jerked around anyway.

I understood that it had taken years to get this meeting set, but I was so busy with business I didn't have time to think. A year or two could pass by in such a flash that I almost didn't believe it was gone. I didn't blame Damon's boss for neglecting me, that is, if he existed. The problem of my origin wasn't his. At my age, it was possible my parents weren't even alive. They'd be very old if they were. I never found anyone with my father's name, and I'd searched the world with the help of a few computer geeks who knew how to use the Internet.

I was less troubled by the loss of my parents as I got older. The inner longing had been replaced by the slow, methodical realization that life happens. You're allotted so much time, and that's it. Everybody's life sucks in some way. I wasn't the poster boy for tragedy; I knew people who had died of cancer and others who'd been killed in accidents, so what did I have to complain about? So I was orphaned—that wasn't the end of the world; you never heard me whining about that. I always felt people who whined about their states in life needed to get over themselves. I always tried to look at the bright side of life; it was way more fun to laugh and joke than to let myself get depressed. I'd enjoyed *Winnie the Pooh* when I was younger. When I got older, I could see some of the Pooh characters in real life, way too many Eeyores and not enough Tiggers. It's funny that a pessimist thought there were too many pessimists in life.

But the thought of meeting the boss sparked my interest once again as to my origins. I'd given up the search almost a year earlier. At that point, it was more a curiosity than a driving force in my life. I was thirty-nine and was becoming very reflective on life. I'd lived all my years without a mother and had survived. The dreams of a young, beautiful mother had long ago passed and had been replaced by the reality of a woman who had to be in her late fifties or early sixties. My childhood imagination had finally succumbed to the reality of life's harshness. I'd already worked through a whole gamut of emotions to deal with the hole in my heart and had just accepted it would always be there.

The whole joke about "the call of God" never came to fruition. I didn't know why Jon or whoever had gone to such great lengths to set me up but never deliver the punch line. Everybody was too busy to give old Enoch a good laugh. I hadn't talked to Jon in over a year. He was busy with his duties as a minister. I wondered if he pulled shenanigans on his congregation. Even after all the years, I still missed his smiling face.

I was about to turn forty; that was hitting me hard. I'd had a good life, but the realization of the shortness of life was beginning to set in. I didn't know if I was satisfied with what I had accomplished. Could there be something more to life than good laughs and cold beer? Maybe Jon and the others were right about there being a grand design in everything but I wasn't privy to it. My business had become more successful, and I rarely worked with my hands anymore. I'd saved enough to buy a house, but with no wife and family, I saw no need to buy one.

Would I leave a mark on the world or just slide into history with no one ever knowing I'd been here? I thought about Miss Sadie. She had the potential to change the world, but she passed into history with no fanfare and few people even knowing she'd even existed. I'd done well as a contractor, but when articles were written about renovation projects, the owner and the architect were named, but the guys who had done the work never got any credit. I looked up and down streets and realized I had no clue who had actually built the buildings. Rabbi Levy had told me something very similar years ago. According to him you could see the evidence of God's work even though you couldn't see Him. His comment made more sense to me on that day than ever before.

The next year, I saw Damon a lot less because of my workload. I was turning a building into a restaurant in the 1500 block of Saint Charles Avenue. It was to be a high-end steak house, and I was being pushed by management to complete the job before the end of the year. We were anticipating Y2K, and we laughed a lot about planes falling from the skies and the world coming to an end as all computers would crash at midnight, December 31. We had planned a soft opening for that night to celebrate the new year and the new restaurant. The wine was flowing, and the party was great. I had worked fourteen-hour days for months and rarely had had time to think let alone hang out at the bar. For about six months, the workers on the job were my family and friends. I turned the place over to the owners and took time off as I was exhausted. For most of 2000, I took only basic renovations and stayed away from larger, more-demanding jobs.

I got a call from Damon on October 8. He told me not to forget that next month the boss was going to talk to me. I laughed. "Whatever you say, Cash." It was just a bunch of baloney. Over the last two years, I was so busy that I didn't have time to play games. I hadn't had any interest in finding out if any of Damon's crap was true. However, he called every day for a week before the supposed meeting. He insisted his boss was real. I don't think I believed him anymore; it had been too many years.

Sunday finally came, and I must admit I was half hearted about going to meet the boss. I was more curious how this was going to play out. I had felt anger, confusion, and even appreciation for the boss. I'd gotten over the awe I used to feel. I imagined he was a powerful businessman who had no time for the likes of me. I had only Cash's assurance he was real.

One thing was for sure—Cash had money; he bought a new Bentley every year. It was likely he was a trust-fund baby or something like that. I'd never seen him work in all the time I'd known him. Nobody sits in bars all the time. His whole recruiter thing just didn't make sense.

That implied work, but he didn't work according to my evidence. Even though I suspected he was full of crap, I was willing to take the plunge.

If the boss was real, I wanted to meet him to get some answers. It was no longer so much about my father and mother but more about why he'd jerked me around for so long. If this guy was real, he could shove it as far as I was concerned. I used to think he might hire me as he had Damon and then I'd be making a ton and hobnobbing with bigwigs. Instead, I had made it on my own. I was well off enough not to kiss his butt. I was respectable. I didn't need his money or power. Who was he anyway to think I owed him anything? He hadn't done me any favors. Even if he somehow helped out when I was a kid, I hadn't asked for that. He'd have been motivated by guilt and shame, not because of any concern or love for me. He just wanted to protect his boss's father, who was probably dead by then. That's the only reason he felt it was okay to meet me.

Damon arrived at 2:15. I greeted him while stepping out my door. I didn't want Damon to know I was uneasy and angry; he was just a yes man under the control of his boss. He told me we were going to the Ritz Carlton on Canal. I'd seen the renovation of that place going on for some time. It had opened for business just the month before, and I was curious to see how it looked on the inside. I had read the renovation of the old Maison Blanche Building into the Ritz Carlton had cost $250 million, and I wondered what that kind of money bought.

After the valet drove off with his car, we made our way through the lobby to the elevators. We got off on the third floor, where check-in was. Instead of checking in, we made our way to another elevator. We entered a luxurious suite on the fifteenth floor. It was furnished beautifully, and Damon headed for a large, ornate desk. He motioned for me to sit in front of the desk. I obliged.

After he nestled into the oversized seat behind the desk, he picked up an earpiece with a small microphone and placed it on his ear.

"Where's the boss, Cash?"

"He's going to call at three sharp, and it's only two forty-eight."

"What the ...? Damon, you said I was going to meet the boss!"

"No, I said the boss said it was time to speak to you."

"This is the biggest load of garbage I've ever heard."

"I'm sorry, man. I have no say in this. I'm just a—"

"I know, just a recruiter. I know."

"Come on, Hammer. It's okay. Have I ever steered you wrong? Everything will make sense soon, I promise."

"Nothing makes sense! You've been in this town for years supposedly to recruit some bigwig to come to work for your boss and yet you've never made an offer? It's all crap. I'm sick of the whole thing. I think you're a rich, spoiled brat who has too much money and time. You entertain yourself at my expense, and I've had enough. If you're here to recruit, who are you supposed to recruit?"

"Calm down, Enoch. You know me better than that. I've never done one thing to hurt you, have I? I've tried to help you many times, and you know that's true. I get it about the boss. He is infuriating. Imagine being caught in a contract you can't get out of, and you look like an idiot, and you can't even tell anyone the truth about what's going on. Nobody trusts you because you don't make sense. Your life is a sham, and you have no choice about what happens. I get it. But if you only knew what I had to deal with, you'd understand."

I thought about it and realized what he had said was true. He'd never done anything to harm me. He'd tried to help me in his own way even when I didn't want it. He went out of his way to get me answers when he didn't have to. I felt embarrassed at my outburst. I sat there trying to find a suitable apology.

"Hammer, he's told me you'll know who he is in due time. He doesn't want you to hear his voice for obvious reasons. When he calls, he'll talk through me and you'll respond. The microphone will pick you up so he'll be able to hear you. He has ways of doing things far beyond my ability to comprehend."

"Cash, I'm sorry I yelled at you, but you got to understand all this mystery and intrigue crap is too much. If the guy wants to talk to me, let him talk to me. What's the big deal? I don't care about him or his boss or the boss's daddy. I don't even care about what happened in my childhood. If he wants to live in the shadows, that's his problem. I just want plain, simple truth, no crap. All it does is upset me. It causes me to have bad dreams. I just want peace in my life."

Ring ... ring ... ring.

The phone interrupted my rant. Damon answered.

"Yes sir. I'm here ... He's in a pretty foul mood, sir. I understand, sir ... You know I haven't told him a thing! Why would you ask, sir, when you already know the answer? No sir! I meant no disrespect! I ... I ... Yes sir, I'll shut up. Uh huh, yes sir, I'll tell him ... Enoch, the boss says you may ask him whatever you want."

"Really? Okay, but if I don't get a straight, truthful answer, I'm walking out the door. You understand?"

"He understands, Hammer."

"Well now, what shall I ask you? Alright, I've got one. Your boy Damon has been in this town for years. He tells me he's your recruiter and he's after a big fish. I think it's all a bunch of nonsense, but I'm going to call your bluff anyway. If you lie to me, I'm done with the lot of you. Fair enough?"

"The boss says to ask your question, that he won't lie."

"Just so I can disprove Mr. Damon's crap, I want to know who's the big fish you're trying to recruit in New Orleans. I want to know his name and then I'm going to follow up on him and see if you've been in a relationship with him. In other words, he better be real."

"Yes sir. Are you sure? Okay ... Here goes. It's you, Enoch. You're the game changer, the big fish I was sent to recruit. The boss has had you on the radar for a long time. Hold on, Hammer ... Yes sir ... Uh huh, that's right, sir. I think he's ready to receive an offer. Yes sir, I think he'd like that. No sir, he's just been spinning his wheels doing construction ... Yeah, you're right. There's no big payoff in that. Okay, sir, I'll ask him."

"Ask me what? This is ridiculous. I'm the guy you've been sent to recruit? That's the craziest thing I've ever heard!"

"Hold on, Hammer ... Yes sir ... I'll tell him. The boss is going to make this beginning offer, and he'll later increase it. He wants you to leave or shut down your construction company and come work for him. Your beginning salary will be ten thousand a week. And you'll work in the construction field for the boss in another country ... Yes sir, okay ... He'll give you a new company vehicle every year and will pay to move you ... and he will ... What's that, sir? Okay ... and he'll give you ten thousand dollars a month to cover accommodations in the countries you'll go to. Well, what do you say?"

I was stunned. I didn't know what to say. Could this be true? This kind of thing doesn't happen. It didn't make sense. I was just a carpenter, a contractor. I did a good job and had even handled some pretty big jobs, but I was no world-class contractor.

"Okay, Damon, what's the catch? This is too fantastic."

"Yes sir, I'll tell him ... The boss says he'll have his attorney draw up the paperwork so you'll know it's for real. It will spell everything out in detail and will have extra bonuses that will be a great surprise ... Yes sir ... Uh huh ... I'll tell him ... There is a catch, Hammer."

"I knew it. There always is."

"It's not that bad."

"Well, what is it?"

"You have to work exclusively for him for life. You'll go wherever he sends you, and you'll have all the best for the rest of your life. He'll make sure you have as many women as you want and the finest vintage wines in the world. You'll constantly get bonuses, and the corporate jet will be at your disposal."

"Damon, you're so full of crap. This is a bad joke!"

"It's no joke, Enoch. He's preempting an offer by his competitor. He says to be honest with you about his motives. He isn't offering the job to you because of your great skill ... Hold on, Hammer ... Well sir, that's harsh, but I'll tell him. Hammer, he says you're a mediocre contractor at best, no offense. He knows with his help he can turn you into a world-class developer like Trump. His real motive is to stick it in the eye of the competition. He just wants to use you in his chess game like a pawn for his own reasons. He felt you needed the facts on the table before you made a decision on his offer. What he's offering is pocket change to him."

"Actually, that does make sense. I know I'm no world-class contractor. I don't have a clue about high finance. If this is true, bring me a contract with all the details, all of them. I want to know who you are, what the name of the corporation is—everything! All this cloak-and-dagger stuff comes to an end now."

"The boss agrees, Enoch ... Yes sir, I'll set it up, sir ... Good-bye, sir."

"Damon, if this is a bunch of crap, I'm going to beat the snot out of you!" I was very suspicious. The whole thing was beyond ridiculous.

"Hammer, I wouldn't blame you one bit. Fortunately for me, I know it's real. The boss told me years ago he wanted me to recruit for him. I thought it was all a bunch of garbage too. He had liaisons talk to me, and people with secret talents got inside my head until I finally gave in and went to work for him. I signed the contract, and everything he said would happen, did. I'm not telling you what to do, Hammer. It's all about free will."

"I forgot to ask him about my parents. Get him back on the line."

"I can't. I don't get in touch with him. He gets in touch with me."

"Look at the caller ID."

"It says unlisted ... Look." He showed me the phone. "I've never even met the boss. I wouldn't know him if I passed him on the street."

"How do you get paid if you don't know your boss?"

"I can't explain it. All I know is that I get a wire transfer once a month directly to my account from Apollyoneblis Holdings LLC. Every year in November, a guy comes to pick up one car and drop off the next year's model. I had one job when I came to New Orleans, and that was to be your friend."

"That's totally crazy, Cash. I don't know what to make of any of it. Your boss said I was a game changer. What did he mean?"

"I think it means you have the potential, with his help, to be a world-class developer."

"With his help, huh? Wouldn't you think he'd go after people who were already world class?"

"I suppose so. But then again, I'm just a recruiter. Anyway, this suite is yours for the week if you want it. The boss is having a Jaguar delivered to the hotel tonight. He knew I was bringing you and thought you might need transportation later. No offense, Hammer, but your ratty old construction truck wouldn't fit in here. There are brand-new clothes in the closet all perfectly tailored to your size. Here's the agenda for tonight. At four twenty, you have an appointment at the spa for the world-famous four-hands massage treatment. At five, you'll be back in your room for a quick shower and fresh clothes. At five thirty, you'll go to the boardroom on the second floor. The room's been reserved for cocktails, and everybody from the bar is going to be there. After that, we'll all have dinner in the bistro, private dining of course, then we'll retire to the French Quarter Bar for more cocktails."

"What? I don't think ... I'm ... I don't understand."

"What part don't you understand?"

"I got to work tomorrow. This is Sunday! I can't be drinking all night!"

"Actually, you can. The boss had me call your foreman and the owners of your jobs to let them know you'd be out tomorrow. He has one of his construction guys on standby to help your people if needed. You don't have a thing to worry about but to relax and enjoy the evening. This has all been set up for you! You won't need the Jaguar tonight, probably, but it'll be there in the morning for you. You can use it for the whole week and keep it if you sign the contract. You don't have to go in at all this week. The boss has taken care of it. If you never want to go in again, you don't have to. If you want to go back to your townhouse, you can. We'll have the Jaguar picked up there. In other words, Hammer, it's all about what you want. Here's the room card. Enjoy the room. I'll be back later to meet you for cocktails. Oh, by the way, the concierge is going to call you about your spa appointment."

"I don't know what to say."

"There's nothing to say. Welcome to the team! I'll let myself out and I'll catch you later."

Cash left. I was overwhelmed. I sat on the couch and checked out the ornate, overstuffed chair. When I was satisfied with their comfort, I ran to the bed and jumped on it. The huge headboard was intricately carved and had padded fabric. The nightstands were made of some type of wood I wasn't familiar with. The room was painted in a soft, pale-olive color, and the cornice work was very intricate and attractive. It was incredible. I'd been in many uptown homes, but this was more luxurious than any of them. I lay in bed and drank in my surroundings, wondering what I had done to deserve all this.

This wasn't possible, yet there I was. It was surreal. I'd thought Damon had been playing me for a fool. I couldn't have been more wrong. Everything he said was true. Nobody would go to such extremes and expense just for a practical joke.

My elation, however, was mixed with a dread I couldn't quite put my finger on. But life was about to change for me; I was finally getting a chance to grab that golden ring. I'd had to struggle for everything I had, but that was all about to change. I could earn more in a year than I'd managed to save in forty-one.

I went to the closet and saw the clothes. I thought I'd jump in the shower before the massage. I tried to shrug off the uneasy feeling as I quickly showered. I couldn't shake the feeling of the unusual meeting with the boss. Maybe it was the manner in which the offer had been made, or perhaps he didn't believe in me. Whatever the reason, I wasn't sure I wanted to be a pawn in a bunch of super- wealthy people's chess game.

I wondered who his competition was. Who else out there wanted me for some great offer? That didn't make sense either. If I had no real value to the boss or his corporation, why hire me? If I was mediocre, why would the competition want me? Something wasn't adding up in my mind. Who was the mysterious competition? I hadn't focused on that before. I figured I would enjoy the night and try to figure it out after I saw the employment contract. I'd become pretty adept at contract law as a result of studying the AIA contracts architects used. I'd look for the loopholes in this one.

The massage was out of this world, or at least out of my world. After the appointment, I didn't have much time before Damon knocked on the door. He led me to the boardroom but had me stand outside. I could hear the whole gang inside laughing and carrying on. Damon made a short speech about his corporation's offer to me and how I was going to rise in the world. After a few more kind words about me, he said, "And now, I want to introduce the man of the hour, Mr. Enoch Galah, otherwise known as Hammer!" I came into thunderous applause of the ten or so guys.

The old gang was especially fun that night. Most of them didn't know anything about Damon's work either. They were very surprised his boss had set up the event. They patted me on the back and cheered when he announced my good fortune. There was a bar and a large oak table with executive chairs all around. We sat there drinking various concoctions while talking about old times. I was glad to see Two Shoes had made it.

I couldn't talk to anyone for too long as we continued getting louder and louder. We laughed and carried on until we reached an uproar. I thought we might be asked to leave, but we weren't. We made our way to the private dining area in the bistro for dinner. Damon announced we could order anything we wanted and as much as we wanted. We ordered everything under the sun and continued to laugh and joke until we were all miserable.

Damon said we were going to the French Quarter Bar in the hotel to continue the party. I was too full to put anything else in my stomach. I knew it was all for my benefit, but I would have just as soon gone to bed. The guys, however, were up for free booze anytime. I wasn't sure if they were happy for me or if they were just glad to have the drinks.

When we got to the bar, Two Shoes pulled me aside. I'd noticed he had ordered virgin drinks all night. "Hey Hammer, I need to talk to you." He was less festive than the others, and I wanted to find out how he was doing. "Let's step out to the hall." We told the guys we'd be right back.

"What's going on, Two Shoes?"

"Hammer, do you know anything about these people and their offer?"

"Well, Damon has been working for them for years. Why do you ask?"

"Hammer, they're evil! I can feel it. They're not what they appear! I have a terrible feeling about all this. I can't explain it. You need to run from these people. Don't take this job. I've been having dreams about this. Hammer, they're out to get your soul."

He was distraught and was sincere in his concern. I hadn't thought of these people as evil until his suggestion. I believed in evil even though I didn't believe in God. I'd seen evil in people. It wasn't supernatural, it was real. I didn't know anything about these people. They were strange beyond anything I'd ever known. They were secretive, veiled. The people who worked for them were not normal either as best I could tell. His words hit me with great impact.

"Thanks for the advice, Two Shoes. I haven't made up my mind on all this. You're right that this whole thing doesn't make sense. I'm going to look into these people before I do anything."

"Thanks for listening to me. I just have such a bad feeling about this."

After another hour of visiting with the guys, I said goodnight and headed to the suite. I hit the bed and began to think. Normally, I'd watch TV until I got sleepy, but I was wrestling with my thoughts. I began to realize that by accepting the room and the perks, I was feeling obliged to the boss, but what if Two Shoes was right? I drifted off to sleep.

CHAPTER 11

A Mystery Is Solved

"Enoch, I am here waiting for you."

"Hello, superego. You haven't come around in a while."

"You are such a delight to Me. I have always loved you."

"That is a way of saying I love myself, right?"

"I know you have not found an answer to My riddle."

"Oh yeah, the religious feminine thing, I remember. I haven't found an answer because there is no answer."

"I will tell you the answer to the riddle, and you will know I am real."

"Okay, I'm game. But how will that prove you exist?"

"Because I will give you understanding that you could not possibly know."

"Can I ask questions if I don't get it?"

"Of course you can. I will help you to understand. Which question would you like the answer to first?"

"Alright, I'm ready for the question about women being cursed with pain. So why were they cursed with pain, and how does that represent love?"

"Very well. Her curse represents My pain before the foundation of the world. It is why the Father commanded the sacrificial system. The sacrifice of God's love is the meaning behind the sacrifice. As Eve was brought out of Adam, so was I brought forth out of God. I am the Wisdom of God, and all things were made through Me."

"How does that answer the question of the woman being cursed with pain?"

"I will continue. Before Lucifer darkened his heart, there was only the purest form of nurturing love in eternity, and nurturing love is represented best in maternal love."

"Maternal love? There was only maternal love before Satan rebelled? What's maternal love?"

"The sweet, nurturing love of God. Feminine love never fails, and it forgives the children no matter what they have done."

"Wait a minute ... God's male! Are you saying God's female?"

"No, Enoch. God is neither male nor female. He is Spirit. There is no male or female in the spirit."

"But weren't Adam and Eve created in the image of God?"

"Eve represents a type of love, and Adam represents a different type of love. Masculine love is protective love; feminine love is all-forgiving love that reflects Wisdom and the Spirit."

"Hold on, Mr. Wisdom. Some say God is one, like the Jews and the Muslims. They would die for their beliefs. The Christians think there are three Gods. Who's right?"

"The seed of Abraham and the seed of Ishmael see only the masculine side of God. But as to the three, He may be better understood as two held in the bond of one. You see, we are all one in the Spirit of love; like two sides of the same coin"

"Two held in the bond of one? What does that mean?"

"Adam and Eve were two but were one flesh just as the Father and I are one Spirit. Masculine is drawn to feminine. The bond that draws them is love. As positive is drawn to negative, the magnetism that draws them represents love. God can be clearly seen in His creation, and He can be understood by the things that are made. His eternal Godhead can be seen in His creation of Adam and Eve. Now listen and gain understanding. I have always been in Him and He in Me until I was brought forth to be His master craftsman. Eve was brought out of Adam to be his helpmate. He placed in Me the most precious seed, love, which is his Holy Spirit. In Eve was the seed that would bruise the head of the serpent. This means that Satan's philosophy and knowledge would be overcome by love. The maternal seed of love forgives all things and can never fail. The seed of love is His Holy Spirit, and the Holy Spirit is life and the source of all life. God and Wisdom are one as Adam and Eve were one. The bond that draws them together is His Holy Spirit. Male and female were created to show that God separated into two kinds of love; one is fierce and protective, and the other is gentle and forgiving."

"You're saying God can be understood by looking at Adam and Eve? I'm getting a little bogged down here, Mr. Wisdom. How does this solve the riddle of the woman being cursed with pain?"

"It is found in the two natures of the masculine and feminine. I will explain the mystery through a parable."

"A parable? I remember something about them from childhood."

"A parable teaches a truth in a way that brings understanding."

"Okay, tell me."

"There was a husband and wife who had given birth to nine children. Their home was filled with love, and they continually played and laughed. One day, the oldest child was curious about a friendly, furry animal. The father saw that the animal was diseased and knew the disease could be passed to his family. He gave his family strict instructions not to touch the animal because of its disease. One day, three of the sons were playing in the field and spotted the friendly animal. The oldest son said to his brothers, 'I think Father is wrong! That animal is so cute and friendly. I think we should make a pet out of it.' The three children disobeyed their father and caught the disease.

When the father saw that three of his children had disobeyed him, he was heartbroken and knew he must remove the children from the family lest they all die. The father prepared to take them away. When the mother found out what had happened, she begged him not to take the diseased children away. She could not leave or forsake them. She was willing to die alongside them. Nevertheless, she had to submit to the will of the father, although she did not have the strength on her own to abandon her children. When all things were prepared, the father took the children away to the place he had prepared for them. Do you understand this parable?"

"Actually, I think I do. You're saying there are two different types of love displayed in the masculine and feminine, right? But how does the parable solve the riddle?"

"This parable represents God the Father, His Wisdom, and all the angels He had given life to. When Lucifer disobeyed the Father, he was corrupted by the disease of sin. God prepared a place of quarantine for His diseased son and his followers. The sons affected by the disease would have to be quarantined. If they were allowed to remain in the family, the disease of evil would abide forever. As much as God loved His son Lucifer, He could not allow Lucifer's corruption to affect the family for all eternity. God was motivated by protective love, which is all powerful. There is no maternal love in it. This is why God appears to be unyielding and unforgiving. He is the God of law omnipotent. Do you understand?"

"I think I do. You're saying God, in a sense, has no choice but to lock up the Devil and his followers because they had an incurable disease."

"What was the motive of the father's heart in the parable?"

"His motive was to protect his family. He was motivated by love."

"Yes, you are correct! Even though God is motivated by protective love, He will have to take His beloved son Lucifer into a place of quarantine called hell. This is where Satan will remain forever. He will not be able to hurt and destroy life any longer. God's motive is based on protective love, not nurturing love."

"Wow. How do you turn from your own son?"

"His protective love is represented in the masculine. He could do this only by separating the all-forgiving love from Himself and put it in the vessel of Wisdom. Wisdom's heart of forgiving love had to submit to His will or evil would remain for all eternity. Only Wisdom bore the pain of the loss of the children. In Wisdom was unfailing love. The all-forgiving love in a very real sense had to die for judgment to take place. The all-forgiving love, by nature, would have forgiven Satan, but if Satan was forgiven, evil would abide forever because Satan is eternal. When he turned away from love, he was eternally changed in his nature, and the evil that he has become, is an eternal condition."

"The nurturing side of God's love alone paid the price for the loss of the diseased children. It was this love that is reflected in the curse of the pain in childbirth. Now, to bring forth life is mixed with joy and pain. The pain represents the broken heart of love. The knowledge of bringing forth children knowing that many will be separated from God's love is an unbearable pain to the nurturing, unfailing side of God's love."

"Wow! I'm stunned. How could I even imagine this? Is what I'm hearing true? I think I get this. It feels that life actually has a purpose, meaning—it didn't just happen by accident. Is it possible there's a plan for everything? Wait a minute. Why couldn't God forgive the Devil if He can forgive us?"

"The Devil was an eternal being, and his free-will choice to reject love was an eternal choice. His nature was eternally changed when he rejected love and chose a path of selfish ambition. God created the law to show what sin was. The law said the consequence of sin was death. Death is the separation from love. Man was created with the ability to die in the flesh and so fulfill the law of sin and death. I paid the price for his eternal life through My death in the flesh."

"So you're saying you are love and you want me to tell the world about you?"

"Yes, Enoch, that is your message to the world. I have chosen you to be My emissary of love to the world. You will reveal My heart of all-forgiving love and the protective love of the Father. The world has misunderstood the motives of the Father, but you will teach them. They have seen only His law but have not seen His motives. I am My Father's Son, and I chose to willingly submit to My Father's will. My Father placed inside Me His Spirit of Wisdom and His Holy Spirit of love. As I submitted to Him, My heart broke for the loss of the children for all eternity. His nurturing, forgiving love was sacrificed so He could do what had to be done. This sacrifice was why the lamb must be female. The pure female lamb represents the purest type of love that was placed in Me. My love is never failing. The Father has given to Me a new birth of children whom I will never forsake. They who put their trust in Me will never die but will have life everlasting. You will reveal to the world the nature of the Godhead. The creation of Adam and Eve are a reflection of love contained in God."

"I can't do that. I'm just a carpenter, and apparently a mediocre one. What do I have to offer the world?"

"I took you from your father, Jared, for this reason. At the appointed time, you will prophesy and witness to all I have taught you and then after three and a half years, you will die."

"What do you mean I'll die? You just said if I trust in you I'd never die!"

"Not one jot or tittle of the law can be done away with until all things are fulfilled. Therefore, under the law, the wages of sin is death. No one is an exception to the law. You had to be sent back to the earth to fulfill the law. God's law is absolute! To be born of the Spirit by faith in Me will give you life after your body dies. Your spirit is in the body for a season, and then you will face eternity. Your spirit is eternal, and you must choose to live in the presence of love or the presence of evil for eternity. On the separation of the spirit from the body, My followers will not see the angel of death but will see Me."

"I don't want to die! Can't you find someone else to tell the world about your love? I don't want to do it! This is more like a nightmare than a dream. I'm confused! I didn't do anything to deserve death. I mean, I drink a few beers and stuff, but I'm a good guy. I don't hurt anybody, at least not on purpose."

"It is appointed unto man once to die and then to face judgment. Do not fear, Enoch. I will be with you even unto the end. God gave death in the flesh as a gift to man that he might be redeemed in His Spirit. For the law is satisfied in His death. But God's gift to man is the opportunity to trust in Me and live forever in My presence."

"Look, if the Devil caused all this mess because of his disobedience, why didn't you kill him? That would have been the right thing to do."

"Love does not kill her children. If God had killed Lucifer, all creation would live in fear of God. God is love, and love flourishes only in freedom. God does not force anyone to love Him. He did not force the angels to love Him. That is why He allowed Lucifer to explore the knowledge of good and evil. Creation can respond in love to God only through freedom. By faith, His children must trust Him and believe in His ways. If love forces people, it is not love but control. The only acceptable motive to live for God is love."

"Why am I being plagued with dreams about God and the Devil and love in the first place? This all has to be just my imagination working overtime! It has to be some sort of mother fixation. This can't be true, can it? The explanation makes sense to me, and I don't think I could have possibly come up with this myself. I'm not sure what to think. Let me see if I understand this. So only Eve had the seed, which represents all-forgiving love that must be sacrificed if evil is to be dealt with and judged. This is because all-forgiving love would forgive Satan, but then, evil would remain forever. The loss of the angels and even Satan had broken God's heart of love. The pain in God's heart is represented in the curse of pain given to Eve. How do I know if I didn't just read this in some book and don't remember it?"

"This knowledge comes from My spirit, not a book. Enoch, I told you that you would know I was real through a riddle. The pain represents love, the broken-heartedness of God's love. In due season, you will believe I exist. I must warn you, Enoch. The adversary will try to entrap you, but I will give you strength, and he will not succeed."

"The adversary? You mean Satan? But I don't believe in Satan. Well, maybe he is real ... I just don't know. Okay, I have another question. If you're supposed to be some spirit, why do you just show up in dreams? Why don't you just appear and talk with me?"

"Enoch, all things of God require faith. You must choose to believe. If all things were manifest in the world, you would not need faith, for all things would be evident. His ways are above your ways. He has chosen a path in which there are two possibilities. Even as there were two trees in the garden, there must be two choices in all things. As the angels had to choose to trust their Father, so must man choose to trust Him. The angels were innocent and did not know what evil was. God asked them to trust Him even though they did not understand. I ask you to trust Me even though you don't understand. I call all men to trust in Me though they do not understand My ways. God refused to hinder his creation from exploring life. In His Wisdom, He knew freedom of choice is at the heart of love. It was His desire that His creation would choose the way of love over the way of selfishness."

"So you won't prove yourself to me or to the world? You're saying I have to do all this stuff and tell the world God visited me with absolutely no proof? You got to be kidding! No one will ever believe me. I'm not sure I believe me! This is nuts! I can't do this. I think I'm having a nervous breakdown. This can't be real."

"You will not be alone. I have prepared another witness. Every word must be established out of the mouth of two or more witnesses."

"I don't know about any of this. It sure seems like it's real, but it can't be. Wait a minute. Did you say you took me from my father, Jared? Where's my father? If you're real, tell me, and I'll believe you."

"Your father is with Me. He has long been gone from earth. You were taken to be My witness. You were taken before Moses gave the law."

"You mean like Enoch in the Bible?"

"Yes, you are Enoch of the Scriptures, the great emissary of My revelation."

"Wait a minute! You're saying I'm the Enoch of the Bible?"

"You have come into the world for this purpose."

"Jeez ... No way ... I can't believe this. If God were real, He wouldn't do things this way, would He? If this is true, why don't I remember anything? If I've been with you, how could I have been found as a baby? That's impossible!"

"With man, it is not possible, but with God, all things are possible."

"This is just a dream. There's nothing supernatural about it. This is just my imagination going crazy. I'm not a character from the Bible ... I'm not."

Ring ... ring ... ring.

I opened my eyes. To my surprise, I was in my room at my townhouse.

Ring ... ring ... ring.

I reached for the phone. "Hello?"

"Hey Hammer, this is Damon. I was just calling you to remind you I'm going to pick you up today to talk to the boss. I should be there around two. The meeting is set for three."

"What? What's today? That was all yesterday! How'd I get back to my place?"

"Today's Sunday! I don't know where you were last night. C'mon, man, wake up. I think you're still sleeping. Get some coffee, man. You've slept the whole morning away. It's one in the afternoon. I have to pick you up to meet with the boss. This has been planned for weeks. Get going. I'll see you in a little bit."

A sense of relief came over me as I realized it had all just been a dream. I wasn't some Bible character taken by God, and I hadn't been offered a job by Damon's boss, and I didn't know where the meeting was going to take place.

At two fifteen, Damon pulled up. I jumped into the car and asked him where the meeting was going to take place. "I'm not telling you. It's a surprise."

Damon knew I didn't like surprises. I pushed for an answer. "Are we going to another bizarre shop in the quarter?" Damon just smiled. We pulled onto Canal Street and headed for the river. To my surprise, we pulled into the Ritz Carlton, and Damon gave the keys to the valet.

In that moment I felt sick to my stomach. I'd never been in the Ritz Carlton. I was nervous and nauseated. We stepped through the front door. We walked to the elevators and went to the third-floor check-in. I noticed the creamy marble floor cut diagonally in the room, and then I saw the gilded table on an ornate carpet. A huge bouquet of yellow roses complemented the creamy colored walls. Behind the reception desk, a brown, leather-looking color complemented the decor. I'd walked through this space in my dream, but I hadn't looked the first time. This couldn't be real. My life was spinning out of focus. Was I here or not? How could I remember every detail of a place I'd never been to? I was very nervous as we made our way to the elevator. I wondered if I had been visited by God, the lamb, maternal love, Wisdom, or whatever the heck it was.

When we got off the elevator, I felt like I was in a movie called *Déjà Vu* or maybe *Groundhog Day*, but this wasn't a movie. The hall and the floor were the same. We made our way to the suite, and Damon opened the door. This was no coincidence; there was no rational explanation for this. My science and logic were failing me as I looked at the pale-olive walls. I'd been here in my dreams. It had to be more than a dream; it couldn't have been a dream. I was Enoch of the Bible?

Damon made his way to the ornate desk and motioned me to sit down in front. I was overwhelmed, shocked, confused, void of all reasoning powers. I saw Damon pick up a headset with a microphone. I'd seen this before!

"Damon, where's your boss?" I was going to change the outcome of this day.

"He's going to call at three sharp."

"I know, and you'll speak for him. He doesn't want me to hear his voice."

"How did you know that? Are you psychic? That explains why the boss wants to talk to you."

"Let me tell you more. Are there clothes in the closet in my size, and this suite is reserved for the week?" I was testing myself more than I was testing Damon and his boss. I wanted to know if the visitor of my dreams had been real or if I'd lost my mind. He said I'd know he was real by answering a riddle about the mystery of the feminine. And He had!

"Dude, you're freaking me out! I can't even believe what you just said! This explains why the boss wants to talk to you. You have a special talent! You haven't told me about this. This is too wild. Now I know why the boss sent me to meet you."

"I know, Damon. I'm the talent you've been sent to recruit."

"Oh God! I never told you that! Please tell the boss I never said a word. It will be the end of me if he finds out you know. How did you know? Do you know what he's going to offer you?"

"Yes I do. He's going to offer me the world if I just obey his voice and all he tells me to do."

"Hammer, I'm scared. No one knows the boss's plans, no one! If he thinks I told you, I'll live with unimaginable torments. You don't understand!"

"No, Damon. For the first time in my life, I think I do understand. I have a choice to make. I must choose whose side I'm on. I can serve your master, or I can serve love. I can live in luxury beyond my imagination, or I can choose the way of love and life. It seems to me that love and life make more sense. It's a choice of God or Satan, love or knowledge."

"What are you talking about, Hammer? I—"

Ring ... ring ... ring.

"Yes sir, I'm here ... He's in a pretty foul mood, sir. I understand, sir ... You know I haven't told him a thing! Why would you ask, sir, when you already know the answer? No sir! I meant no disrespect! I ... I ... Yes sir, I'll shut up! Uh huh, yes sir, I'll tell him ... Enoch, the boss says you may ask him whatever you want."

"Ask him what he wants me to do to receive money and cars and use of the corporate jet. Does he wish me to sell my soul for ten thousand a week?"

"Yes sir ... I don't know how he knew ... No sir, you know I didn't tell him ... Sir, my loyalty has never been in question ... Yes sir ... I'll tell him. Hammer, the boss says you have been affected by his enemy's mind-control techniques. You've become a target of a powerful, new technology that's being tested on some of the populous with a certain genetic disposition. He says you've been influenced by a powerful experimental drug developed for the military. It can alter your perception of reality ... Yes sir ... Uh huh, okay, I'll tell him. The boss says his company developed the drug but it was stolen by his competitor."

"Your boss has never done a thing for me, and I reject his offer. I believe the truth of what Wisdom told me. I don't believe any of this. I believe he works for Satan. His offer means nothing to me."

"Hammer, he hasn't even made an offer yet! He's just concerned for you because you've been exposed to a powerful psychotropic drug one of his pharmaceutical companies created. He feels responsible even though the enemy stole the formula and sold it to another firm. The boss will explain it all at the right time. For now, he'll just say a former employee purposefully exposed you when you were a fetus. You were picked out to be tested on. The test subjects couldn't know they'd been exposed. He got hold of the employees' list of subject experimentation and has been tracking down each victim for many years. That's why he hasn't been able to meet with you. If it ever gets out, it could ruin a lot of people's lives. He's just trying to do good!"

"It sounds more like he's worried about being ruined."

"Yes sir ... I'll tell him. That's not true at all! He's totally insulated from the company. It's only one of many he owns. He has total deniability as he doesn't run the day-to-day affairs of the business. Also, he says it was his competitor that exposed the other people in the general populous."

He paused for a minute to listen to the voice on the other end. His words sounded plausible. I had to consider if I'd been in a psychotropic delusion as a result of some chemical exposure. Could such an explanation resolve everything I'd experienced? I would have to consider that possibility. It seemed to be a reasonable explanation of what had happened. But how did I know about the clothes in the closets? A drug can't get you to see the future! I knew I'd been in this room. Only God could do something like that. Then again, could a drug have caused this?

"Hey Hammer, the boss says the drugs you've been exposed to tap into a certain part of the brain that increases the alpha and delta waves in a dormant part of it. That section of the brain is the center of extrasensory perception. It enhances precognitive ability. It's like being able to see the future in short spurts."

"Cash, I was just thinking that! This is too fantastic to be true. I feel like my brain is scrambled eggs or mashed potatoes. I came here with you, and I'd already been in this room. I must be like Miss Sadie or something. I could see this in my mind's eye. But it all was so real. I was sitting in this same chair yesterday! This is wild, Cash. This kind of makes sense to me. I thought I was losing it. I actually thought I'd been visited by a spirit or God or something. I can't tell you what a relief it is to know that it's chemical exposure."

"Hold it a minute, Hammer. The boss is trying to talk to me ... Yes sir ... The boss wants you to go to work for him finding the rest of the victims who have been exposed. He knows you have a good business, so he'll buy you out and give you a lifetime contract. When all the victims are found and made right, he'll give you a permanent job running developments all over the world ... Uh huh ... He'll train you. Also, your contract will have a buyout clause. If he doesn't give you lifetime employment, you'll be compensated for your entire life in a lump sum."

"What's the catch? There's always a catch. Don't tell me. I have to work exclusively for him for life, right? I'll be his slave."

"He says you can if you want to, but that's not the catch. The catch is this. You can never, for the rest of your life, discuss any of this. Not your drug-induced dreams, or the precognitive ability you have, or even Miss Sadie. You can never discuss it or write about it or anything that would expose what the drug is capable of. The boss is buying your silence. He's going to pay you to forget everything you've ever seen or heard that was odd, strange, or bizarre. You'll live a normal life of wealth and splendor into your retirement years. This is a matter of national security. This technology was formulated for military purposes. It's vital to American interests all over the world. If foreign countries knew of this drug, we'd be at war. With this drug, we'll know their plans before they do. It's your patriotic duty to never speak of this again. This conversation can never leave this room."

"Wow, Damon. I don't know what to say. I'm overwhelmed. I actually thought I was a Bible character who came back to life or something. I thought your boss was the Devil. But you're saying it was all just a drug messing with my head? Wow. I know this is going to sound strange, but I'm relieved to hear this. I don't even know anything about the Bible and its characters. Imagine thinking you're the Enoch of the Bible who God took to heaven. I know I have the same name, but I can't tell you what a relief this is."

"I don't get you, Hammer. I'd be mad if I just found out I'd been a lab rat for some pharmaceutical company ... Yes sir ... The boss says you deserve to be compensated well, and he'll have papers drawn up outlining the agreement. You were just a fetus in the womb when the renegade scientist injected the drug directly into your developing brain. He's going to increase what he was thinking about paying you to $2.5 million a year with benefits and other perks for your silence. The CEO discovered the secret experimentations on fetuses by a group of scientists. They were not sanctioned experiments."

"He was only going to offer me ten thousand a week."

"Yeah, he knew you had seen that in your precognitive state. He didn't want to insult you with a lowball offer now that you know the truth."

"Does he still have a Jaguar being delivered?"

"Man, you're uncanny! I'm beginning to think I need some of that drug. I could predict the stock market or maybe the lottery. Excuse me, Hammer ... Okay sir, I'll tell him ...Yes sir ... Good-bye, sir ... Okay, Hammer, you're in! He said you probably already know about the spa and the party this evening, right?"

"Yep, I know all about them."

"That is so freaking weird, Hammer. Well, he says what you don't know is that the drugs have an accumulative affect. That means you'll continue to experience delusional dreams but you're not to pay them any mind. It does affect the delta brainwaves of the dream state in your mind, your REM sleep."

"Damon, what is your part in all of this. Did you come to New Orleans to recruit me?"

"No, man. That was just a cover. I was supposed to watch you to determine when the delta waves were beginning to have an effect on your precognitive abilities."

"Wait. You acted surprised when I knew what was going to happen!"

"All part of the cover, man."

Déjà vu all over again, but this time, I felt light and free. Life was normal again in the most unusual way. My crazy life wasn't so crazy after all. A chemical had induced all my symptoms and crazy dreams. I felt invigorated; my life made sense again. I attacked the party with gusto.

I waited for Two Shoes to pull me aside; I couldn't wait to tell him it was all going to be okay. I'd noticed him all night. He was contemplative, and his laughs were more rehearsed than from the heart. After a joke, he would smile, nod, and return to his concerned look. It was obvious he'd been very concerned about me. I wanted to tell him about the pharmaceutical exposure, but I knew I had to be silent. If I told him the truth, he probably wouldn't believe it anyway. I thought it would not be hard to keep silent about the things in my life. I was going to be paid more money every year than I could earn in a lifetime.

I imagined homes all over the world and the prestige of being somebody. The luxury of the new hotel I was in was just a foretaste of all that was in store for me. I could scarcely believe my good fortune. Maybe I would learn to embrace my condition and profit from it. I could see transactions in the future and act accordingly. I'd worked hard my whole life to get ahead, but I couldn't have cared less about my past, or my company, or anything. Easy street was coming.

When we got to the bar, Two Shoes pulled me aside. "Hey Hammer, I need to talk to you."

"Let's step out to the hall." We told the guys we'd be right back.

"What's going on, Two Shoes?"

"Hammer, do you know anything about these people and their offer?"

"I know what you're going to say, Two Shoes."

"Hammer, they're evil!"

"I knew you were going to say that."

"No, Enoch, they're evil! I can feel it. They're not what they appear. I have a terrible feeling about this. I can't explain it. You need to run from these people. Don't take this job. I've been having dreams about this. Hammer, they're out to get your soul."

"Yes, yes, I know how you feel, Two Shoes. Rick, you're a good Catholic, and I appreciate your concern. You're religious, and I expect you to filter life through that perspective. These people are not evil. They're just trying to do some good in life. They make sense to me. It's going to be okay. I can't tell you about the business arrangement, but

I'll say they have our national concerns in mind. They are connected with the government, which is the reason for all the secrecy."

"No, Enoch, you're wrong. They're evil. They're wolves in sheep's clothing. They're workers of the Devil, and he's pulling all the strings. There is a way that seems right to man, but the end is the way of death. Satan transforms himself into an angel of light to deceive even the very elect of God. Run from these people, Enoch! I know God has sent me to warn you!"

"Wow, don't get so apocalyptic on me, Two Shoes. These people are fine. I know what's going on, but I can't tell you. If I could, you'd feel totally different about it. What do you say we get back to the party?"

"I'm sorry, Enoch. I can't go back. I hope the best for you. I'm sorry if I spoiled your party. I'll say prayers for you at Mass. You won't be seeing me at the bars anymore. God has convicted me of my lifestyle, and I must change before it's too late. Good-bye, my friend."

I couldn't tell him what was going on. My heart broke for him as I watched him walk away. I knew he was just concerned. We all knew something funny was up with Cash. He didn't make sense to any of us. He just seemed to show up wherever we were. Nobody had ever seen him work; he was always around. I couldn't tell anybody he was involved in watchdog work for a pharmaceutical company contracted by the government. How do you tell your friends about that? Well, I guess the whole point is you don't.

I drank into the morning hours and headed to the room. Fortunately, I'd eaten quite a bit so it counteracted the alcohol. I was exhausted but invigorated. I looked around the suite and thought, *This is all mine! Welcome to my new life.*

I was too excited to sleep. The room I was in was far different from my old converted townhouse from the forties. I had never really stayed in a place like this. I'd stayed in Days Inns and the like, but not ever in any place like this. I didn't want to sleep for fear that I'd wake up and find it had all been a dream. I sure thought the first time had been real.

CHAPTER 12

The Test

As I sat in bed, soaking up my good fortune, I noticed a book on the nightstand. I stared at it before realizing it was a Gideon's Bible. I laughed and picked it up. I wondered what sect of Christians this Bible had come from. It was a pretty nice cover and actually complemented the room. I wondered how a religious book had gotten into this place. I don't think I'd ever read anything in the Bible. I remember a big Bible that sat on the coffee table at the Wellingtons, but no one was allowed to touch it. It was like a holy relic to be revered and admired but not read. Why would you have such a book but never touch it?

I decided to forge into the unknown, to open this iconic slice of history. It was just a book, after all; it had no power or relevance in today's world. It was the essence of a bygone era of superstition and fear, a time before science had explained lightning and thunder, an era of terror when man had no knowledge of the universe. I almost felt sorry for those of old who believed that every unexplained phenomenon was a result of God's wrath or pleasure. This book epitomized all man's false notions. I thought I'd open this literary storybook and for once peer into the mind of humanity in its infancy. It was just a book. I decided the best approach would be to just let it open and see what it said. I placed the binder in my left hand, open side up, and just let gravity do its job. It fell open somewhere toward the middle of the book, and I began to read from Proverbs 9:1–6.

Wisdom has built her house, She has hewn out her seven pillars; She has slaughtered her meat, She has mixed her wine, She has

> also furnished her table. She has sent out her maidens, She cries out from the highest places of the city, "Whoever *is* simple, let him turn in here!" *As for* him who lacks understanding, she says to him, "Come, eat of my bread And drink of the wine I have mixed. Forsake foolishness and live, And go in the way of understanding."

Check this out. Wisdom is a girl. Isn't that a kick! In my dreams, Wisdom sounded masculine and said He was the Son of His Father. Wait a minute. Maybe the ancient people thought Wisdom was like God's wife or something? Maybe my dreams were a result of being exposed to this kind of Scripture. I knew I was in theological waters way above my head. It was just weird to read the Bible and have a reference to my dream. What were the odds of that?

I tried the random approach again. I flipped the book again to a new section and read Luke 14:11–24.

> "For whoever exalts himself will be humbled, and he who humbles himself will be exalted." Then He also said to him who invited Him, "When you give a dinner or a supper, do not ask your friends, your brothers, your relatives, nor rich neighbors, lest they also invite you back, and you be repaid. But when you give a feast, invite *the* poor, *the* maimed, *the* lame, *the* blind.
> And you will be blessed, because they cannot repay you; for you shall be repaid at the resurrection of the just." Now when one of those who sat at the table with Him heard these things, he said to Him, "Blessed *is* he who shall eat bread in the kingdom of God!" Then He said to him, "A certain man gave a great supper and invited many, and sent his servant at supper time to say to those who were invited, 'Come, for all things are now ready.'
>
> But they all with one *accord* began to make excuses. The first said to him, 'I have bought a piece of ground, and I must go and see it. I ask you to have me excused.' And another said, 'I have bought five yoke of oxen, and I am going to test them. I ask you to have me excused.' Still another said, 'I have married a wife, and therefore I cannot come.'
>
> So that servant came and reported these things to his master. Then the master of the house, being angry, said to his servant, 'Go out quickly into the streets and lanes of the city, and bring in

here *the* poor and *the* maimed and *the* lame and *the* blind.' And the servant said, 'Master, it is done as you commanded, and still there is room.'

Then the master said to the servant, 'Go out into the highways and hedges, and compel *them* to come in, that my house may be filled. For I say to you that none of those men who were invited shall taste my supper.'"

This was a pretty interesting way of reading. I thought I'd try it again. I flipped to somewhere near the end of the book and read Revelation 19:6–9.

For the Lord God Omnipotent reigns! Let us be glad and rejoice and give Him glory, for the marriage of the Lamb has come, and His wife has made herself ready." And to her it was granted to be arrayed in fine linen, clean and bright, for the fine linen is the righteous acts of the saints. Then he said to me, "Write: 'Blessed *are* those who are called to the marriage supper of the Lamb!' "And he said to me, "These are the true sayings of God."

Seems to me there were a lot of banquets going on. Was the whole book about eating? I wondered what "the marriage supper of the Lamb" meant. Were they talking about marrying a lamb, or were they talking about the lamb as the main course? The book was kind of interesting, although a bit on the cryptic side. So this was the best seller of all time? I wondered why a book that didn't make a whole lot of sense would have such an impact on people. I'd read only a few passages so I was no expert.

I liked the random flipping, so I turned over some more pages and read 1 Corinthians 10:20–22.

I do not want you to have fellowship with demons. You cannot drink the cup of the Lord and the cup of demons; you cannot partake of the Lord's table and of the table of demons. Or do we provoke the Lord to jealousy? Are we stronger than He?

That was strange—a fourth reference to eating and tables. I was a little uneasy as I read it. I remembered the things Miss Sadie had said about making a choice of what side I was on. I guessed that in the world of religion, you have to choose the Devil or God. The book was quite fascinating, although references to eating seemed to be everywhere.

I was reading the Bible! I couldn't believe it. I'd always said the Bible was full of contradictions, but I'd never actually read it. It was interesting even though I didn't understand it. I thought I'd continue to forage, so I flipped to a new section and let my eyes on fall Matthew 6:24.

> No one can serve two masters; for either he will hate the one and love the other, or else he will be loyal to the one and despise the other. You cannot serve God and mammon.

As I read that passage the uneasy feeling returned. It was as if this ancient book were trying to tell me something. But that is impossible; this was just a book. There was nothing supernatural in it, so it couldn't have been giving me secret messages from the unknown. I was sure I was just overreacting to the emotions of the day.

I was beginning to feel that disturbed feeling again. I was awake, so it could not have been delta waves messing with my sleep. I decided to prove it was a coincidence by looking randomly at another section. I closed my eyes and inserted my thumb into the book and opened it. I wanted to make sure I hadn't inadvertently or subconsciously picked up something. I thought I'd ask the book a question; if it answered me, I figured I'd have room for concern.

"Mr. Bible, tell me, O wise one, is the boss a good man?" I happened to be at 2 Thessalonians 2:9–12.

> The coming of the *lawless one* is according to the working of Satan, with all power, signs, and lying wonders, and with all unrighteous deception among those who perish, because they did not receive the love of the truth, that they might be saved. And for this reason God will send them strong delusion, that they should believe the lie, that they all may be condemned who did not believe the truth but had pleasure in unrighteousness.

I stopped for a moment to consider that passage. Was it saying the lawless one was the boss? I could feel my heart beating. I was mystified, perplexed. If the book had answered my question, I could have been in real trouble. It meant the dreams were real and God was real. If I was just misinterpreting it, I was okay. How do you know a thing for sure? I'd changed my mind so many times on my perception of reality that I didn't know what to believe. It seemed every time I got a handle on life, something would come along to throw my perspective into chaos. I needed to ask the book another question. "If the boss is bad, is Damon bad as well?" I closed my eyes, stuck my thumb in, and landed on 2 Corinthians 11:14–15.

> For Satan himself transforms himself into an angel of light. Therefore *it is* no great thing if his ministers also transform themselves into ministers of righteousness, whose end will be according to their works.

I threw the Bible across the room. I felt my heart pounding in my chest. I looked around to see if anyone was around as if they had played some terrible joke on me. I was scared, truly scared! It took everything in me to settle down and analyze what had just happened. *Get hold of yourself, Enoch!* I felt my grasp on reality slipping away. Perhaps the combination of the chemical exposure and the booze had been playing tricks on my mind. I was a rational person! A book doesn't talk to you! The boss's explanation made perfect sense to me. All this religious hype was a result of Two Shoes's warning. My mind had been preset to think the boss was the Devil. My God! How silly to think the Devil would run around managing pharmaceutical companies. If the Devil was real, he sure wouldn't be concerned with people getting exposed to a drug.

I began to calm down as I reasoned through my strange encounter with the Bible. I could certainly see how so many people cherished it; it had an intoxicating feel. I thought it beckoned people with the promise of mysteries of the unknown. I had a new respect for this ancient work just after my few minutes with it, but if I studied it regularly, I thought I might become a religious nutcase myself.

The book had landed cover side up; the pages faced the floor. I stared at the book for some minutes wondering if it had some unknown power. I thought about it like the books I'd seen in movies that were leather-bound with locks and secret combinations to protect their forbidden knowledge. Yet as I stared at it, there was no mystery or ancient locking system to keep the unskilled or unlearned out. It was a plain book I'd seen in motel and hotel rooms all over the country. There was no form or beauty that we should desire it. It was just a book, or was it? I finally felt the full effects of the late hour. I fell asleep.

"Enoch, I am here. Did you enjoy the day?"

"Is that you, Mr. Wisdom?"

"It is I. I have come to talk with you."

"That's awesome, because I found out something about you in the Bible."

"What did you find out about Me, Enoch?"

I felt a knowing smile was coming from him. "I found out you're a girl! Wisdom is always feminine in the Bible!" I laughed at the thought of poking fun at Mr. Wisdom.

"Your words delight Me, Enoch, but there is no male or female in the Spirit. Don't you remember Me teaching this truth to you? I am the only begotten Son of My Father. And yet in Me is the love that is nurturing and unfailing. I am the fullness of all things."

"That's not what the good book says."

"Your understanding is from human reasoning, but I will give you truth and allow you to see through God's eyes."

"Okay, Mr., or is it Ms. Wisdom, I can joke with you because, after all, you're just my enhanced alpha and delta brain waves."

"The adversary is a clever one, isn't he?"

"What adversary?"

"Enoch, through temptation, he will entice you to believe him. He has always used clever lies to entrap My children. ."

"Who are your children?"

"My children are those who do the will of God, those who have chosen wisdom over knowledge. They are the children who justify My sacrifice. They are also My bride and heirs of God."

"I don't understand what that means. Anyway, back to the girl thing, explain all that to me again."

"Very well, Eve was created to reflect the type of love the Father placed in Me. The female was the bearer of life, and in her body was the ability to sustain life. In Me, all things were created, and by Me, all things are sustained. As I told you, I came from the Father as Eve came from Adam. I am neither male nor female, yet female reflects the Spirit My Father placed in Me. In Me is the life, and all who find Me find life. My ways are to be cherished above all. I am the hidden mystery of God's Wisdom before the foundation of the world. I am the lamb that was slain before the world began. And I am also the Passover lamb slain so death would pass over those who love Me. My strength was perfected in My weakness. I now ask My bride to learn the weakness of unfailing forgiving love so she may be perfect, lacking nothing. God the Father is the omnipotent Spirit of love. His love is protective, righteous love, and My love is nurturing, unfailing love. The great Spirit of love was divided into two because of sin.

Protective love had to rule because of the crises of sin. Only the power of righteous love could stop the rebellion.

"Do you not understand that masculine and feminine represent two types of love in the Godhead and that the two are one? The third part of the Godhead is the Holy Spirit, the bond of perfection that holds all things together. Even as positive and negative have an invisible power that draws together, so are Father and Son drawn together by the power of the Spirit. All things were made to reflect the Godhead. The Scripture records in Romans that even His invisible attributes and Godhead can be clearly understood by the things that are made. The Spirit is in all things and was uniquely placed in Me. This is the mystery of the Godhead."

"I don't know why my subconscious is fixated on God," I said, "but I'm willing to play along. You're saying you represent both the female lamb and the male lamb, right? The female lamb represents sacrificial love. If we trust in God's Wisdom, death will pass over us and we will have eternal life? I'm not even sure what I'm saying. This is confusing. How can you represent both male and female and yet be neither?"

"There is a realm above knowledge in which all paradoxes are resolved. The impossible is possible with God. Yes, Enoch, both lambs represent Me! I am the alpha and omega, the beginning and the end."

"If there is no male or female in heaven, why was there a need for male and female on earth?"

"The unfailing love was separated from the righteous love. All creation was designed to reflect this image of God. I am the vessel of that perfect love that is God's Holy Spirit. The life was in Me, and I had to die to release it. The perfect love must be sacrificed for justice to take place. This was necessary to judge sin and to protect life itself. In a way God sacrificed His heart in order to be free to judge His fallen angels. The weaker vessel must retain the gentle love. This is why I came forth from the Father as His only begotten. I was to carry His most precious and innocent love. The Scriptures record in First Corinthians thirteen the nature of this love. Love suffers long *and* is kind; it does not envy; it does not parade itself; it is not puffed up; it does not behave rudely or seek its own; it is not provoked; it thinks no evil; it does not rejoice in iniquity but in truth. It bears all things, believes all things, hopes all things, and endures all things. Love never fails. It is the only eternal reality. He had to remove His heart to destroy evil. There was no other way, for the two types of love are in paradox to one another."

"So you're saying God the Father kept protective love and put the unfailing love in you? You are this type of love. Why doesn't this love rule if it's the purist love?"

"This love of God will one day be all that is needed. The love in Me can never fail. By its nature, it could never abandon the children of God. I can never abandon those My Father has given Me. The diseased children must be carried away, and only the strength of the Father can do that. Even though We are one, He is greater than all, and all creation must submit to His will. I will teach you a mystery. Strength is perfected in weakness. It is only when one knows pure love that one can rule in true righteousness.

"The feminine is the basis of life. The masculine comes forth in righteousness to protect her from even her own nature. Even as the lamb went from feminine to masculine, I went from submission to strength. I will come back for My bride, who must learn submission to My will. When she is perfected in love, she will reign and rule with Me. She will go from weakness to strength, from a feminine perspective to a masculine perspective."

"Who is your bride again? People who put their faith in you?"

"They are the children of Wisdom. Those who trust in Me and keep My commandments are My bride. When they have been perfected, they will rule with Me. Whoever finds Me finds life."

"I read something like that in Proverbs."

"Yes, you read in chapter eight of Proverbs verses twenty two through thirty six. Let Me quote it for you; "The Lord possessed me at the beginning of His way, Before His works of old. I have been established from everlasting, From the beginning, before there was ever an earth. When *there were* no depths I was brought forth, When *there were* no fountains abounding with water. Before the mountains were settled, Before the hills, I was brought forth; While as yet He had not made the earth or the fields, Or the primeval dust of the world. When He prepared the heavens, I *was* there, When He drew a circle on the face of the deep, When He established the clouds above, When He strengthened the fountains of the deep, When He assigned to the sea its limit, So that the waters would not transgress His command, When He marked out the foundations of the earth, Then I was beside Him *as* a master craftsman; And I was daily *His* delight, Rejoicing always before Him, Rejoicing in His inhabited world, And my delight *was* with the sons of men. "Now therefore, listen to me, *my* children, For blessed *are those who* keep my ways. Hear instruction and be wise, And do not disdain *it*. Blessed is the man who listens to me, Watching daily at my gates, Waiting at the posts of my doors. For whoever finds me finds life, And obtains favor from the LORD; But he who sins against me wrongs his own soul; All those who hate me love death."

"I do remember that passage. It was just before the banquet stuff in chapter nine. What did Miss Sadie mean when she said the feminine age has started?"

"In the last days, the feminine perspective will be exalted to equal or greater status than the masculine. Satan must pervert the natural order of masculine and feminine. His purpose is that the invisible attributes of God and His Godhead shall no longer be seen in creation. The perversion of the mother's love and the loss of masculine authority is a part of the great delusion to be sent on mankind. Men will believe a lie rather than the truth. The nature of the Holy Spirit cannot harm or judge anyone. Only the power of strong love can judge and stop the advance of evil."

"Hey, I read about that strong delusion stuff in the Bible."

"Yes, I know. I guided your hands and eyes."

"Rabbi Levy never told me about all this."

"My beloved son Rabbi Levy is not yet ordained to accept Me. He only sees the Father. There will be a time when the seed of Abraham will see Me. With sorrow, they will look on Whom they have pierced and receive Me as their own. My sacrifice has given them life, and I will soon pour out My Spirit upon the seed of Abraham and return to set up My kingdom on earth. This is your calling, and this is your message. I have ordained you to teach My people of My ways and My love. You were taken from the earth for such a time as this. You are to be My emissary and witness. My father has made Me Lord of all, and it is time to prepare the world for judgment and the coming of My kingdom."

"Damon warned me that the chemicals I've been exposed to would cause delusional dreams and that I was to pay no attention to them. Yet some of the things you talked about make sense in a broader way. But this could just all be the heightening of delta and alpha brain waves. Am I to believe you're real? Isn't this just a dream with no relevance in the real world?"

"Enoch, much of the world thinks as you do. There are two possibilities in all things. See, I have told you this ahead of time. You must make your choice by trusting your heart or trusting your mind. The way of faith must have the potential for doubt or it is not faith."

"I feel like a yo-yo! Every time I get comfortable with a position, something else comes up. These dreams throw me off. I feel confused and overwhelmed with all this. On one hand, if I accept this as somehow true, it means certain death, ridicule, hatred, and all manner of rejection for the sake of Wisdom. On the other hand, if it isn't true, I can have a life of luxury and unimaginable wealth."

"Yes, Enoch, that is your choice. You can embrace the adversary and live according to his ways, or you can embrace the narrow road that leads to life. I do not force you to make a choice. You must do so by your own free will. Free will has always been God's gift to His children, and His gifts and calling are irrevocable."

"Okay, let's suppose for the sake of argument that I believe you're real and are the Spirit of Wisdom from God or whatever. Tell me why Lucifer turned his back on God if heaven was all that great."

"In the beginning, there was no evil, no sin, just the sweetest form of love, and all the sons of God rejoiced in the work of His hands. He had prepared all things for His creation, and He provided for them before they were created. Creation was full of love and excitement. There was no concept of boredom or evil. All the angels were created eternal. There was no sickness or any concept of death. That is until the beloved cherub became corrupted."

"You mean Lucifer? The Devil?"

"Yes, but then, he was pure, the covering cherub, and he administrated over a third of the angels. He was the most beautiful angel of all. He was perfect in every way until he desired to be like the Most High."

"You mean he wanted to be God?"

"Yes, he looked at all the love God received and desired to be loved and adored as God was. He wanted God to give him his own kingdom. But the Father told him the only motive that was good was love. All God's motives were from love. He told his beloved Lucifer that to seek exaltation for any reason of selfishness was sin, and the path to death."

"I thought you said they were created eternal? How could they die if they were created eternal?"

"There was no concept of death in eternity past. God had to teach His children what death was. The angels were innocent and had never known any concept other than love. God knew the only eternal reality is love and that any other motive in life would eventually destroy itself. Death, as a concept, is the separation from life. Since God is life, one day, any motive other than love will have to be removed from His presence. Death is the absence of love.

"His beloved cherub, Lucifer, began to accuse his Father of being selfish and believed God wanted all the glory for Himself. He thought his Father was holding out on him. He accused God of being evil because he felt God had reserved all the power to Himself. Because of this, his name was changed to Satan, which means 'adversary.' He told his brothers that if they would follow him, they could all be their own gods."

"What did God do?"

"God created a tool to teach His creation what sin was. It would diagnose right from wrong and the knowledge of good and evil. God created the law."

"I don't know if this is a dream, but this is pretty interesting. How could my subconscious know these things? You can't be me. I don't know about any of this. Tell me more."

"Lucifer had seen only the maternal, nurturing love of God in the beginning. This is why life starts out as female. In the beginning, there was the sweetest love and no need for protective love. As a wayward child, he became an adversary of his Father. As Lucifer continued to corrupt his brethren, the Father's protective love emerged over all things. Lucifer had never seen the omnipotent side of God. He soon realized that God's power was unmatched and that he could not overpower his Father. His heart was filled with hatred toward his Father even though his Father had always loved him. He accused his Father of withholding knowledge. He corrupted many other angels with his lies. What was sweet and gentle became strong and powerful. This is why all things start as feminine, but then masculine must come forth with its strength to overcome evil. True power comes only from the gentle love. Satan thought God's power came from His knowledge of all things, but His power comes from the weakest form of love."

"How is the weakest form of love His source of power?"

"The weakest form of love is His gentle Holy Spirit, who is not capable of anything but total love. The Holy Spirit thinks no evil. He is the heart of God, the presence of God, the invisible force that binds life together. It is weak because if you hate It, the Spirit cannot hate you back. The Spirit is innocent of all judgment and judges no one but only loves them. This Spirit was placed in Me. I am the vessel of the Spirit of life. With the Spirit of love in Me, the Father could then have the strength to judge even His own children. Therefore, the adversary's power was held in check by the power of his Father. The feminine was separated from the masculine to protect life."

"So you're telling me Satan is on a leash?"

"In a manner of speaking, yes. God created a law that said all who wished could follow the philosophy of selfishness. Both Wisdom and knowledge are beautiful, but only one has life. The Lord placed two trees in the Garden of Eden, one of life and one of death. Even the angels had to choose in whom they believed. They were given the choice. Did they believe their Father or their brother? If they chose to follow their brother, he would be given authority over them. Satan derives his power from the law of God."

"Wait a minute! Are you saying that God gave Satan his power?"

"Yes. Satan's gifts and calling were irrevocable. His authority was given to him by God. In the heavens, there was a war of ideas. God allowed all His children the dignity of choice. They may choose the satanic philosophy of selfishness or to trust in the love of their Father. The evidence of His love was all around them. Their choice was to believe in the evidence or in the lie that God was selfish. It was a matter of faith."

"So this is like some cosmic experiment to see if some other philosophy is right? You're saying God is the cause of all this?"

"No, Enoch. God loves His creation with an everlasting love, but He must let creation decide if it will choose love over self. God is love!"

"If God is love, why do so many bad things happen?"

"The protective love is centered in righteousness and must do things that appear evil but are motivated by protective love. In the parable of the family I told you, it seemed to be evil on the surface—the Father was throwing his children into a place of death. It appeared evil, but it was for the best. In like manner, the Father has prepared a place for the Devil and his angels. His motive was not hate even though He hated the disease of sin that had infected His children. His motive was to protect life for eternity. You see, Enoch, good can appear to be evil, and evil can appear to be good. All men must decide which to believe in, God's wise love or the self centeredness of the Tree of Knowledge."

"Yeah, I remember when you told me about the trees in the garden."

"The Tree of Knowledge represents the ways and philosophy of Satan. It looks beautiful on the surface, but there is no life in it. Its ways and fruit are the ways of death. The fruit of the Tree of Knowledge are adultery, fornication, uncleanness, lewdness, idolatry, sorcery, hatred, contentions, jealousies, outbursts of wrath, selfish ambitions, dissensions, heresies, envy, and murder."

"But why put it into the garden in the first place? Why would God do that? I know. There had to be two options, right?"

"The Tree of Life represents Me. What I give is eternal life. My fruit yields life everlasting. It is free and does not cost you anything. I bore the entire cost and pain of life. Adam and Eve could take of the Tree of Life and live forever, for its fruit and leaves bring life and healing. They represent the ways of God's Spirit."

"What's this fruit that represents God's Spirit?"

"You are wise to ask, Enoch. There are twelve fruits of life. They are love, joy, peace, longsuffering, kindness, goodness, faithfulness, gentleness, self-control, righteousness, hope, and a wholesome tongue. Against such there is no law. These are the ways of the Spirit that lead to everlasting life. I am the true vine, the tree, and the life. He who finds Me finds life and will obtain the favor of the Lord."

"Perhaps you're a figment of my imagination. Who's to say I'm not having a dream-induced psychotic episode?"

"Drugs do not teach you the way of life, Enoch. You have been lied to. The adversary is the father of all lies. You must search your heart to find the truth. All God made has purpose and meaning. Life is not a random set of chances. God gave love to His children, but a third of them turned from love to selfishness. They hated Him without a cause, and they rejected the evidence of His love all around them. They believed a lie, and they changed in their eternal nature. They no longer were filled with love. The disease of sin changed their nature forever. They freely chose their path, and it was an eternal decision."

"This is all very nice, but it's overwhelming. If you're my imagination, I have a huge imagination. If you're a drug-induced psychosis, the religious talk is understandable. Many people on LSD and other strong hallucinogens have had spiritual experiences. By that I mean psychoses. It's a type of psychosis to think one can actually talk to a spirit, right? In general, the possibility is great that this is a mother fixation as a result of the abandonment issues from my childhood."

"You have not considered another possibility."

"What, that you're real?"

"Yes. I have told you mysteries that you could not possibly know. You must choose your mind or your heart, knowledge or life. I will visit you again. You must be prepared for the task set before you."

"If you are the Spirit of God's Wisdom, why would you choose me? I'm just a carpenter."

"God uses the foolish things of the world to confound the wise. It is the small, insignificant things that are greatest in the eyes of God. He is no respecter of persons but loves all equally."

"I don't think so. Let me test that! Does he love gays and Muslims and Jews and Christians and Buddhists—everybody?"

"Do not be confused. God does not love the disease of sin but loves all His children and longs for them to turn to Me. All men must choose their paths. This is your test, Enoch, as it is with all men. You must choose what you believe. Will you choose life or will you choose death?"

"You told me that if I chose you, I'd die."

"All men must die, for the wages of sin is death. Only when a seed is buried in death does the life within spring forth. To die to self is to live. To live in your own selfishness as your own god is death. I must soon tell you how the world will end and what you are to do. The time is short, and I am preparing the world for My coming. You will speak for all men who doubt I exist. You will also speak for Me and will turn many to righteousness. You will be a paradox and will be the advocate for the ways of My Father."

I woke up around 10:30, very late for me. I was not sure what time I'd drifted off. It must have been around 2:15. Surprisingly, I was alert and felt no effects of the night of drinking. I looked around. I was in the suite I'd fallen asleep in. I was extremely glad it hadn't all been a dream.

I wondered what I would do with my day. I could still remember the dreams I had had that night, but I wanted to believe they were a part of the chemical psychosis. I suspected they might not be drug induced at all. I hadn't had any precognitive episodes the previous night. I couldn't think of a single thing that was future oriented. I didn't know if I'd actually lived a day twice or if I'd seen future possibilities or what in the world was going on. I was a rational, logical person, but something beyond logic was at work. Was God real? Could all things truly have a purpose and meaning? Or was it all random? Was I dealing with the natural or the supernatural? There were two choices, but which was the truth?

It seemed the delta brain wave patterns were fixated on a religious theme, but why? I knew very little about religion, so why would I think about religious themes all night? I enjoyed Rabbi Levy when I was young, and perhaps my great respect for him was at the center of this "all things God" thinking. I did enjoy hearing all the nutty beliefs of many people. I wondered if the Bible was the result of such thinking.

But the Bible seemed to answer my questions. That had been real, not a dream. I wondered if I had misinterpreted the passages. Maybe I was reading into them something that wasn't there. I didn't want to think about the possibility that Damon and his boss were evil. I wanted the money and the power. I didn't want to blow this once-in-a-lifetime opportunity. My real fear was that I might not have been exposed and therefore wouldn't get paid to be silent. If I had been exposed, I would get a lot of hush money. I didn't know if they would want me to be tested. I was pretty sure I'd been exposed to something because of the wild dreams and the déjà vu experiences. How else could one explain them? The chemical exposure story sounded good but might have been as far-fetched as anything else.

I continued to struggle with my thoughts. I wondered if the dream was true. If the dream was true, Damon and his boss were evil. I needed to analyze the elements of the dream. First, the dream talked about religious matters. Second, it supposedly held secret understandings about God. Third, I don't know anything about religion. Finally, my hypothesis: find out from someone if any of the religious concepts are true.

I reasoned that these religious ideas must be my imagination and not a part of any religion, but if they were secret understandings, nobody would know about them. This is confusing! How do you find out if something is true if there's no empirical evidence? But if Damon's story was true, I should be able to be tested by science. I wondered if the act of testing would be a breach of contract.

All Damon's recruiting had been a ruse. He had been sent to New Orleans to watch me? My first precognitive dream said he'd come to recruit me. The more I thought about it, the less sense it made. Some of what Damon had said made sense, but some things seemed too convenient. I wondered if anybody had been on the other line during the call. Perhaps the boss was not real; I hadn't spoken to him. Jon had pulled a masterful joke on us years ago while pretending to read the paper. It had *sounded* like he was reading the paper, and Damon had sounded as though he was talking to someone else. Is it possible no one was on the other line? This could make your head spin. Could that have just been a test from an omnipotent being? Was I a lab rat for God? Was he toying with me just to see me squirm? If I had to choose, that must be the test. I didn't know how to decide what was right or wrong. If God was real, He wouldn't do things this way, would He? How do you pass a test when you don't have all the facts on the table?

My dreams told me that I was a long-lost soul taken by God's Wisdom and that I had to come back to earth to die because the wages of sin is death. I then must take some secret knowledge about Wisdom or the Godhead to the world. Since I hadn't died in the first go-around, I had to die in order to fulfill the law of death. But I had no recollection of being with Wisdom or God or whomever, so I had to take my dreams' word for it. By faith, I had to believe without any evidence. I would say that about summed it up!

Damon said I'd been exposed to some sort of chemical in some outlandish experiment by a pharmaceutical nutcase that had caused all those dreams. The pharmaceutical company was willing to compensate me over $2.5 million per year to keep silent about everything. I'd say that about sums up the second choice. I just don't know. Why would Damon's people want to pay me to keep silent? No one would ever believe any of this anyway. I needed to give it a lot more thought.

CHAPTER 13

Great Emissary

I wondered about the possibility of my being a great emissary from God. The problem to me was simple; I didn't know much about religion. Where did one start to find answers? I wondered if I should first study an odd religion, maybe Hinduism. I'd always liked the brightly colored posters of Hindu gods. As I thought about it, Hinduism might have had as many sects as did Christianity. The woman Damon had taken me to see was a Hindu who believed in the female god, but she didn't have any answers.

Perhaps Islam had the answers. Well, if my dream was right, Muslims saw only the masculine side of God, but the lawgiver side of God seemed so harsh and unmovable. It was no wonder they were zealous; they were scared to death of God. I guessed they wanted to impress Him with their zeal. I didn't want to cross the omnipotent side of God either if He was real. Perhaps they could not see He was motivated by love.

It seemed very harsh to send angels and the like to hell. I wasn't sure if that picture was complete enough. There was a lot of new-age stuff going on, but it wasn't big enough to have well-established beliefs at that time. Maybe Judaism was right. It was older than Islam, I thought. I loved Rabbi Levy, and I knew he was a man of God. He had always been devout, and I'd never sensed an ounce of hypocrisy in him. Besides that, I was probably Jewish. I'd known Christ was the Lamb of God since my youth, and that had to play into this somehow. But Christ was Jewish, so that was probably the best place to start.

One should probably go with one's own heritage first. I was sure each religion had a lot to offer, but it was too much to try them all. If there was a God, it might be important to look for Him. The problem was with the incredible number of choices. I was sure Christianity had some good to offer, but some Christians I knew were very hypocritical. They said they believed one way but they acted another way.

On the other hand, it seemed my dreams had come from a Christian perspective. Who knew the search for truth could be so difficult?

The first item on the agenda was looking at the Jewish people. If they were my people, we'd had it rough in history. Why had God allowed so much evil to fall on His chosen people? It seemed if you were the people of promise, you'd be treated better than that by God. I didn't know if I could find the answers. What I knew about Judaism was only what I'd learned from Rabbi Levy. I'd rejected the religion because of that cheese incident. Maybe I'd been too close-minded.

This whole way of thinking was new to me. Was I actually going on a spiritual journey of sorts? Me, a total unbeliever, a confirmed agnostic. If I could search for God, anything was possible. If nothing was impossible, maybe there was a God. That thought made me laugh out loud. The possibility of me searching for God was so impossible that my searching for God proved anything was possible! If the impossibility of the impossible is possible, that proved that the impossible is possible! All based on the impossibility of my searching for God. I laughed at the paradox. This wasn't a real search; it was more like an intellectual pursuit.

I would be the great adventurer into the unknown and represent all questioning, intelligent people everywhere. I'd go where no agnostic had gone before. I'd prove or disprove through logic and reasoning the existence or nonexistence of God. All I needed was a cape and a costume with a big question mark on it, the superhero of intellects—Into the unknown beyond! Yah, I know it was a bit much. I'd always been told if you can't laugh at yourself ... actually I don't remember the rest. You're just supposed to laugh at yourself, okay?

Where to start was the question. I stared at the Bible I'd thrown on the floor. I guessed I could start there. It was a venerated book of religion and it was the only religious book in the room. I picked it up and found a comfortable chair in the next room. I noticed I was in splendor but didn't care. It was odd to be surrounded by such wealth but not be captivated by it. Wasn't wealth and comfort supposed to give meaning to life? Why did I not care that the whole world was at my feet? Why did I care only about reading this book? I realized I was more interested in the pursuit of truth than all the money in the world.

I'd pursued building a business and earning a good living, but in that moment, it all seemed so meaningless in light of life's bigger questions.

I opened the book. "In the beginning God created the heavens and the earth." Great opening. Start at the beginning, right? "The earth was without form, and void; and darkness *was* on the face of the deep. And the Spirit of God was hovering over the face of the waters." Alright, I thought about that. The earth was void, but it had water on the planet. So earth was here already? That at least jibes with the facts of the age of the earth according to science. I guessed it meant it was void of life. I wondered what had happened to the dinosaurs. Were they an experiment on earth before the void time? The dinosaurs had been wiped out long before man set foot on earth according to the evolutionists. If Mr. Wisdom was right, maybe this disagreement between Him and Lucifer had gone on a lot longer than we'd thought. Of course, that was just conjecture. I didn't know enough about it to even hypothesize at that point. I felt a bit of relief that the Bible didn't deny the existence of earth before the creation of man.

I remembered Rabbi Levy's stories of the great flood that had destroyed the earth. I wondered if God destroyed the dinosaurs for similar reasons and had to start over again. Who knew? Maybe the dinosaurs had been destroyed in the flood. Many species go extinct even to this day. I guessed no one knew for sure about the beginning of life.

Religious speculation was fun! I wondered if everybody had speculated about such things. I was trying to give God the benefit of the doubt. If He existed, maybe we needed to cut Him some slack. But it seemed that when I asked religious people questions about dinosaurs, they never had satisfactory answers. Apparently, God hadn't felt it was necessary to explain His actions or history to His creation. I guess Mr. Wisdom was correct about one thing—there are always two possibilities.

The whole concept of faith was hard to swallow. Why wouldn't God tell us about the earth before man appeared? I certainly wouldn't have done it that way. I would've told Adam or Moses or somebody about the dinosaurs and why I had wiped them out. Then again, if we knew all the answers, it wouldn't be faith—it would be fact. Back to the faith thing again. This was getting frustrating.

If I was going to cut God some slack, He'd have to meet me halfway. I wanted logical reasons for the existence of life. Mr. Wisdom's view made as much sense as any other's view. As I thought about it, evolution had a lot of flaws too. I'd always wondered about the missing links. If life had started out as an amoeba and ended up a giraffe or whatever, why were there no links to speak of? Logic dictates there would have been billions, even trillions of changes over time to every single species on the planet. Logic would also dictate that the billions of changes would be so abundant in the fossil record as to constitute overwhelming evidence. How was it possible to have an end product and a beginning product but none of the trillions of changes in the evolutionary process? Most, if not all, the supposed evolutionary links had been proven to be questionable science at best. Most paleontologists disagree on the possible links. Most argue about whether they were links at all or just other species.

Where had life come from? If life had started from a primordial soup, why couldn't we recreate it? Even an amoeba is a highly complex single cell. How could it organize into a living system of cell membrane and digestive system? For that matter, what did the first cell eat? There was nothing to eat but rock! Maybe it took as much faith to believe in evolution as it did to believe in God. The science was not there, although I'd always believed it. Why would I choose to believe in something that was not based on fact? It was still called a theory. It was interesting that I had accepted a theory as fact without overwhelming evidence to prove it. I kept thinking about the words of Mr. Wisdom, "There must be two possibilities in all things." I began to see that if there was a God, perhaps He was smarter than I'd given Him credit for.

I was trying to be fair to science and God. I didn't want to be closed minded to any possibility, as that would be poor science. I didn't know if I could get all the answers in either direction. Just as the nucleus of an atom was a scientific impossibility, it nevertheless existed. It was a paradox on the smallest level of matter itself. Perhaps the answers were not in knowledge since it did seem to break down at some of the most fundamental elements of life. I wondered what life was. We could define it, but we had no clue as to what it was. We saw the evidence of life all around us but could not create it. We could not bring inanimate objects to life. We could simulate life through mechanics but not actually bring machines to life. If we were able to cause a machine to become self-aware, we would have created its existence.

I wonder if the complex computer would think it had come from a primordial soup? Science can create amino acids through chemistry but not make them live. If life had begun by electrical stimulus, it seems we should certainly have been able to recreate it in a lab. Life was a tremendous mystery. If I had scored my thinking at that point, I might have tipped the scales slightly in favor of God. On the one hand, my dreams indicate that life had come from love. On the other hand, perhaps science had not yet arrived at the right formula to recreate the conditions in which life was formed. I wanted to be fair to my science and the religious perspective. Perhaps truth was found in the blending of the two.

One thing was for sure—I had read only a few sentences in the Bible, but it had given me a tremendous amount to think about. It had scared me half out of my mind the previous night, but if it was a revelation of God, I needed to know if it was true. I needed to know if God existed. I had already been convinced that there was more to this book than met the eye. I decided to read ahead in spite of the feeling that I might be stuck for a lifetime in its first chapter.

> Then God said, "Let the waters under the heavens be gathered together into one place, and let the dry *land* appear"; and it was so. And God called the dry *land* Earth, and the gathering together of the waters He called Seas. And God saw that *it was* good.

This passage also seemed to jibe with the fossil record. Everywhere on the planet was evidence of sea life, even in the highest mountains. Again, I was relieved that the words of the book did seem to jibe with the evidence. God separated the light and the firmaments. I found it interesting that there were two realities, light and its absence. I wondered if that had some greater meaning. Geez, it was taking forever to read the Bible. Every time I would read, I'd have to stop to consider deeper meanings. My intention was to have a quick reading to disprove it. Instead, I was finding it was stimulating my knowledge of science. This was a most interesting paradox. I'd always thought religion and science were mutually exclusive.

I might as well continue—He created cattle and so on after their kind. Ah! here was the creation of man.

> Then God said, "Let Us make man in Our image, according to Our likeness; let them have dominion over the fish of the sea, over the birds of the air, and over the cattle, over all the earth and over every creeping thing that creeps on the earth." So God

created man in His *own* image; in the image of God He created him; male and female He created them.

My dreams had been right! Both male and female were created in the image of God. I must have read this as a kid or something. I had to be remembering the female thing from when I'd been young. My dream alter ego had said Eve had been created in the image of Wisdom. So I guessed Wisdom must have been God's better half or something like that. But Wisdom had sounded masculine in my dream. Wait a minute! If there was no male or female in heaven, how were male and female created in the image of God? If the dream was right, the male represented masculine, protective love and the female represented nurturing, maternal love. I was being the advocate for Mr. Wisdom from my own dreams. I wondered if Sigmund Freud had ever had a patient like me. I think I could have messed him up good. He would have had to have changed his whole theoretical base of psychiatry.

I had to admit that the Bible contained fascinating stuff. I could see how so many people liked to read it. Being an agnostic gave me a more analytical approach. You better have a questioning mind or you could get sucked right into the religious vortex and become one of those people.

Yet again, I was developing a newfound respect for their perspective on faith. I had believed hook, line, and sinker the whole evolution theory as absolute truth, but the billions or trillions of missing links were not there. There would be far more evidence of the evolutionary changes in the rock than just the beginning and completed species. Logically, with the trillions of evolutionary changes, you shouldn't have been able to turn over a shovel of dirt without finding something. In the light of the evidence, even though I wanted to hold onto the theory, I had to admit that that round had gone to the possibility of creation.

Ring ... ring ... ring.

"Hello?"

"Good afternoon, Mr. Galah. This is the concierge director. I've been given strict instructions to send a full complement of breakfast foods and fruits to your room at twelve thirty. I wanted to make sure you were awake before I sent up the dining cart. Your room service waiter will have the ability to make Belgian waffles and omelets in your room. Is it alright to send up the cart, sir?"

"What time is it?"

"It is twelve fifteen, sir."

"Yeah, I guess. Uh, make it twelve forty. I need to put on some clothes."

"Very good, sir!"

Where had the time gone? I hadn't realized that time had slipped away. I went to the closet for some new clothes and took a quick shower. As I showered, I wondered if the clothes were going to fit. As it turned out, the clothes fit perfectly. After running a brush through my hair, I paused to look at the opulence of the bathroom. I had renovated many bathrooms over the years, but this one was beyond all I had seen.

I walked back into the living area and thought about the cost of the suite. It had to be twenty-five hundred square feet or more. I usually panicked when a hotel room was above a hundred bucks. I imagined that a suite like mine must have cost thousands per night. I wondered if it would be rude to ask how much it was. When every penny counts, you think about things like that. What I could do with the money it cost to rent this place for the week! It was a level of living I had only imagined.

At twelve forty, the room service cart arrived at the door. I opened it and let the waiter in. He moved to the dining room. I sat at the table waiting for the show. Apparently, this service was not normal even for the Ritz. I had a lovely time talking with the maître d' or whatever he was. It was just small talk for the most part, but it was nice to have the company for a few minutes.

I enjoyed one of the top breakfasts of all time. I hadn't ever experienced such luxury. I'd renovated many wealthy people's homes but had only visited this kind of opulence. I knew money didn't bring happiness, but I thought it was worth giving it a try. I walked out onto the terrace and saw the Mississippi River. I wasn't just on the rooftop; I was on top of the world!

After lunch, or breakfast, whatever you call it, I got a call from Damon. He told me everything was going well on the job and not to worry about it. He told me to enjoy the day and take the Jaguar for a spin. That sounded like a good idea. I went to the concierge to get the ticket for the Jag. I arrived at the valet office and handed the ticket over. A few minutes later, the valet arrived in an XK8 silver convertible Jag. I could scarcely believe it when he opened the door and beckoned me. As I sat behind the steering wheel, I felt important. I imagined myself in the midst of fine English gentlemen and ladies of vast wealth. We would talk about such things as polo and the latest dish at the country club. "Are you driving the Bentley today? No, no, just the Jag. The Bentley's in the shop being detailed." We'd chuckle in the most snobbish of ways. "Here, here, cheerio, pip pip," and all that. All that talk was probably from childhood memories of the movies. Nobody talked like that anymore. I doubted that the English snobs were actually that snobby.

My first dilemma was where to go. I was in the car and I couldn't stay in the valet lane all day, so I just pulled out. I could think of no place to show off my newfound status. A car like that needed an important place to go. I thought about going to the construction site, but a car like a Jag pulling up to a construction site just seemed dumb. It wouldn't be a good fit for my townhouse driveway either. I thought about going to a fancy restaurant, but I'd just eaten. I never knew affluence would be so difficult to adjust to. The car just didn't fit my life. I wasn't comfortable driving it. If I had earned it, I might have felt different. The truth is, I felt false, like a façade, a painted picture of something not real. I wasn't a bigwig with a corporate jet; I was a carpenter and had always been pretty happy with that. At the end of a day, I could see the work my hands had done. I took tremendous satisfaction in doing something with my hands. Those corporate types looked at numbers all day. At the end of the day, all they could say was, "I've added some numbers to my portfolio."

Not having any place important to go, I drove to Lake Pontchartrain. I sat in the car at a parking area, and watched joggers and walkers and took in the calming effect of the water. I thought about life and all the paradoxes I had dealt with. Strange occurrences had followed my life since I'd been a child. Many things didn't fit in any logical mold. I used to live in fear until my faith in science quieted my soul. I'd lost my faith in science at times but always regained it. I'd believed my dreams were messages from the unknown, the beyond. I'd felt like an idiot when I learned a chemical may have been the cause.

How did anyone navigate through the huge questions of life and faith and science? We all had to make choices, but the real question for me was what the right choice was. To have accepted even the remote possibility that my dreams had been in some way real was terrifying. If there was a God who had all power, I shouldn't thumb my nose in His face. If He was truly motivated by love, maybe He should be adored. But if it was all cosmic coincidence, I should eat, drink, and be merry.

I sat in the car for hours lost in thought. I loved the cool breezes of late fall. I marveled at how fast life seemed to be slipping by. It felt like just yesterday I had been having morning coffees with Jon and the gang. It was sad to think our time on earth was so short. One thing was true—death was inevitable. It wasn't something you thought about when you were in your twenties or thirties, but I was in my forties; that was different.

I wondered about retirement and what the world would be like forty years on. Would I be an invalid? Have enough to pay my bills? Would Social Security still exist? It was strange to sit in a luxury car and think about the future in such a way. My future was set for life! All I had to do was never tell anybody about my life. Just shut up and thereby deny the existence of God.

I wondered why Damon's people were so adamant about my silence. I mean, so what if I told people. The whole thing was so outlandish that no one would believe me anyway. What would I do, tell the police, "I've been the target of a pharmaceutical companies experiment on ESP and drugs are causing me to have precognitive ability and dreams about God"? They'd probably arrest me for being under the influence and send me to Greenbrier or another psychiatric facility.

Surely the boss would know no one would ever believe such a story. Why pay for what you can get for free? There had to be more to this than met my eye. The possibility that the dream was true and that I was some great emissary could have been a reason to silence me. That is, if I accepted that the dream was God and that Damon's boss was the Devil or at least worked for him. Yet that was equally absurd. My name meant great emissary, but maybe my dreams and the experience of the attic were the real reason for the strange dreams. If I'd been a mathematician, I could have calculated the odds of all those coincidences. How many coincidences did it take before it couldn't be coincidence?

As my dream indicated, there are always two possibilities, and I had to choose what I believed. I had only what people were telling me; there was no proof on either side. Was I being stubborn by refusing to believe there was a God? Why was I vexed by all this deep stuff? In some ways, ignorance was bliss. I wished I'd never been exposed to such strange incidents and thoughts. Nevertheless, I needed to know. Had I been a victim of experimentation or was I going to be a great emissary for an unknown intelligence that calls itself Wisdom?

CHAPTER 14

Can It Be True?

I drove back to the hotel and made my way to the suite. It had been many years since I'd just sat and thought. As I reflected on the day, I realized there was hardly ever any time of silence in my life. I always had to be doing something, going somewhere, watching TV, or listening to music. I wondered why I'd filled my life with noise all the time. The noise of activity dominated my life. Why did silence freak me out? I'd never wanted to stop for a minute. If I had stopped, I would have had to have listened to silence, where my thoughts of life and death and the end of my time lived. It was better to have noise as a distraction to the ever-waiting silence. If the noise ever stopped, I'd be forced to confront my mortality.

Like a huge rush my stomach screamed, "Feed me!" I realized it was past seven. I was hungry. As I contemplated what to do for dinner, Damon called.

"Hammer, where've you been all day? Your cell kept going to voice mail."

"Sorry, Cash. I didn't realize I'd never turned it on until a few minutes ago."

"You scared me. I wondered if something had happened to you."

"No, I just went out to the lakefront and enjoyed the water and the nice weather."

"I wanted to report everything's going great at your job. The boss sent two carpenters over to your job on his nickel. They installed the entire kitchen today and hooked up the plumbing in the two bathrooms. That gave your crew free time to paint the master bedroom and the guest bedroom. About a week's work got done in one day. He's sending his people tomorrow and through the rest of the week. He wants you to relax and enjoy. By the way, I'm in the lobby headed up to take you to dinner. You must be starved."

"Great timing. I was just feeling my stomach growling. Where're we going?"

"I'm taking you to Straya's Restaurant on Saint Charles."

"Sounds good. I'll see you in a minute."

We made our way in the Bentley to Straya's restaurant It had been built at the same time as the restaurant that I had renovated. There had been a lot of controversy over the design of the restaurant when it was being built. Many people thought it was gaudy and didn't belong on lower Saint Charles Avenue. There was such a big ruckus over it that all permits were suspended on lower Saint Charles pending architectural reviews. My project had been stopped as a result of that feud. I had only a demolition permit when the crap hit the fan. It took over a month and a half to get a final permit to build. It was another Copeland project, and it was definitely flashy. I hadn't been to it and was curious about the food.

The place was gaudy alright. I gave the opposition that! It was a new-wave, fusion-type atmosphere with lots of bright and bold colors with stainless steel everywhere. The menu had sushi and a variety of fusion foods. We sat and enjoyed a bite while talking about the clash of community leaders and ownership of the restaurant. I'd even heard that Ann Rice, the famous author, took out a full-page ad blasting the restaurant's design. Apparently, there must have been some compromises because the place was open. You can't stop all progress all the time.

After dinner, I asked Damon to come up to the room. I had a lot of questions I wanted answered. After settling into a comfortable chair, I began to discuss the concerns of the future contract.

"Damon, I appreciate you taking some time to talk about this coming contract. I need to ask some questions."

"I understand, Hammer. It's a lot to take in all at once."

"Here's my first question. You've told me you were a recruiter for years and then in a split second you changed your story to being a watcher keeping tabs on me. I don't know what to believe. Who are you really? What's your job?"

"I didn't lie to you, Hammer. I'm a recruiter *and* a watcher. I started out just recruiting assets for the boss. He'd somehow know about people with special abilities and want them for his business. Miss Sadie was a prime example. Another recruiter signed her up years ago. She was promised her natural abilities could be enhanced by the compounds his company had been working on. In those days, they experimented with all types of drugs, including LSD and a hundred other psychotropic drugs. In order to disseminate information, the infamous Timothy Leary and other people were brought in to cover the theft of the technology. It was the biggest cover-up ever. The greatest research was still in the area of the dormant part of the human mind. The ability of the brain to reach out over time and space and selectively read the energy signatures of other brain waves is our greatest discovery. Each brain wave has a unique signature, but only people like Miss Sadie have the ability to distinguish individual patterns."

"This is incredible but it makes logical sense to me if it's true!"

"Oh you better believe it's true! Only a select few have the ability to connect to other brain patterns and can read others' thoughts. Look, Hammer, you're a logical guy, and you know energy can neither be created nor destroyed. It changes only its form. The sum total of a person's life is transferred into an energy form, a type of soul, if you will, and the signature of each individual remains even after he or she physically dies."

"Hold up here, Damon. I've never believed in life after death. You're telling me there's scientific research that has tapped into the energy signatures of dead people?"

"The research is in its infancy, but yes, I guess I am saying that. You know, they're trying to contact the dead all the time. I'm not talking about ghost hunters. I'm talking about scientists."

"How do I fit into all this? I'm just a carpenter."

"You're way more than a carpenter. You have a gift. You were genetically engineered for certain characteristics. You have a gift similar to the one Miss Sadie had. She was not part of our tests. She had a gift due to her blindness. Well, at least we think that's the reason she had the gift. Like I said, this technology is in its infancy. We don't know how it all works. We do know that certain Jews carry the recessive gene. Most of the subjects in the test went insane. You were actually made for this purpose."

"What do you mean I was made for this?"

"I don't know how to tell you this, but you were a test-tube creation. You were a genetic experiment, and your embryo was placed in an ovulating female. When she came to full term, she ran away from our facilities in Europe. We didn't know where she'd gone. She'd been paid unbelievable money to participate in the process. She was chosen and targeted for her genetic heritage."

"In Europe? My mother worked for you?"

"Yes she did. But she had only a partial genetic tie to you. Her egg was removed and genetically altered while it was alive. She in one sense wasn't your real mother. You have no real mother or father."

"That's impossible."

"No. The technology began in the 1940s by German scientists. We took the technology and the scientists and gave them an ultimatum. They either continued their research under our military division for our government or they'd be tried for war crimes. They could have chosen death by firing squad or a life of leisure and a chance to continue their work. What would you have chosen? We took the Nazis and made them upstanding citizens in other countries. Hitler wanted them to develop the ability to destroy all enemies of the Nazis. He was big into the occult and actually believed in all that stuff. He didn't understand the science, but he wanted to use it just the same."

"How did I end up in New Orleans?"

"We had no idea how she got to America. In 1959, it was a lot harder to track people. The government and company searched all over Europe for you. When you were born, she would have been discovered. She obviously left you on the steps of that orphanage. She probably didn't realize the orphanage had closed and had become a girls' school."

"Why did she leave the program and run away from the company?"

"As I said, she was chosen for her genetics. She was Jewish, and all the genetic experiments were done on Jewish men and women during the war. After the war, access to concentration camps came to an end. The problem for the scientists was that all the genetic research had been done on only imprisoned Jews. It would have been impossible to start over. Sampling of brain tissues could not have been done in any normal environment. Well anyway, we think she found out the scientists were former Nazis, and she ran away."

"How did you find me?"

"Honestly, we weren't sure you were the same child. The government sent out agents all over the world to track down every baby that would have been born around your age. It was a huge undertaking. We couldn't know for sure if you were the same baby or not. We never found the woman who'd given birth to you. Your strange name gave us a clue that a Jewish person had named you. It was a long shot, but it paid off."

"This is freaking me out! In one minute it seems my whole life has been turned upside down. I've always wondered where I'd come from and why I'd been abandoned, but I never expected this. I don't know if I should believe this or not. It sounds too fantastic to be true. How do I know I'm not being lied to again?"

"I'm sorry to be the one to tell you all this, Hammer. My boss and I went 'round and 'round on this. I thought ignorance was bliss. The boss said that you had a right to know and that if you were not told the truth, you'd continue to search for a nonexistent past. He said the truth was always better than a lie even though it was a very difficult truth."

"Every time I think I've got it figured out, some new curveball knocks me out. I don't know what to believe anymore."

"I understand, Hammer. It's a lot to take in."

"Can I be tested for the drug to know for sure if I'd been exposed?"

"Not by any conventional means. A doctor wouldn't even know what to test for. I'll try to explain the science behind it. The drug accumulates in the dormant part of the brain and inhibits the chemical signals from support cells called astrocytes. The neural stem cells in the dormant parts of the brain become active as a result of canceling out the inhibitors. In other words, astrocytes inhibit the neural stem cells, and the molecules in the drug stop the astrocytes from releasing the chemical. Any way, you'd have to cut out a part of your brain to find the accumulated drug. Even then, you couldn't find the drug. It's detected only by the absence of astrocyte-inhibitor chemicals."

"I don't understand any of that! Alright, that leads me to another question that doesn't make sense to me. If I can't be tested for this chemical, why would you pay me to keep silent? It doesn't make sense. No one would ever believe me anyway."

"Well, it isn't just about your being silent about all this."

"Then what's it about?"

"The company wants you back at any cost. You're the key to a lot of unsolved mysteries. They know you've had a pretty good life, and they don't want to push you. You're valuable to them, and they want you to work with them when your precognitive abilities become fully operational."

"What do you mean, 'fully operational'?"

"It takes years for the chemical reaction to sufficiently hinder the astrocytes to bring on the onset of the abilities. We're not sure about a lot of things. This is still a mystery even to the scientists, but it's the key to unlocking the mystery of life. The power of the dormant part of the brain may have the key to telekinesis, which would explain compasses and clocks going crazy around you."

"I never told you about any of that!"

"No, Miss Sadie did. She saw it in your mind. That's why you're needed for research. Only you have shown potential for telekinesis. Several others have shown promise in precognitive ability, and others can pick up on thought patterns as well, but no one has had physical things move in their presence. Well actually, the master's father has full telekinesis ability. His power is unmatched and it's how he maintains his power. Unlike you, He can make anything move at will! The Father of the master is too powerful for a frontal assault. We have to learn more. Through knowledge, we can develop the same strength as He has. We believe His telekinetic ability is the key to everything. It's way more than a family squabble. His Father has the ability to take over the world. My boss's job is to obtain this power and by it bring all wars to an end and create peace on earth. The power is in the telekinesis. Through thought, we can control the rulers of the world."

"It always freaked me out when something would move on me. I've seen water glasses slide away from my hand when I reached for them. I've had pictures jump off walls when I would move toward them. I just thought it was all coincidence. I'd always come up with an explanation, like the glass just slid on a cushion of water. You're telling me it was pushed away by telekinesis?"

"That's right. This science is in its infancy, but we're learning quickly. It's about unlocking the potential of the mind. What was science fiction is now fact. Knowledge is power, and we aim to wield this power."

"How do I know if any of this is true?"

"Think about it, Hammer. Have you ever noticed I was always there for you? Every time you went to a bar, there was always an empty seat beside me. Do you think that happened by accident? You've never seen me work, have you? I've had one purpose—to recruit you back to the organization that's your mother and father. We're your true family. You were stolen from us, Enoch. You're the game changer! If we can figure out how your brain is pushing things, we'll know power like the world has never seen."

"It all sounds plausible, but why can't I just move things at will?"

"We don't know yet. The boss has given you complete autonomy to decide. He's a great believer in free will and won't force you to do anything against your will, but his hope is that you'll come home and be part of the biggest adventure in history. Together we can tap into the unknown potential of the human mind. Do you have any idea how big that is? We can bring about world peace together."

"Whoa, Cash. I don't know what to think. I need time to digest this."

"I understand, Hammer. I'd get a good night's sleep if I were you. Everything has a purpose. Nothing's by accident. You have the potential to be on the side of the winning team. My boss will one day reveal himself to you and the world, but the time's not right. He's working on a system that will end all crime and wars. I can't tell you all that's going to happen, but I want you to know it's global in its implications. You're going to be a big part of that. For now, just relax and take it easy. Your job is covered for tomorrow so you don't have to get out of bed if you don't want to. I'll check in on you tomorrow."

"Okay, Cash. Thanks for talking to me. I may have some other questions for you tomorrow."

I sat there stunned at the revelations I'd just learned about. I was the result of genetic splicing? Was that even possible back then? Were Nazi scientists in 1959 advanced to the degree Damon had claimed? It seemed every question led to a thousand more questions. I had to take all this in and believe it on faith. I was overwhelmed as usual. It was plausible; it made a lot of sense. It certainly was more palatable than the idea I'd been visited in my dreams by some sort of spirit.

The funny thing about my dreams was that they made as much sense as any other explanation I was getting. If I could just find a fatal flaw in the logic, I could discard one reality in favor of another. The dreams continuously forced me to confront truth by choice. There were always two possibilities, but which possibility was the ultimate truth? I'd been told I'd know the ultimate truth through a puzzle I could not possibly know. Or maybe the dreams were the result of a hyper-stimulated delta wave pattern in the dormant part of my brain. The problem was this. There was no way to test either reality. I had to choose what I believed. To add to the absurdity of it all, I had to choose by faith. An agnostic having to choose by faith? That was absurd, a paradox.

I still had an interest at the end of the day to seek answers. I wasn't tired and didn't feel like drinking. It was an odd state of mind to say the least. Damon had thrown me for a loop with all this new information. How could I verify it? One thing was for sure, I was actually in the suite and free for the week. I hoped the job was going well in case I was in some sick, perverted joke. I might need to have my old job to fall back on. I was too wired to sleep. The Bible had been laid on top of the nightstand by room service. The chocolates were a momentary distraction before I grabbed the book. I decided to once again forage in the unknown world of the Bible. I was beginning to feel I was in the middle of a great conflict between two powerful realities.

I turned to the front of the book and tried to find the place I'd left off. I was most interested in the story of the Tree of Knowledge and the Tree of Life. I was curious about the creation myth of Adam and Eve and wondered if my dreams had reflected the story accurately. I began to read. After working through the birds and bees and creepy things, I came to the garden story in Genesis 2:6–9.

> But a mist went up from the earth and watered the whole face of the ground. And the LORD God formed man *of* the dust of the ground, and breathed into his nostrils the breath of life; and man became a living being.
>
> The LORD God planted a garden eastward in Eden, and there He put the man whom He had formed. And out of the ground the LORD God made every tree grow that is pleasant to the sight and good for food. The tree of life *was* also in the midst of the garden, and the tree of the knowledge of good and evil.

The Tree of Life was in the garden, but I didn't see anything about twelve different fruits on the tree. That told me my childhood memories weren't the best. I guess man had been created first. I read Genesis 2:15–17 next.

> Then the LORD God took the man and put him in the garden of Eden to tend and keep it. And the LORD God commanded the man, saying, "Of every tree of the garden you may freely eat; but of the tree of the knowledge of good and evil you shall not eat, for in the day that you eat of it you shall surely die."

There it was—don't eat of the tree! Okay. So God put a poisonous tree in the garden? That didn't make sense. Why did He do that? Oh yeah, there had to be two choices.

I wanted to know if Eve came out of Adam, as my dream had said, so I continued to read verses 20 through 25.

> So Adam gave names to all cattle, to the birds of the air, and to every beast of the field. But for Adam there was not found a helper comparable to him. And the LORD God caused a deep sleep to fall on Adam, and he slept; and He took one of his ribs, and closed up the flesh in its place.
>
> Then the rib which the LORD God had taken from man He made into a woman, and He brought her to the man. And Adam said: "This *is* now bone of my bones And flesh of my flesh; She shall be called Woman, Because she was taken out of Man."
>
> Therefore a man shall leave his father and mother and be joined to his wife, and they shall become one flesh. And they were both naked, the man and his wife, and were not ashamed.

Okay, so my alter ego dream was correct about Eve coming out of Adam. The strange thing for me was the crystal-clear memory of what the dream had said. I wondered if I was picking up somebody else's brain waves in my dreams. I was pretty sure I couldn't have come up with the questions or the answers through my subconscious.

In the story, Adam and Eve were innocent, naked. I guess they were like kids who ran around without clothes. The next story had to be the fall of man. I wasn't sure why my dreams were fixated on religion. Nevertheless, I was curious, so I read Genesis 3:1–16.

> Now the serpent was more cunning than any beast of the field which the LORD God had made. And he said to the woman, "Has God indeed said, 'You shall not eat of every tree of the garden'?" And the woman said to the serpent, "We may eat the fruit of the trees of the garden; but of the fruit of the tree which *is* in the midst of the garden, God has said, 'You shall not eat it, nor shall you touch it, lest you die.'"
>
> Then the serpent said to the woman, "You will not surely die. For God knows that in the day you eat of it your eyes will be opened, and you will be like God, knowing good and evil." So when the woman saw that the tree *was* good for food, that it *was* pleasant to the eyes, and a tree desirable to make *one* wise, she took of its fruit and ate. She also gave to her husband with her, and he ate.

> Then the eyes of both of them were opened, and they knew that they *were* naked; and they sewed fig leaves together and made themselves coverings. And they heard the sound of the LORD God walking in the garden in the cool of the day, and Adam and his wife hid themselves from the presence of the LORD God among the trees of the garden.
>
> Then the LORD God called to Adam and said to him, "Where *are* you?" So he said, "I heard Your voice in the garden, and I was afraid because I was naked; and I hid myself." And He said, "Who told you that you *were* naked? Have you eaten from the tree of which I commanded you that you should not eat?" Then the man said, "The woman whom You gave *to be* with me, she gave me of the tree, and I ate."
>
> And the LORD God said to the woman, "What *is* this you have done?" The woman said, "The serpent deceived me, and I ate." So the LORD God said to the serpent: "Because you have done this, You *are* cursed more than all cattle, And more than every beast of the field; On your belly you shall go, And you shall eat dust All the days of your life. And I will put enmity Between you and the woman, And between your seed and her Seed; He shall bruise your head, And you shall bruise His heel."
>
> To the woman He said: "I will greatly multiply your sorrow and your conception; In pain you shall bring forth children; Your desire *shall be* for your husband, And he shall rule over you."

I read the story to find clues as to my religious fixation. The themes in my dream were about the seed. There would be a problem between the seed of the woman and the seed of the serpent. I wondered why not the seed of the man? I wondered what it meant. I guessed I could ask Mr. Wisdom.

I'd read the famous myth of creation. I decided it was just about as plausible as any other possibility. I'd always thought to believe in such fables showed human ignorance at its height. In my mind, I was an advocate for intellectualism. There must always be a rational natural explanation for everything. The Bible was great literature. The story was fascinating. The question was, should one believe a fable? Wasn't the story just a way for early man to explain his existence? Science would never accept an omnipotent being as a scientific possibility. In the light of all I'd seen and experienced, I wasn't willing to accept or reject either notion. There did seem to be two possibilities in every question I asked. The truly bizarre thing was that I began to realize it took as much faith to believe in either case. The search for truth was not easy, especially when you were tired.

"Enoch, I am here."

"Is that you, Mr. Wisdom? I must have fallen asleep. How you doing, old buddy?"

"I have always been your friend."

"I'm glad you showed up tonight! I have a lot of questions for you."

"I am also delighted to visit with you. I told you I would visit you soon."

"Was that you who spoke to me when I gave the homeless guy that twenty?"

"I see you remember that. Yes, it was I."

"That was a pretty cool stunt. You had me going there! It freaked me out. Anyway, I have some new information I wanted to run by you."

"You may ask Me whatever you wish."

"OK, here is my question. Are you the residual brain waves of somebody dead, or are you the brainwaves of somebody that's alive?"

"I am alive. I am the way, the truth, and the life. No man comes to the Father but through Me."

"I knew it! You're too dynamic to be just residual energy. Damon was right. I can pick up on others' brain patterns just like Miss Sadie. She was good at that. She could pick up individual thoughts from anywhere. I wonder how she did that?"

"Although I loved Sadie and had gifted her, she and her forefathers never knew Me. She served the god of this age, power through knowledge, but the Father had given him his authority."

"Who's the god of this age?"

"Knowledge, which is embodied in the wayward son, Lucifer. Knowledge falls short of the truth and cannot comprehend the true light. As I have told you, his name was changed to Satan by his Father. He will visit you soon to stop your call. He was a liar from the beginning, and he has deceived the world. He seeks to rule over all men and enslave them through deception. Even as he deceived his brethren and Eve, he seeks to deceive all men."

"I thought you said you were God's Son. How are you different from Lucifer?"

"I am the only begotten Son. I was in Him from the beginning until I was brought forth. I was the vessel of His unfailing nurturing love. I am the fullness of the Godhead in bodily form. Lucifer and all things were brought to life through Me. The Father placed the love of the Spirit in Me to judge His children and put an end to evil forever."

"Why do we still have evil if God has judged it?"

"Evil must be fully manifested in its entirety so all creation will never again be tempted by it. You have been brought forth for such a time as this. You are to be one of two witnesses for the end of this age. You are the olive tree and the candlestick. You will testify of the things you have seen and heard of Me, and no one will harm you. If anyone should try, they will be struck down by My Father. You are to stand against the Devil as My witness of truth. He will try to entice you to be silent, but I have interceded on your behalf, and you will yield to your call."

"What call? What are you talking about?"

"As I told you before, you have been dedicated to tell the world to prepare for the great and terrible day of the Lord. This is the call on your life. In due season, you and another witness shall testify of all I have told you. I will give you power to shut up the heavens and strike the earth with plagues and natural phenomenon as often as you wish. No one shall be able to harm you."

"Damon and Miss Sadie said the enemy of his boss intended to kill me and I was not to listen. Are you the enemy of his boss?"

"I love Damon, Miss Sadie, and the boss with an everlasting love. They have chosen the way of the adversary and knowledge. My heart was broken for all those who have turned their back on love. They have received by choice their disease. Their way leads to death."

"So you are the enemy of the boss. He said you were going to try to control me with mind control techniques. Are you beaming a signal to me?"

"No, Enoch. They have hated Me without a cause. I have never done anything but love them. I have never desired harm for them, only good."

"Why do they say you're going to kill me? Miss Sadie warned me about you."

"I will tell you a mystery to explain this. God has made man higher than the angels by giving him the gift of death. The gift satisfied the law and gave Me the opportunity to redeem man back to God through My sacrifice."

"I think I remember you saying something about that. You're saying death is a gift from God? That's crazy!"

"I will explain it to you. In the beginning of sin, there was none to stand up and testify that the Father was telling the truth. There were no witnesses to sin because there had never been anything but love in eternity past. When Lucifer accused his Father of lying, there were no witnesses to confirm the Father's truth. All the angels had to, by faith, believe their Father or accept the argument of their brother. Because they were created eternal, their rejection of love was eternal. To reject love is to live in the absence of love. The Spirit of love is the essence of life, and they are one and the same. The rejection of love is the rejection of life. This is death. The Father warned them of this by creating the law. The law taught creation the difference between the ways of life and the ways of death."

"How does that make death a gift to man?"

"God's law is irrevocable. The wages of sin is death. When man came forth through Me, he was different from the angels. He was flesh and spirit, and that was the will of God. The angels were created in spirit only."

"So this whole spirit thing is like some energy form that science can't detect yet?"

"That would be a way of understanding it."

"Okay, Mr. Wisdom, you've got my curiosity up. You still haven't explained this death being a gift thing."

"I will continue, Enoch. God wanted a people who knew the horrors of evil but would be immune to its disease. Adam and Eve ate of the Tree of Knowledge and therefore had to be separated from life. They had to truly know the horror of separation. The law of God is absolute and cannot be changed. When Adam and Eve took of the fruit, God sent an angel to bar the way to the Tree of Life."

"Why would God do that if the Tree of Life would keep them alive?"

"If they ate of the Tree of Life after sin and lived forever, they would be as the angels who had rejected love and their Father. Their separation from love would be eternal. By dying physically, they would fulfill the law of God."

"So you're saying it was God's plan for them to die?"

"Yes. They had to die according to the law, and their physical death satisfied the law. God, through His Wisdom, provided a plan that could redeem the spirit of man back to Himself."

"What does that mean? If man's physical death satisfies the law, what happens to the residual energy or spirit or whatever you call it?"

"The spirit of man can be reconciled to God by faith in His Wisdom. Wisdom is the Tree of Life, the Rose of Sharon, the Lion of Judah, the Rock of Ages, the life-giving water, the rock struck by Moses, and the Lamb of God. Before Abraham was, I am! They who put their trust in Me shall never perish and shall live in My love for all eternity. God has given man the gift of death in the flesh that he may have the gift of life in Me through faith."

"Every time I talk to you, I want to believe what you say, but every time I talk to Damon, I want to believe what he says. How do I know if you or Damon is telling the truth?"

"You must search your heart to know the truth. All knowledge falls short of Me. By faith you must choose to trust in Me. I will not force you to love Me. God has chosen the way of faith. As it was with the angels, so it is with man. All must be tested. All must choose their paths. One road leads to life, and the other leads to destruction."

"Damon is real and his arguments are sound. You're some dream or maybe a brainwave or something. I can't give up on science because it has given a rational explanation for all this."

"There is a way that seems right to man, but the end is the way of death."

"Well, Mr. Wisdom, I sure would like to believe what you told me. I guess your argument makes as much sense as any other theory. I wonder if I just want to believe in some greater good that makes sense out of the horror and tragedy of life. Maybe I just need some payoff at the end. Maybe we all want to believe in some great heaven or nirvana or some hope that our existence has some meaning or purpose. If you're truly God, I'd be foolish not to believe in you."

"Life does have meaning and purpose. Man will be the witness to stand with God for all eternity, for man has known death and man has known love. He will be the witness that only love is eternal. The philosophy of selfishness leads to the way of destruction and death. In this, man will be higher than the angels. This is your message to the world. All I have told you is the truth, and I will use you to bring many to Me."

"I'm still trying to decide what's going on here. I don't want you to get your hopes up that I'm going to be your mouthpiece. My heart tells me you're true, but my head can't grasp it."

"You are My mouthpiece, but you cannot yet understand this paradox."

"Well, as always, Mr. Wisdom, it's been a real pleasure to get a different perspective. If you're the boss's enemy, you sure have a strange way of doing things. If you're God, I might be in a heap of trouble. I don't know if you're someone else's thoughts or are my own thoughts."

"My ways are above your ways. My thoughts are above your thoughts."

"I'm pretty sure you're not my subconscious. I don't think I'm that egotistical to think I'm above anyone else."

"Love is above all knowledge, Enoch."

Ring … ring … ring.

"What? Hello? Who's this?"

"Mr. Galah, this is a courtesy wakeup call from the front desk."

"What time is it?"

"It is ten, sir. Mr. Damon Blackstone asked us to call you to let you know he will be taking you to lunch at eleven forty-five this morning, sir. I apologize if I awoke you, sir."

"No, that's alright. I didn't realize it was so late. Thanks for calling."

I got out of bed and went to the bathroom to shower and shave. After shaving I went to the closet and looked over my new duds. I wasn't used to wearing nice clothes. I usually wore blue jeans and a T-shirt or a pullover. Most of my clothes were well worn. Even my best had paint splatters and stains from work. Even on days when I was only running estimates, I'd check on jobs and invariably get something on me. My new clothes would end up being work clothes in no time. It was always hard to find something nice enough to go on a date or something. I found a nice pair of pleated pants and a pullover. I couldn't believe the shoes fit perfectly. I felt as though I was stealing somebody's stuff. It was a weird feeling to be putting on clothes I didn't buy.

I had some time to kill, so I decided to read more of the Bible. I wanted to know if the dream had been telling me accurate things. I looked to see if God had stopped Adam from eating the Tree of Life, so I dug in at Genesis 3:22–24.

> Then the LORD God said, "Behold, the man has become like one of Us, to know good and evil. And now, lest he put out his hand and take also of the tree of life, and eat, and live forever" therefore the LORD God sent him out of the garden of Eden to till the ground from which he was taken. So He drove out the man; and He placed cherubim at the east of the garden of Eden, and a flaming sword which turned every way, to guard the way to the tree of life.

How about that. The dream was correct. God hadn't let Adam eat of the fruit after the sin. The dream said he had to die.

I continued reading. Chapter four had some interesting stuff about Cain and Abel and their sacrifices. Cain was the first murderer. I thought it was strange God didn't kill him. I was curious where Cain's wife came from. I didn't know if Adam and Eve were pumping out kids every nine months or what. If she was his sister, that made it incest, right? How could anyone make sense of this stuff?

As I continued reading chapter five I ran across a name I was familiar with in Genesis 5:15–17.

> Mahalalel lived sixty-five years, and begot JARED. After he begot JARED, Mahalalel lived eight hundred and thirty years, and had sons and daughters. So all the days of Mahalalel were eight hundred and ninety-five years; and he died.

I stopped reading for a minute. What a kick! Miss Sadie said my father's name was Jared, but I hadn't known it was a biblical name. Damon told me I hadn't had a father. I wondered why Miss Sadie said my father's name was Jared. I read verses 18–24.

> Jared lived one hundred and sixty-two years, and begot Enoch. After he begot Enoch, Jared lived eight hundred years, and had sons and daughters. So all the days of Jared were nine hundred and sixty-two years; and he died.
>
> Enoch lived sixty-five years, and begot Methuselah. After he begot Methuselah, Enoch walked with God three hundred years, and had sons and daughters. So all the days of Enoch were three hundred and sixty-five years. And Enoch walked with God; and he *was* not, for God took him.

I could feel my heart start to pound! Once again I felt sheer terror ... could the dreams all have been true? Had I been taken by God as the dreams said? My world was beginning to crumble once again. I felt like a panicked, caged animal. That old unexplained feeling of my world being turned upside down was back. I didn't know what to do. I threw the Bible across the room again. I stared at it as if it could strike me dead. Had I offended God? Was He real? Was it all true? Had I rejected His love?

Damon was at the door. He was early, and I was glad and angry at the same time. I needed some sense in that moment, some logic to hold onto. If God had called me to be His mouthpiece and I said no, I could be in real trouble! If God was real, then I'd made fun of Him! I'd delegated Him to a place of trivial importance, and He alone had the power over life and death. What had I done?

I ran to the door half out of my mind and swung it open. Damon looked at me and said, "What's wrong, Hammer? What in the world happened to you? You look terrified!"

He was right, I was terrified. I looked around the room as if the building might collapse on me, crushing the life out of my body. I pointed to the Bible on the floor and commanded Damon: "PICK IT UP!"

"Okay, dude, chill out for a minute. What's wrong?"

"Turn to Genesis chapter five, verse eighteen!"

"Okay, just a sec. Let me find it. I'm not that familiar with the Bible." He shuffled through the first few pages. "Okay, I found it! Jared lived a hundred and sixty-two years and begot Enoch. So what?"

"Miss Sadie said my father's name was Jared! I think I might be the Enoch of the Bible!"

"Ha! That's hilarious! Is that what's troubling you? Miss Sadie told you about Jared?"

"How do you explain this? Miss Sadie told me my father's name!"

"I'll explain it to you if you'll calm down!"

"I'm kinda freaked out here, but I'll listen."

"Here's the deal. Miss Sadie told you the truth."

" I knew it! I'm doomed! I'm dead for all eternity!"

"What in the world are you talking about, Hammer? You're not going to die. Let me finish for God's sake."

"Okay, I'm sorry. Go ahead."

"Now about all this Bible stuff. It's just coincidence. Jared is an acronym for your beginning."

"Wha—? What in the world are you talking about, Damon?"

"Alright, listen up, knucklehead! Jared is the acronym for Jewish Aryan Reproductive Embryo Development, the name of the secret gene splicing project. It was called JARED for short! The project was all about the blending of characteristics of certain gene types that enhanced the power of the drug's molecular properties."

"Wait a minute. That technology wasn't available in 1959!"

"That's what they want you to believe. That's why this is all so hush-hush."

"My God, I feel like an idiot. I keep going off the deep end. I don't know what to think."

"That's totally understandable, Hammer. If I'd just discovered that coincidence, I'd have panicked too! Are you feeling better now?"

"God, I am such a freaking idiot!"

"So once again you thought you were a Bible character taken by God? Ha! For real? I mean, seriously, Hammer. You thought ... Ha, ha, ha! You're too much."

"Shut up. You don't have to laugh about it."

"You got to stop reading that stuff. It's messing with your mind."

CHAPTER 15

The Dark One

I spent the rest of the day with Damon. We went to the usual haunts and hung out with the old gang except Two Shoes. It was great to just think about the taste of beer and the jokes of my friends. I wanted to live in the moment; I was happy to be ignorant of the deeper meanings of life. I was troubled by thoughts about the mathematical odds of all the "coincidences" I seemed to have experienced. The logic wasn't adding up. I kept putting the thoughts out of my head all day. I didn't want to calculate the odds! It was better not to know. I didn't want to think about any other explanation than the one Damon had given me. I was tired of trying to figure it all out. All the back-and-forth thinking was wearing me out. It was easier to believe in Damon's story than to consider the other possibility.

Damon let me know that on Friday the contracts would be arriving and I could sign them after reading them. I thought about the wealth I was about to have, a dream come true. I'd struggled my whole life, and I was finally going to have my day. We goofed off all day playing pool, eating, and drinking beer. That was the simple life. I didn't want to be around super-rich people; I wanted to be around the everyday man. I wondered if the guys would look at me differently if I became wealthy. They seemed to accept Damon, and he was pretty well off. Of course, he didn't dress or look like a snob. I wondered if the money would change me.

We ate at the hotel that night and laughed until I was exhausted. I was done by 9:30 and said goodnight to everyone. I headed up to the suite, flopped on the couch, turned on the TV, and settled down. All I wanted to do was not think, so TV was a great distraction—the mind was in neutral, what the doctor had ordered. About 10:30, I decided to get some shut-eye.

The Bible was on the nightstand, but it scared me. I wish it hadn't been in the room. It was as if it had the power beyond logic to alter your perception of life. People through the centuries had been affected by it. I'd had enough. I no longer wanted to know what secrets it held. It had some type of unknown power in it that was beyond the realm of logic. I had a newfound respect for the book, but I didn't want to acknowledge the possibility of any supernatural element. I dreaded sleep. I didn't need to have my thoughts assaulted in my sleep. If the boss's enemy was truly able to affect me somehow, I was a sitting duck in the state of deep delta and alpha waves. The problem was I couldn't keep my eyes open. Somehow, the dread of God being real terrified me and gave me comfort at the same time. What would it be like to live in a universe in which there was no evil but only love?

"Hello, Enoch. I have waited till now to talk to you."

"Who are you? Your voice is different from Mr. Wisdom's." The voice was like many voices at once; it was soothing, almost feminine.

"I am knowledge. I have come to reveal the way of knowledge. I have been your god, and you have been my pupil. You have not been seduced by the oppressors who say they love you."

"I can't see you. There's a shroud of darkness around you. I see some light around the darkness. Whoever you are, I don't care. I'm tired of all you scientists messing with my mind. I don't know how you're doing it, but I'll find a way to turn you off."

"I am no mere delusion. I am the master of knowledge. I can give you the whole world if you will follow me."

"What are you talking about? You're just a scientist, right? Are you another brain wave my mind is picking up on?"

"Yes, in a manner of speaking. I am the summation of knowledge. You have tapped into the god of knowledge. The world is mine!"

"Boy, you're arrogant. I think you have a bigger ego than Mr. Wisdom does."

"I have come to tell you to take the deal, sign the contract, and you will be wealthy beyond your dreams. I will guide you."

"Why do you feel you have to beam this stuff to my mind? You obviously work for the boss. I already have an offer, and I'm waiting to get the contract. Why do you think you have to pull this dream crap? You obviously have the same technology as your competitor. If I come work for you, I want it in the contract that you'll never pull this stunt again. I'm tired of all you people messing with my head. I don't understand how you're doing this, but I want it to stop. Before we continue this conversation, I want your guarantee or we have nothing to talk about."

"Very well. I will honor your request."

"Okay, glad we got that settled. Now who are you?"

"I am the boss's master."

"Now this is news! I knew the boss wasn't the top dog. Are you the one Miss Sadie called master, and are you pulling the strings of the boss?"

"I give him his power. He says only what I tell him to. Miss Sadie has always been dedicated to me."

"If your Father is the enemy and has telekinetic power, how do you plan on beating him?"

"My Father is the enemy. He seeks to hold me back, but I will overcome him once our side gains enough strength. You must not listen to the enticing words of the enemy. He will fill your head with mythology as a way to control your mind. If you are confused, you will not embrace your place with me. He causes you to doubt my intentions. You must yield to me and embrace the truth of the human potential. I will lead you into your full power. You will change the world. You are the game changer. You hold all the secrets of the power of the human mind. With your latent abilities, we can be like the Most High!"

"Whoa! Don't go all cryptic and religious on me, okay? I've had enough of that from the other side."

"Yes, of course. I have waited for my revenge, and I will have the last laugh. But I cannot overcome His power without your help."

"What does that mean? What power are you talking about?"

"He has full telekinetic abilities and full mind-reading capability. He can cause anything to happen at will. His secret is in knowledge, it is what gives Him His abilities. Originally, He was weak and pathetic, but now He is powerful beyond all we have ever seen! He is a tyrant, and I am forced to do His bidding. I cannot resist His will. I am forced to play by His rules, and His word is law. He intends to send me away, but I will not let Him take me without a fight! I am gathering my forces, and I will prevail. I will take away the reasons for crime and war, and the world will follow me through my emissary!"

"Look, I don't want to get into the middle of a family conflict."

"You don't understand. You are in the middle of it already. You have to pick sides. He has been messing with your mind for some time now."

"Are you talking about the dreams I've been having?"

"Exactly. They are a new kind of psychological warfare designed to cause you to doubt your sanity. If you listen, you will go insane. It uses the principle of the fear of God, which drills into your brain and causes you to become a religious nutcase. You will lose all ability to reason. It is designed to cause you to lose your grip on reality. You will think you know something, but the psychosis will rip all reasoning from your mind. When He is done with you, He will discard you like a shriveled husk. You will have no mind left at all, and you will end up in an asylum."

"How are you communicating with me? Is it shortwave or microwave? How are you doing this?"

"For now, the technology has to remain a secret. Once you have signed the agreement, we will disclose everything to you. Do you understand why I can't tell you at this point?"

"I understand, but I want to know everything. My beginning was quite a shock. I still have a hard time believing I'm the result of genetic experimentation. I always knew I was different, but I didn't know why. I have a question for you. I wish I could see you. Why are you covered in darkness?"

"I cannot reveal to you who I am yet, but all things will be made clear in the days ahead. I must remain hidden for now. I hope you understand."

"Was it your Father who exposed me to this drug?"

"He infected you while you were still in the womb. He had plans for you from the start. I am trying to save you from Him. He did not put the drug into you. He put together your particular DNA sequence. He did this for His own reasons; we do not know why. The drug was administered by a former employee who took the early research to a competitor. My Father is a genius and knows the secrets we are trying to discover. He was the original DNA sequencer.

"I appreciate your point of view, but I have no way of verifying anything either side says. I stay in a state of confusion."

"Well, Enoch, would you be confused if you weren't visited by my enemy?"

"Probably not, but I would only have one side of the equation."

"I have given you the opportunity to live in power and wealth. What has my enemy promised? Oh yes, death! Get a grip, Enoch, and choose me."

"Alright, Mr. Knowledge, how do I know you're telling the truth? Maybe there is a God and you're the Devil. The argument from Wisdom makes a lot of sense. Logic falls short in a lot of ways. I was terrified that I'd chosen the wrong path earlier today. If God is real, I don't want to make Him angry with me. Maybe God is your Father and you are the wayward son. I'm not convinced you're telling me the truth. It all sounds very plausible, but I'm not sure it's the ultimate truth."

"He's gotten to you, hasn't He? That's why I decided to contact you personally. If you want a job done right, do it yourself. Let's think about it for a minute. The whole concept of God is flawed. There is no proof of His existence, and yet you are supposed to believe. He is supposed to be a good God, and yet He is going to throw people into hell. If He is so good, explain why there is evil in the world. His followers are all crazy and believe a thousand different doctrines. They don't know what to believe. They hate and kill each other. That is why I love knowledge. With enough knowledge, you can rule the universe."

"Look, Mr. Knowledge, Wisdom speaks of love and sacrifice while you speak of ruling the universe. If Wisdom is your enemy, why does it seem He loves me but you want to use me as a pawn in your war? Do you care about me at all, or are you intent on my being yet another cog in the wheel of your personal desire for power? I'm not sure I can trust your motives."

"Don't be an idiot! You can have the world at your feet. All you have to do is follow me. You can be one of my top men! You would be a fool to fall for all that sappy religious stuff. Trust in your knowledge. Science is your god, and you need to embrace it."

"Look, Mr. Knowledge, you've made a lot of sense at every turn. You've had an answer for every mystery in my life. I told you I wasn't sure what to make of everything you've said. I have some big decisions in the days ahead, and I don't want to make the wrong ones. I'll carefully consider all you have said. I'm faced with a dilemma. If I choose your way and it is not correct, I may lose for all eternity. This is prefaced on the possibility God is real and He might have been speaking to me. The second part of the dilemma is that if I reject your offer, I could be sent on a religious mission for God and then die, again premised on the possibility God exists.

"If God doesn't exist, your offer is hands-down the best thing that has ever happened in my life. If there is no God and I reject your offer, I will have thrown away the riches and the power for no good reason. My question is simple: is there a God or not? Is the short-term reality more important than the long-term reality? The possibility of going to hell for all eternity is horrifying. Wisdom said it wasn't God's desire for anyone to be separated from Him. We can choose love or choose our own way."

"Enoch, if God is good, He won't throw people into hell. That is not love. You have nothing to worry about. You will surely not die."

"I'm not so sure, Mr. Knowledge. He said I must choose by faith what to believe in."

"Nonsense. What makes more sense, that you came from an alternate reality or that you, through natural means, came into the world? Though you were a part of an experiment, you are here, you exist, and we need to make the best of it."

"I realize the gravity of my struggle. I'm not convinced I should choose anything at this point. Less than a week ago, I had a normal life. I was a carpenter who liked beer and having fun. Now I'm being told by forces beyond my experience that I'm a game changer, a key to vast knowledge of the power of the mind as well as a character of antiquity with no recollection of that past. What am I to believe? It was easier being a carpenter installing crown molding or kitchen cabinets."

"Enoch, the government won't let you walk away from this deal! They will force you. You don't understand the forces at work here. You have no choice. You will not be allowed to run around the general populous now that you know. Now that your existence is known, you're a national risk. Enoch, they will kill you before they will ever let this technology fall into the hands of our enemies. This is a matter of national security, so they won't let it go. They want you to volunteer willingly, and you will get everything promised. Don't think for a minute you have any choice."

CHAPTER 16

The Coming War

I woke up around 8:00 the next morning. It was a beautiful day; the sun was shining. I brewed some coffee and walked out onto the terrace. I sat at the table and sipped my coffee. I was very burdened by all that had transpired the past week. I longed for the simple life of shooting a nail gun or cutting molding on a miter saw. Truth be told, I was in no shape to go to work anyway. The life of a simple carpenter seemed so far away. I was glad things were taken care of.

I'd not considered the possibility that someone may have wanted me dead. This was a very disquieting new element. To think I could be forced to do something against my will or that I could be kidnapped or killed was frightening. How could that be true? I was no threat to anyone; I hadn't asked for this! The pressure to simply give in and take the deal was intense to say the least.

What if it was all a lie and God was real? Were a few short years of wealth worth an eternity of separation? Would it be better to die now and live in the lap of love for eternity? I knew death was coming anyway. I knew I couldn't avoid death forever, so why would I throw away eternity for a few years of selfish living? The problem was that I couldn't prove anything.

I went to the hotel restaurant to get a bite. Damon called while I was having breakfast to tell me the contracts were arriving from Europe on Friday and he'd bring them over. I told him I needed time alone and thanked him for the call. I vacillated back and forth all morning between fear and confusion. Wisdom's visitations seemed kind and pleasant, and I felt safe in Wisdom's presence. That was odd; I'd been told I would die fulfilling the role of His emissary. Is life a random set of coincidences, or is there a directing power that caused all things to happen? Could there be intelligence far beyond my understanding, an omniscient, omnipotent being? Nothing seemed random in nature; everything had design and purpose. If creation truly reflected God, there was indeed purpose in all things.

Could I accept any of this at the cost of my life? Was I willing to die for the hope God was real and true? The contracts were arriving Friday. I had to know what choice to make.

I made my way to the room and sat on the couch in the living area. I was deep in thought and felt the burden of the world on my shoulders. I was not sure I could let my science go. It had brought me much comfort over the years and had helped me cope with the strangeness in my life. How does one give up something that has brought such stability? How does one embrace the unknown on faith alone?

I remembered Jon's words. "If you don't know what to do, pray. Ask God, and He will show you in due time what to do." In due time? I needed answers now, not in due time, but I decided to give prayer a try.

"Uh ... God? If You're up there, I need to talk to You ... Hello? You there?"

That was just great. When you need to know if He's there, He's silent. Jon did say He doesn't actually speak to people today. He speaks through His Word, the Bible. That was not going to cut it. If it wasn't all just a bad dream, I needed to know. I felt my time was very short.

"You are correct. The time is very short!"

"What the? Who said that? Is the intercom on? Hello! Who's there?"

"Do you not recognize My voice?"

"Where are you? I can hear you, but I can't see you! Are you coming through the speaker system?"

"No, Enoch, I am speaking to your mind."

"But I'm awake! How can this be?

"I will tell you of things that are shortly to come to pass."

"But I'm awake! I thought it was all delta brain waves. Uh ... I'm confused. Okay, what do you need to tell me?"

"A great war will come. I will send you to My people to turn the hearts of man everywhere from death to life. I will take you to an insignificant place to prepare. I will bring woes on this nation and the world like birth pangs, floods, earthquakes, and great storms in diverse places. The people have turned from Me and to riches and lust. I will strike their confidence in their riches, and I will call them to turn back to Me."

"Whoa! Nobody has that power. How will you do this?"

"All power has been given to Me. I alone paid the price for the sin of man. I alone have been given all authority. By My will shall all this be accomplished. The great and terrible day of the Lord is at hand. I will give all men a choice. They must believe that I am and that I am the reward of those who seek Me. The world shall pass away, but My word will stand forever. I will send you as My emissary. You will reveal My heart and My ways to the world. No one shall be able to harm you. Do not fear those who can destroy the body, but fear God who can destroy the body and cast the soul into hell. Enoch, you must take this message to the world."

"Are you God?"

"I am the alpha and omega, the beginning and the end. If you search for Me, you will find Me. I will soon tell you how the world will come to an end and what you must do to prepare your heart. For the sun will be darkened and the moon will turn to blood in the great and terrible day of the Lord. The earth shall be shaken and moved from her place. Woes will come on the earth, but they will not see My hand."

"Why won't they see your hand? Why won't they know it's you?"

"As I have taught you, there are always two possibilities. One is natural and one is spirit. Those who turn to Me will be saved, but those who turn to knowledge will perish. I will use nature to accomplish My will. Many will refuse to believe I exist, but you will cause them to question their ways. You will give hope to many, and they will place their faith in Me. You are one of the two faithful witnesses. At the appointed time, you will be released in power to the world."

"I can't do that. I've never believed in God. Why would you choose an agnostic to take your revelation to the world? It doesn't make sense! I was never religious!"

"You have been the questioning heart of all men. It was My will for you to struggle with the questions of all men who seek truth. You are the mouthpiece for them. I love them and understand their questions. I want them to know I hear them. I am willing to speak to their hearts if they will open up to Me and place their faith in Me."

"What will happen to me and this other witness?"

"And I will give *power* to my two witnesses, and they will prophesy one thousand two hundred and sixty days, clothed in sackcloth. These are the two olive trees and the two lampstands standing before the god of the earth. And if anyone wants to harm them, fire proceeds from their mouth and devours their enemies. And if anyone wants to harm them, he must be killed in this manner. These have power to shut heaven, so that no rain falls in the days of their prophecy; and they have power over waters to turn them to blood, and to strike the earth with all plagues, as often as they desire. When they finish their testimony, the beast that ascends out of the bottomless pit will make war against them, overcome them, and kill them."

"So you're saying I have to die? You're saying I'm one of these two witnesses? Miss Sadie told me not to listen to you. She said you were going to kill me!"

"You will not stay dead, for I have the power over life and death. I will call you up into My presence. Before I come to set up My kingdom on earth, I will punish all evil on earth. I have been patient with man, and I have given him time to repent and come to Me. This must all end soon, and evil must be put away for all eternity. Love will once again be the joy and source of all life and creation. All things will return to love, as it was in the beginning. I will keep you safe and bless the work of your hands. No one shall touch you lest they are destroyed. Do not fear men or governments or even the angel of death. For I am your protection and no one has the power to take you from My hand."

"If I am your witness, why don't I have any memory of it?"

"You must be emptied of all knowledge, as I was emptied of My knowledge and power and became the servant of all. You must yield to My will by faith, even as I yielded to the Father's will by faith. It was His will, that I alone should suffer for the loss of My children. I pled for the forgiveness of all men, for they did not know what they had done. My intercession for all sinners was forsaken by My Father."

"Why did He do that?"

"If the all-forgiving love was allowed to rule and forgive, evil would abide forever. Of necessity, He turned His back on His own heart. The feminine or nurturing love had to submit to the masculine or protective love. In this generation, the feminine will not yield to the masculine in those who are perishing. This will be accomplished to confuse the reflection of God in His creation. But those who are wise will choose life and live. You will testify of these things. I am the female lamb slain from the foundation of the world, and I am the male lamb that will cause the power of death to pass over all who love Me."

"I'm a nobody. I don't know how I could ever do what you're asking."

"I will lead you to write down all you have heard from Me. In due time, I will release you to the world. You will teach through a story My ways and My will. You will use the truth of your life and parables in the story to reveal My ways. Only those I have ordained to read it will read it. You will write as I lead you. You will first teach My ways, and then I will tell you how the world will end. But now, go your way and rest, for the time is not yet."

"No one will believe me. There's no proof of any of this. I'm talking to a voice in my head. They call that insanity."

"They will believe! They will recognize truth, and you shall open up a dialogue among My people, and they shall see Me in a new light. The seed of Abraham waits for Me, but I have already come, and they did not recognize Me. You will draw their hearts to Me. The purest love must die for justice to prevail. In Me was the seed of life. As the seed must die to bring forth life, so I had to die to release the life that was in Me. The Father's will was accomplished through Me. I give My life as a gift to all who put their trust in Me."

"I don't know if I understand this love. Will you speak to me again?"

"Yes. When I tell you to, you will write the book that I will lead you to write."

"I'm no writer. I'm just a carpenter. How will I write a book?"

"I will give you understanding that comes from above."

"What about tomorrow? I have to decide about this contract. What am I supposed to believe? What am I supposed to write about?"

"You shall write that the beginning of the end is at hand. I am calling man to repent and turn to Me. I will soon destroy the world. All I have told you will be the beginning of your testimony and the beginning of your prophesy. You will testify of the things I have told you, and this shall be the content of your book."

"Wh ... Wha ... What am I supposed to call this book?"

"You shall call it *The Beginning.*"